D0041070

The *Killing* of MONDAY BROWN

Also by Sandra West Prowell

BY EVIL MEANS

The *Killing* of MONDAY BROWN

A Phoebe Siegel Mystery

Sandra West Prowell

WALKER AND COMPANY ✺ NEW YORK

First published in the United States of America in 1994 by Walker
Publishing Company, Inc.

Published simultaneously in Canada by Thomas Allen & Son Canada,
Limited, Markham, Ontario

ISBN 0-8027-3184-8

Printed in the United States of America

*This book is dedicated to a
Miniconjou baby girl
picked up on the battlefield at Wounded Knee
December 29, 1890, by my ancestor,
Kate Bennett, who named her Cleo
and raised her as her own.
She died in 1904 of tuberculosis.
This one is for you, Cleo, in the hope that you fly on
Raven wings with the spirit of your people.*

The *Killing* of MONDAY BROWN

Prologue

The Yellowstone River is a great gray ribbon of water that is born high in the mountains near Yellowstone Park, nurtured each year by the melt of alpine snowpacks. At Billings it gradually drifts to the northeast, where it eventually joins the great Missouri just inside the North Dakota border. Grizzlies, as big as houses, roamed here once, as did mastodons and primitive peoples veering off the Great North Trail. Buffalo herds were so vast some say it took weeks for an entire herd to pass one point, so powerful they could knock a train off its track if they were stampeding.

Cowboy Country, Big Sky, Land of Shining Mountains, they all fit. Calamity Jane called Billings and the banks of the Yellowstone home for a brief time, and Custer spilled his blood and that of the Seventh Cavalry a mere sixty miles east of here. We boast the Bloody Bozeman Trail; you can still see the ruts from wagons loaded with dreams, and settlers, and hard times a few miles to the south. Montana has had its share of copper kings, courtesans, and gold so plentiful you can see it sparkle in the mortar of the old brick buildings in Helena. Depending on your tastes, you can still get a taco for forty-nine cents, a hooker for twenty bucks, and two quarters will get you a game of keno.

But the truth runs as deep and as old as the Yellowstone itself. This is Indian Country. Lewis and Clark knew it, so did Jim Bridger and John Colter. Colter ran naked across the plains of Montana near Three Forks on a bet with some Blackfeet Indians. The stakes were his life, and he won.

American Gothic wasn't painted here. But *Montana Gothic* was. You can see it any day of the week on Minnesota Avenue. No pinch-faced, bespectacled farm couple holding a pitchfork, with fertile farmlands stretching as far as the eye can see, a white clapboard house standing in the background. It's a too-young Indian woman leaning up against a decaying, vacant building being hustled by a toothless, horseless cowboy in town on another binge. This is Indian Country. Their names roll off your tongue and tickle your throat: Oglala, Assiniboine, Arikara, Kootenai, Salish, Blackfeet, Blood, Cheyenne, and Crow. This is Indian Country all right. I just never looked for it. Until the day it came looking for me.

1

I could hear them before I could see them. The Dodge van stopped at the end of the lane that led to my house. It was a class act, painted a deep cherry red with black and silver detailing and tinted windows all around. It was a knockout piece of vehicle and didn't belong to anyone I knew. Yet.

I walked over to the spigot on the side of the porch and turned off the water, dropped the hose I was holding, and squinted against the sun to see who was inside the van. No one was getting out, and it was making me nervous.

My house sits in an isolated area; my nearest neighbor is a good half mile away. It had been vacant for many years and had the reputation of being a hangout for beer busts and God only knew what else. Six months ago I moved in and had the cops out every weekend for the first month. Reputations are easy to earn and die hard, even for one-hundred-year-old three-story houses.

I was about to turn and walk into the house when the door on the side of the van slid back, and several Indians piled out. Two young boys and a girl bolted toward me, ran past, and disappeared into the trees to the right of the house. A tall man, over six feet, with long, traditional braids, a John Deere duck-billed cap on his head, wearing Tony Lamas, Levi's, and a pearl-buttoned western shirt, strode toward me. His hands were tucked into the pockets of his jeans, and his face, the color of earthen clay, showed no emotion as he covered the ground between us with long strides.

A brooding younger man, eighteen, maybe twenty, leaned against the van and listened with a deaf ear as a young woman chewed on him about something I couldn't make out. He reached in through an open window on the passenger side and brought out a can, lifted it to his lips, and drank. The young woman looked at me quickly, a flush of embarrassment on her face.

I didn't see the two women on either side of an old, old woman until they were almost upon me. No one said a word until the old woman was led to the stairs going up to the porch and gently sat down. The man standing a few feet from me spit chew on the ground and looked me dead in the eyes. I could hear the kids, squealing and laughing as they ran out of the woods and bounded up the stairs onto the porch. Immediately, all three were on the rail, using it as a tightrope.

I took a step toward the porch, prepared to rescue, or maim, whichever came first, one or all of them. "Hey! You could get—"

"Kyle Old Wolf is my cousin. He said we should come to you."

"Who? He said what?" I was doing one of those head turns that you see only at a tennis match, trying to give equal time to the kids and the man who was talking to me. Then the phone started ringing inside the house.

"Could you wait just a minute?" I reached the phone on the seventh or eighth ring. If I didn't sound out of breath or hysterical or both, it was a miracle of self-control.

"Phoebe," the familiar voice said bluntly. "I thought I should call."

"You're a little late, Kyle. All, and I mean *all,* of them are here."

He laughed. "The whole family came, huh?"

"Oh, I don't know. It could be two, maybe three families for what that's worth. What's going on?"

"Been reading the papers?"

"Only my horoscope and 'The Far Side.' "

"Have you followed the news about the woman down on Twenty-seventh Street South and Montana Avenue who reported a body that fell across the hood of her car while she was stopped at the light?"

"Who hasn't? I thought they deep-sixed that because they couldn't verify anything."

"They did. Until she gave them a positive ID on the guy and he turned up missing."

"And?"

"Monday Brown."

"Monday? I just saw him a month ago."

"You may have. As it stands . . ."

"You think it was him?"

"I don't know. But they've been holding a twenty-year-old cousin of mine, Matthew Wolf."

"You've got a lot of cousins, Kyle," I said as I turned around and looked out the door. I could hear the kids but couldn't see them. The muscles in my neck had tied themselves into little knots.

He laughed again. "A couple of hundred or so."

"I'm almost afraid to ask. What are they doing here?"

"Is one of them a big, tall guy with long hair?"

"It is."

"That's Matthew's father. Is there an old woman?"

"Old, Kyle? You call that old? I'm not even sure she's alive."

"That's Matthew's great-grandmother, Anna. And you've probably got his brother and a couple of his sisters and a few nieces and nephews."

"Wait a minute. Did you say Matthew Wolf?"

"Right."

"Isn't he the kid who came back from the Gulf all decorated? They had a big write-up about him in the paper. He's involved with some radical Indian group that's been working the reservations in the state. It was quite an article. Bright kid."

"One and the same."

I felt someone standing behind me and turned. My eyes widened, and my breath caught in my throat when I saw the raven-haired little girl cradling Stud in her arms. "Jesus! Kyle, hold on a minute." I stretched the phone cord toward her. "Honey, that cat hates people. He'll scratch your eyes out and peel off your cheeks."

I could hear Stud purring from where I stood. The girl said nothing as she nuzzled her face in the yellow fur that covered his twenty-five-pound body. She stroked his back as his tail switched back and forth in an upside-down arch. All I could do was shake my head as she walked around me and sat in a chair. I couldn't remember Stud ever looking so content.

I lifted the phone back to my ear and craned my neck to see what was going on outside. "Kyle, maybe you should be here."

"Can't do it, Phoebe. I just wanted to let you know what was going on."

"How does Matthew Wolf figure into all this?"

"They popped him three days ago down at the Arcade."

"For what?"

"Suspicion of murder."

"Let me guess. Monday Brown?"

"Right."

"When did they find Monday's body?"

"They haven't."

"Kyle . . ."

"It's complicated. I've got a feeling on this one. Could be a major setup. They have to release him tomorrow morning, but that doesn't mean the heat's off."

"Roger should have the names of a few good criminal lawyers. I'll get ahold of him and—"

"Just hear them out. I'll owe you one."

"You don't owe me anything. I just don't have the time. I'm busy fixing this place up, landscaping, all of that."

"Landscaping? You? How much does it take to lay down Astro-turf?"

I had to hold the phone away from my ear while he laughed.

"Right. Me. You've got connections and probably more than a few chips out there to call in."

"Not on this. They've already given me the word to stay clear. I've gotta run."

"Don't you dare—" The line went dead.

I stared at the phone, hung it up, and looked around for the kid. She was nowhere to be found. "Little girl?" Nothing. "Let's go back outside. Okay?" Still nothing.

Stud has a killer reputation and suffers from severe mood swings. He can stare someone down, flex his stiletto claws in warning, and then roll over, fall asleep on his back, all four legs spread out, tongue lolling out the side of his mouth. Or he can attack without warning. Stud and I have a lot in common. We both prefer backs and thighs; mine on chicken, his on people. He had a rap sheet at the Cop Shop, Animal Control, and had left a trail of urine-stained poodles back in the old neighborhood. My kind of cat. The girl would have to take care of herself.

When I walked out to the porch everyone was right where they had been when I'd gone in to answer the phone. They stared up at me with eyes so black you couldn't see the pupils. Curled up on the porch swing beside the girl, his motor still running, was Stud. Still content. The old woman was just below me on the middle stair.

Unexpectedly, she lifted her left arm up, bony fingers extended, and reached for my hand. Instinctively I leaned down, placed my hand in hers, and helped her to her feet. Her grip was as strong as any male handshake I had ever experienced. Without loosening her hold on me, she turned and looked up into my face.

Her eyes were clear, not covered with the milky film of age. There was a brightness, a twinkle dancing through them. She was diminutive. The pressure on my hand increased as she lifted her right hand and shook it in front of my face. Clipped words spilled from her mouth in a high-pitched jumble of unintelligible phrases. Her other hand moved in quick, soft strokes, first on the right side, then in the middle, and finally to the left of my head. My eyes were riveted on that incredible face. Time was drawn there. A dark, ancient mask, etched with the history of a people that I knew nothing about. It held secrets, mysteries, and for a split second I was pulled into those eyes. My breath caught in my throat as an icy finger trailed down my spine.

It was over as subtly as it had started. The two women were at her side almost immediately as she let go of my hand, turned, and allowed them to lead her back to the Dodge. I watched as she walked away. Her dress was a simple, crimson cotton, long-sleeved smock that was gathered at the waist by an impressive silver conch belt. Soft leather moccasins covered her feet and legs up to her knees. She shuffled over the grass, held up between the two women, and disappeared into the van.

Feeling increasingly uncomfortable, I managed a self-conscious smile, ran my hand through my hair, and turned toward the tall man, who was watching me.

"What was that about?"

"She just wanted to touch you, bless you."

"Catholic, huh? I've got a mother that would forever be in her debt."

He laughed quietly, looked down at his feet and then back at me. The bright, twinkling eyes must have been a familial thing. He was amused and knew that I wasn't.

"She's a very wise old woman. She likes you. Was that Kyle on the phone?"

"Yes, it was."

"Will you help us?"

"Look, Mr. . . ."

"Wolf. John Wolf."

"Well, Mr. Wolf. Kyle may not have told you, but I'm only taking on a limited number of clients this year." I swept my hand toward the house. "This has been quite an undertaking. It was built in the late eighteen eighties, and the walls are plaster and cracking, and all the . . ."

I was rambling. He was letting me. I dropped my hand and looked at him. He smiled broadly, revealing a startlingly white set of teeth. He reminded me of Kyle.

"Plumbing bad?"

I looked at him curiously. "As a matter of fact, it is. It has those boxes above the toilets. Why?"

"I do construction, and I've had some experience with these old places and their pipes. Are you taking it down to the lath?"

"The what?"

He laughed again. "How about we talk and maybe we can work a deal?" He looked up; his eyes scanned the house. "I got good references and lots of them."

"Really?" Clawhammers, wrenches, and saws, along with crochet hooks and knitting needles, added up to the same thing with me, instruments of danger and doom. The words slid out of my mouth. "Come on in."

He followed me up the stairs and stopped long enough to shake the porch support. "Good wind and this will be history," he said. "Those stains running down that front wall mean you should consider tightening up this porch roof. You've got some leaks."

I was impressed. "I'm not promising anything, Mr. Wolf."

"Call me John."

He turned when he reached the doorway and signaled the others waiting by the van. The little girl stayed on the porch swing with Stud. One by one, the others filed past me. The last was the older of the two boys. He stopped, looked up at me, and grinned. His foot came down on my instep, and his eyes locked on mine. In the same clipped speech his great-grandmother had used, he said something to the other boy. Pain shot up my leg as I reached out to grab him and missed when he ran into the house.

I shoved boxes, piles of papers, and books aside, clearing debris

from the tops of chairs in the music room, which I had earmarked for
my office. The kids didn't stay put long. Within minutes I was watching them through the bay window that overlooked the side yard. One
of the boys was scaling a cottonwood, cheered on by the other boy
and girl. No one seemed too concerned.

I turned toward the family. "Kyle told me your son was arrested
in the Monday Brown deal."

John nodded and said nothing. I shifted in my chair behind the
sprawling desk, picked up a pencil, and nervously tapped it on the
desktop.

"Maybe we better get down to some basic facts here. You tell me
what you want me to do, and I'll tell you whether I can."

"Matthew didn't kill Monday." John's voice reflected no emotion,
just a blunt statement of fact.

"They must have had some reason, something to go on, or he
wouldn't be in custody."

The young man who had been leaning against the van earlier
glared at me. I tried meeting his stare, but he turned away with a
disgusted shrug and a shake of his head.

"Matthew's Indian. That's reason enough." The young woman
whom I had seen chastising the young man piped up. "They don't
need no reason better than that."

I opened my mouth to answer, couldn't think of anything to say,
and looked back at John Wolf.

"We asked Matthew when we went to the jail to see him if he
killed Monday, or if he knew where Monday was," John said.

"And Matthew said no." I didn't exactly have to channel on that
one.

"Why would he say anything else?" The brooding young man
leaning against the wall shifted his position and continued to glare as
he spoke. He reeked tough and hateful, and on some level he scared
the hell out of me. I was beginning to understand how Custer felt.

"Grandmother asked Matthew. I was with him, and so was my
son Steven." John tilted his head toward the young man against the
wall. "If Matthew told Grandmother he didn't do it, then he didn't
do it."

"Then why was he picked up?"

"Matthew and a couple of others were at the Arcade a while back.

Monday came in drunk and gave the boys a bad time. A fight started, and he beat them pretty bad."

"*He* beat *them?* Three of them?"

"Some cops came and broke it up and pushed the boys outside."

"The cops beat the shit out of James." Steven was standing now and leaning down toward his father.

John's face tightened as the words flew from his mouth. The chopped sentence in Crow was enough to cow and silence the young man, who retreated against the wall and looked out the window. I could see the muscles in his jaw twitching.

"One of the boys, James Eagle, ended up at the emergency room and had to have stitches in his head," John continued. "Matthew was pretty angry. James is a brother."

"His real brother."

"This kind of brother." Steven raised his arm with his fist clenched in a macho solidarity salute.

John said, "They take care of each other."

"It doesn't make sense that the cops would arrest Matthew based on a fight at the Arcade."

The young woman spoke up again. "After the fight, Matthew told a lot of people he would kill Monday. He was drunk, and he was mad as hell. Other people have said that to Monday Brown, and they don't end up in jail."

Silence fell over the room. Visions of Monday and his reputation tripped through my mind. They were right. The line could have formed behind Matthew any day of the week.

John said something to Steven. I heard the words, again in Crow, form and fly across the room. Steven answered. It wasn't hard to see he was in disagreement with whatever John had said. John's anger was apparent. He reached out, held his hand open in front of Steven, and said something else.

Steven reached inside his shirt and pulled out a flat brown package. John took it from him, stood, and laid it down on the desk in front of me.

"What's this?"

"We found this under the front seat of Matthew's car last night."

"If it's drugs . . ." I pushed the package back toward John and raised my hands in the air.

"No. It isn't."

My response didn't seem to affect John one way or the other. It bothered Steven. He laughed cynically and looked back out the window as he mumbled something under his breath. The young woman jabbed him in the side with her elbow.

"Open it," John urged.

I pulled the package back toward me, gingerly opened the mouth of the bag, and pulled out the contents. My mouth dropped open. They were exquisite. The necklace was beautiful in its simplicity: a stiff piece of rawhide cord adorned with small, elongated, ivory-colored pieces of what I supposed to be horn or bone. They were varied in size, small, delicate, and knobbed on each end. Multicolored pony beads separated them.

The purse was another matter altogether. I ran my fingers over the minute glass beads that formed a geometric pattern on the front. It was the size of a small clutch purse and hung from a piece of braided leather. Four long strands of hair adorned each side. The purse bulged slightly. Both pieces were obviously museum quality. The thought crossed my mind that these two items were how they intended to pay me. God, I was tempted.

"These are just gorgeous. I love this stuff," I said, struggling against my conscience as my fingers traced the geometric design. "We can work something out, maybe a payment plan."

"They don't belong to us," John said.

I gingerly picked up the necklace and placed it around my neck just to get a once-in-a-lifetime feeling. I gently twisted the long strands of red hair on the purse around my fingers. "I've never seen hair as red as this. Whoever made it must have used some natural dye to get this color. Horsehair?"

"Scalp locks," Steven answered. I looked up and saw the malicious grin he directed toward me.

"Pardon me?"

"It's a scalp-lock bag. Very old. Not Crow," John explained.

It didn't take much to know that Steven was enjoying this tremendously. I tried to recover as best I could. Something was crawling over my skin, raising all the little fine hairs to attention. The necklace felt like a lodestone hung around my neck. I touched the bottom of it as I looked at John. He read my raised eyebrows and open mouth.

"That?" he asked. "Finger-bone necklace. Not Crow."

Steven continued to stare, grinning. I raised the necklace over my head, placed it on the desk by the bag, and rose slowly from my chair. My voice was high, shaky. "Could you excuse me for a minute, please?"

I didn't wait for confirmation but walked, probably a little too stiff and erect, from the room. Laughter erupted behind me. I could hear Steven, in his clipped Crow speech, say something. Whatever he said, it brought more gales of laughter. This wasn't going well.

2

When Roger, a former lover, now friend-sans-sex, pulled into the driveway that night and staggered through the front door loaded down with his briefcase, a stack of legal briefs, and a couple of sacks from Colonel Sanders, I was struggling with my own overload. The Wolf family had piled two hours of information on me, and I was having a helluva time sorting it out.

Being the homemaker that I am, I put a couple of paper plates on the coffee table in the front room, served up the coleslaw, mashed potatoes, and chicken, and sat on the floor to eat.

"How'd the day go? Get a lot done?"

"Right. A lot," I answered absentmindedly. "How's the painting on your house going?"

"Fine. Thanks for putting me up for the night. It sure beats the hell out of a motel room. Sure you won't be a little uncomfortable with me here?"

"You'll be comfortable."

"Me? I'm talking about you. What's up? You seem a little out of it. Did something happen I should know about? Toilet overflow? Roof blow off?"

"Speaking of roofs"—I perked up a little—"I think I found someone to work on the porch roof."

"Who?"

"Who? Who what?" I asked and tried to beam back down. "I'm sorry. This guy that stopped by the house today."

"What's going on, Phoebe? And, don't say 'nothing.'" Roger looked around the front room. "Where's Stud? He wasn't out on the porch to snag my pants when I came up the stairs."

"Out catting around. Probably on a search-and-destroy mission.

Haven't you noticed the lowered population of mice these last couple of weeks?"

"Never let it be said that I doubt his killer instinct." Roger dug through the white box and withdrew a chicken leg. "Now, what's on your mind?"

"What have you heard about the Monday Brown thing?"

"Odd you would bring him up. What about him?"

"You tell me first."

"I grabbed a cup of coffee at the cafeteria in the courthouse and overheard a couple of guys sitting behind me talking about old Monday. Seems there's some foreign interest in him."

Roger loved baiting me. My attention was immediate. "How so?"

"I didn't get it all. When I left I recognized one of the guys talking. I've seen him in court a couple of times."

"In leg chains?"

Roger laughed. "No. He's an attorney. Anyway, they were talking about some German that approached a law firm here in town and wanted representation with a claim against Monday's estate."

"Estate? Christ. They don't even have his body. For all they know, he isn't even dead. None of this is making much sense." I stopped in midbite. "Or is it?"

"Your turn," he said and bit into his chicken leg.

"I was working out front this morning when this van full of Crows pulled up—"

"They're not really Crows, Phoebe. They're Absarokee. It means large-beaked bird. Crow is just a bastardized version of—"

"We're trying to have a conversation here, Roger." I waved my chicken leg toward him. "Not a lesson in linguistics, damnit."

"Sorry. I've done some pro bono work for the tribe, and in this day and age of political correctness, I just thought—"

My shoulders slumped. "Please, Roger . . . don't think, just listen. They wanted to hire me."

"What the hell for?"

"The man's name was John Wolf. I liked him, Roger. Liked him a lot."

"And Matthew Wolf is his kid."

"How'd you know that? Sometimes your powers of observation amaze me," I said as I smiled.

"Let's see how good I am." Roger put his index fingers to his

temples, closed his eyes, and leaned back against the couch. "It's coming . . . it's coming . . . I've got it. Matthew Wolf is *in*- . . . in-some-
thing . . . innocent!"

Roger's sense of humor falls somewhere between W. C. Fields and
an Oompa Loompa. Usually it just falls between the cracks.

"Roger, they were fascinating."

"The family?"

"All nine of them, including this old woman that looked like she
stepped out of the last century."

"Phoebe, I don't think it would be a good idea—"

"Damnit, Roger. Stop interrupting me. What if he's innocent? Isn't
that how it works? Innocent until proven guilty?"

He shook his head and resumed eating. "You're right. I apologize.
Are you going to take it on?"

"I don't know. They already knew about the German. He showed
up at the jail and tried to make Matthew an offer he couldn't refuse."

"No . . ." Roger loved to drawl his N-O's.

"And, get this. He had an escort. Two Feds worked a meeting with
Matthew and this German in a private room. No through-the-glass
telephone conversations for these guys."

"I suppose now you're going to tell me they roughed him up."

I sucked the chicken grease off the tip of my finger and shook it at
him. "No. Nothing that subtle. They spotlighted him and drilled a
few teeth."

"Nasty," he said and laughed.

"The German offered him fifty thousand dollars and the best defense money can buy. If . . ."

"If what?"

"By the way, before he talked to Matthew, the German asked the
two Feds to step out of the room."

"So no one heard this offer. Let's get back to the *if what*."

"If"—I paused long enough to be effective—"if Matthew told him
where the *items* were that Monday was supposed to have had with
him the day he dropped out of sight."

"Items?" Roger dipped his chicken leg into his mashed potatoes.
"The missing booty?"

"Uh huh. Two of which I think just may be in on my desk." I
picked up another piece of chicken and munched into it.

"You're kidding, of course."

"Would I kid you, Roger?"

Roger's chicken leg bounced like a rubber ball on the coffee table as he threw it down. "This time you'd better be kidding. Damn. Do you have any idea of the trouble you're setting yourself up for? Or me, for that matter? You're smarter than this."

"Smarter than what? Someone who has the disgusting habit of dipping fried chicken into mashed potatoes?"

He stood and started walking out of the room.

"Where are you going?" I asked, shocked at his outburst.

"To your office. Where the hell else?"

Both the bag and the necklace were in his hand when he walked back into the room.

"Good-looking stuff. They're both illegal in most states. You can get in trouble for having body parts."

"You know what they are?"

"Sure, a scalp-lock bag and a finger-bone necklace. What did you think they were?"

"I knew what the hell they were." My eyes tracked onto the red hank of hair.

"They're on the list, Phoebe."

"What are you talking about?" I stood and got a sinking feeling in my stomach. "What list?"

"If you had let me finish, I would have told you."

"I hate it when you do this to me Roger. What damn list?"

"Our firm took the German on. He's got a list, a *long* list, of items. He also has a receipt that says he prepaid for all of them. There are six, maybe seven of these bags and a couple of necklaces like this one." He held it up in front of me. It seemed like sacrilege to bat it away, so I sidestepped the swinging digits. "Plus, a picture of one of Custer's scouts that was previously thought to not be in existence, a few maps, and the awl that was supposedly the one that a Sioux woman used to pierce Custer's eardrums. That particular item ended up in a Sioux medicine bundle. It's quite a list. You've got to call the cops, Phoebe. Now."

"I don't have to do shit. This is privileged information between me and my clients."

"You're covering. Call the cops."

Saved by the bell. I bolted out of the room and picked up the phone on the fourth ring.

When I walked back into the front room, Roger was turning the bag over and over in his hand. "Damn, they did exquisite work."

"Scalping or the beadwork?"

He frowned up at me. "Both. Who was on the phone?"

"Stud."

"Who?"

"Stud," I repeated.

"Right. And what did Stud want? Condoms?"

"He's visiting friends and won't be home until tomorrow."

"Knock it off, Phoebe. Who was on the P-H-O-N-E."

"S-T-U-D. He's in P-R-Y-O-R."

"You're kidding."

"Would I kid you, Roger?" Actually, I was stuffing down a block of anger at the catnapping. It had never occurred to me to frisk the little girl when the Wolfs left. Thinking back, I hadn't even seen her leave. She was already in the van. "He hitched a ride with friends. They'll bring him home in the morning."

"How the hell did that happen?"

"Don't ask, Roger. Just don't ask. Let's get this mess picked up." I started clearing off the coffee table.

"Whoa. We need to talk."

"Sorry, Roger. I wouldn't think of breaching client confidentiality."

"You're putting me in a helluva position here. I assumed you hadn't told them you'd take it."

"Never, never assume."

"When did you tell them?"

I looked at my watch. "About three minutes ago."

"Phoebe, for God's sake, think this over. Just what is it they want you to do? Wouldn't a good defense attorney make more sense?"

"He's got a public defender. Big guarantee there, huh, Roger?"

"What do they want you to do?" Again, he articulated slowly, purposefully.

"Give them an edge with the system."

"Holy Mary, Mother of God . . ." Roger leaned back and threw his arms up in the air.

"You're acting papal, Roger. Invoking all those religious names." I raised my voice to near soprano. "And you know I hate that."

"To talk any sense to you is impossible. 'You're acting papal,

Roger,' " he mimicked. "I just hate it when you do your . . . those damn Phoebeisms. This is serious."

"So is an Indian kid up on suspicion of murder. To leave him to the justice system is suicide. You know that and I know that. Hell, they don't even have a body. Maybe Monday is pulling some disappearing act."

"Right."

"You never know. These items showed up in Matthew's car. The Wolfs want to know where they came from and who would want to stash them there. If I find the goodies, chances are, if someone *has* recycled Monday, we'll know who it is."

"And if that someone turns out to be Matthew Wolf?"

I didn't answer. I had other things on my mind: the bag and the necklace that were staring up at me from the table.

3

My dreams were vivid that night. I could see her running across the plains, draped in calico, her long, red tresses, or what was left of them, trailing in the wind behind her, her bloody hands, held high in the air, minus a few fingers. Poor thing. Never again able to knead bread, no knuckles to wear down on those washboards, and no hair. Bony fingers started boring deep into my shoulders. I woke up in a cold sweat. Maybe Roger was right. But now it was too late.

I threw the covers off, got out of bed, followed a shaft of moonlight to the open bedroom window, and stared down at the grounds below. A grove of cottonwood trees, wild rosebushes, and willows surrounded the house on three sides. It was almost impenetrable but for the narrow paths that wound through it. Beyond the trees I could catch glimpses of moonlight reflected in the Yellowstone River as it flowed silently through the night.

My mind wandered. It must have been a beautiful house in its heyday, a dream come true for whoever conceived the setting, bought the land, and built the towering structure. From what I could research, it had been built as a family dwelling for a wealthy banker making his bucks from hardscrabble ranchers and railroad workers.

Over the years it had been sold several times. The walls had heard the laughter of gamblers and bootleggers paying for the services of the *soiled doves* who probably worked out of this bedroom. The piano had been replaced with an organ and the laughter drowned out with dead silence when a mortician paid the back taxes, put Big Betty out of business, and started one of his own.

In the sixties, it was rented by the unsuspecting estate to doped-out hippies who sold macramé, tie dye, and pot off the front porch.

The seventies threw it back into family life until the repairs far exceeded the family's budget. It had been empty since then. It had a history, just like me. I liked to think it was akin to a lady of easy virtue who had since found religion. All the memories were intact, but there was such hope for the future.

I looked hard into the night and tried to imagine what it had been like long before the house was built on bottomland, wondered what it had been like, way beyond then, when the Wolf family's ancestors had roamed, owned, this area.

Indians had always fascinated me. I had no childhood memories of wanting to dress like Dale Evans. I had spent the better part of a summer trying to start a fire behind the house by rubbing two sticks together. It didn't work. I remembered the movies, at least a couple of hundred Saturday matinees, always shoot-'em-ups, and wanting the Indians to win. They never did. Would Matthew Wolf win this one? Should he win this one? I wasn't sure, but I knew I had to find out.

Something caught my attention. I wasn't sure what. I cocked my head and strained to listen through the darkness and stillness of the house. The phone was ringing. Roger was asleep in the next room, and the last thing I wanted to do was wake him. I ran on the tips of my toes across the room, walked out to the hallway, down the stairs, and toward the phone. The closer I got, the louder it rang. This time it couldn't be Stud.

The grandfather clock at the end of the hall was just striking the half hour after three in the morning.

"Hello?" I heard myself whisper.

"Were you sleeping?"

"No, Kyle. I was working out."

"Why are you whispering?"

"I don't want to wake up Roger."

Kyle was silent for a moment. "Roger? Is that on again?"

"No. He's having his house painted, so I offered him a room."

"Sure, Phoebe," he said and chuckled. "I thought you might want to know they just pulled James Eagle out of the river not too far from your place."

"James?"

"One of the kids from the fight at the Arcade."

"Shit. When?"

"I just hung up the phone. The call probably came in a good forty-five minutes ago. Seems like a couple of guys were doing some night fishing down there and got more than they bargained for. I'm on my way down now. Meet me?"

"Sure. Give me time to get dressed."

"Do you know the spot they call Agate Bar?"

"Yeah. I can take a path behind the house and be there before you pull your pants on."

"Phoebe?"

"You don't need to say it, Kyle. You didn't call me."

"Thanks."

By the time I got dressed and tiptoed out the back door, the moon had risen higher and was shining directly on the tops of the trees. I headed down the path and wondered briefly why the hell I was even out there. Growth on either side of me was shoulder high and higher. A slight breeze had come up and teased the tips of branches, bending them toward me. The closer I got to the river, the thicker the air became. It wasn't unpleasant, just heavy and fishy. There was rain coming.

I turned to the right and followed the rocky riverbank east. In the distance I heard muffled voices and could see the beam from a lone flashlight moving toward me. I stepped off the path and stood still, pressed up against a tree. Something moved behind me. I jumped and turned toward the sound. I had tried Girl Scout camp once, and after twenty-four hours and several refrains of "Row, Row, Row Your Boat," I knew it wasn't for me. Woodsy Owl I wasn't.

They had zoos for a reason: to separate man from beast. And there I was, standing against a tree in brambles and brush that had stickers sharp enough to penetrate my Levi's. All I could think of was Roger telling me he had seen what he thought were cat tracks. Not Stud's. Cougars roam through the area once in a while, and as far as I knew one was salivating right overhead or behind me.

The beam of light came closer and closer and swung from the edge of the river to the edge of the trees. I started to duck just as it caught me in the face.

"Hold on there," the deep voice shouted. "Step out and put your hands above your head."

The voice was unmistakable. Bud Sullivan was the biggest deputy in the county. Not noted for superior intelligence, he was still one of the nicest guys you could find. He'd attended cop school with my uncle John and had been around the whole time I was growing up.

"Hey, Bud. My retinas are slamming shut. Can you point that thing in another direction?" For a minute, no one said anything.

"Who is it?"

"Phoebe."

I felt caught in the middle of a knock-knock joke, my personal favorites. If he had said *Phoebe who,* I probably would have peed my pants.

"Phoebe Siegel?"

"It's me, all right. But I'm still blind until you move that damn thing out of my face." I could hear the edge in my voice.

"Oops, sorry about that, honey. What are you doing out here this time of night?" he asked as he lowered the flashlight and moved toward me. He offered his hand as I stepped through the brambles and onto the gravel.

"Right now I'm probably bleeding to death through my thighs," I said and winced. "You scared me, Bud. I guess I could ask you the same thing. What are you doing out here?"

"We got a kid on the bank up there."

"Dead?"

"Definitely dead."

"Didn't make it across in a midnight swim?"

He started back the direction he had come from. "Unless he was swimming with his hands tied behind his back. Looks like someone put a bullet in the back of his head and slid him in."

"Threw him off the bridge?" I had to lengthen my steps to keep up with him.

"Nope. Bridge is out, under construction. Must have driven him down somehow . . ." Bud scratched his head. "He doesn't look like he's been in that long. He's still got his eyes. Fish didn't get them."

"Jesus, Bud . . ."

"That happens, you know. Fish just go right in there and nibble on—"

"I know. I know." I tried to silence him.

"And he doesn't look like he got snagged on anything. I think he just caught a current and washed up on the bar."

"Who ID'd him?"

Bud turned cop immediately. "What makes you think he's been identified?"

"Nothing, Bud. I just wondered if anyone knew who he was."

"That isn't how you asked that, Phoebe, now is it? What did you say you were doing down here?"

"Looking for my cat. He got out, and it scares me around this river. I heard there was a cougar roaming around."

He loosened up. "Aw, hell. They aren't going to mess with a house cat. Then again . . ." He scratched his head. "Did you find him?"

"No. I didn't. He'll show up. Probably in the morning," I said and conned my way forward. "Do they know who he is?"

"Young Indian. No more than twenty if he's anything. Shit, they have it hard, end up in the damnedest situations. Just can't figure it out. They die young for some reason." Bud reached over and held my elbow, assisting me over a large beached piece of driftwood. "A guy from the city PD is down there. Said the kid's name was James Eagle. He broke up a fight at the Arcade a while back and recognized the kid from that."

"Who's the cop?"

"Clint Beemer. Know him?"

"Sure do."

Everyone knew Clint Beemer. Why he was still on the force nobody could figure. He was big, mean, and verbal about how he held the Indians in contempt. Steven Wolf was probably right: If Beemer broke up the fight at the Arcade, he probably worked the kid over. He was an asshole, and that was giving him the edge.

We reached the group of men standing in a semicircle at the edge of the river. Kyle looked up as I neared and furrowed his brow. I stayed back from the group. In a moment he walked over to me.

His voice was low and secretive. "This wasn't such a hot idea."

I looked toward the body on the ground as the group standing around it parted.

"You better get on back. I'll get ahold of you in a couple of hours. They're picking up all kinds of stuff."

"What stuff?"

"A couple of necklaces. Some trade points. But I sure as hell don't need anybody wondering why you're here."

"This is getting a little crazy, Kyle. You told me to meet you," I whispered back.

He said nothing.

"Kyle—"

"I'll call you." He walked away and joined the others.

I turned and headed back toward the path that would lead me home. Stepping carefully, I looked down at the rocks and picked my way along, cursing under my breath.

"Why the hell call me in the first place?" I mumbled. Kyle and his family were proving to be a pain in the . . .

Something glinted on the rocks below. I backed up one step and knelt down. A silver chain coiled down between the rocks. I reached out and lifted it. A pendulous weight pulled the chain taut. I cradled something smooth and brought it up close to my face, turning so the moon could illuminate it.

It's an odd feeling when you know things. Like who's going to be on the other end of a phone when it rings. Who's at the door. Or when someone is following you. The flashlights and the voices had faded behind me. It happened as I was trying to make out the shape that I held in my hand.

For a split second I looked up. Iridescent lunar light created a strobe effect against the tree line. A shape, ghostly and quick, slid in behind a thick-trunked cottonwood. I stopped and stared, trying to penetrate the darkness. I had two choices. Forge on or go back to where I knew there were people. Could Roger have followed me? Probably not. Maybe the cops had come down this far or had come in another way. Again, probably not. I opted to keep on going.

The bottoms of my feet ached. Walking on the rocks was difficult at best. I'd abused my feet earlier in the year when I had just moved into the house and discovered the edge of the river. I'd wandered up and down the banks for hours, communing with Mother Nature and finding out she talked back to me by bruising the hell out of *my* feet on *her* rocks.

The night sky darkened above. I could hear the roll of distant thunder. Clouds pushed against the moonlight until it was obliterated. The heavy, damp odor still hung in the air. Fishy. Rotting wood. Everything around me stood mute in the pitch blackness. The breeze had picked up and carried the faint scent of rain on its chill.

It was hard to tell where I was. I turned left where I thought the path should be and cautiously changed my course into the woods. The packed bottom soil felt like a soft massage on my aching soles.

The wind picked up and sang through the tops of the trees, slamming branch into branch, sending leaves sailing helplessly to the ground. Something snapped behind me. I turned as lightning broke above, lighting the path. The figure of a man flashed, silhouetted only for an instant, and disappeared into a curtain of darkness.

The pain in my feet was swallowed by the power rush that coursed through my legs as I flew over the ground, hoping to hell I had picked the right path and not one that wound endlessly downriver. My arms flew up to protect my face from willows that lashed out at me. The rain started coming down in sheets. I stumbled once, fell to my knees, and got up. My hand was empty. I looked behind me, saw nothing, and sank to the ground. I brushed across the soil frantically searching for whatever it was I had found. It was there, wet and muddy, in my grasp again.

I could see the back porch light in the distance as I neared the break in the trees. The grass was wet, slick. I went down again for only a second, found my wind, and raced for the back steps. I don't remember my feet touching the weathered wooden planks, or the feel of the metal handle on the screen door, but I was inside. I slammed the kitchen door behind me and leaned against it, panting. Shoving the object into my pocket, I reached up and brushed my tangled hair from my face. I could taste the dirt on my hands.

"Where the hell have you been?" Roger practically screamed as he stood in the doorway leading to the dining room. "I've looked all over for you."

"Like that?" I said as my chest heaved and I fought to catch my breath. Roger stood before me, in his underwear, his hands on his hips. Hysteria started rising in my throat. I bit my lip to keep from laughing.

"Well?"

"Taking the garbage out," I answered.

"At this hour?"

"I've been trying not to put things off like I usually do. You should be impressed."

"You look like you fell in the Dumpster." He tried his best to sound angry.

"That's it, I . . . uh, was looking inside and fell in. God, it was filthy and stinky and—"

"The damned phone was ringing and I got up to answer it. Whoever it was hung up. You weren't in your room so—hell, I'm going back to bed, Phoebe. It's damn near five A.M. Maybe I can get another goddamned hour."

"You go on up, Roger. I have to lock up and get this yuck off my face."

He disappeared around the corner. My hand went immediately to my pocket and pulled out the object that pressed against my leg. It was a flat stone, carved into the image of a fish. The detailing was deep and ornamental. A hole was drilled through the eye. I turned it over and over in my hand. Whatever kind of stone it was, it was as smooth as a bar of soap and about the same length. I pushed it back into my pocket, turned out the kitchen light, and looked out the slender, rectangular window just to the right of the back door.

My breath caught in my throat as my heart went into a charley horse. A tall figure stepped from behind one of the trees, arms outstretched. Another lightning flash lit the sky. The jagged light glinted off the rain pelting his naked chest. A thunderous clap shook the windows. I leaned forward, rubbed at the moisture forming on the pane, and looked out into the night. I could have sworn his face, if it was a face, was painted black. On the next lightning strike, he was gone. Gone like he'd never been there.

4

By eleven o'clock that morning Stud had not shown up, Kyle hadn't called, and I was wearing a path between the front and back doors. Periodically I stared into the trees at the rear of the house wondering whether my eyes had played tricks on me. The garish, black-painted face and outline of a half-nude man had been only a split-second glimpse at best. A figment of my overactive imagination? Maybe. But the body on Agate Bar wasn't.

I finally worked up enough courage to walk out the back door and down the stairs to get a better look at the tree line across the backyard. Sure as hell, there it was: a blackened scar on one of the century-old cottonwoods. Lightning had probably removed and then cauterized the massive limb. I felt foolish, just a little neurotic, and a lot relieved. The phone ringing off the wall in the kitchen pulled me back into the house.

"Phoebe—"

"Damnit it, Kyle," I said into the receiver. "This is a couple of hours?"

"Sorry about that. God, you're whispering a lot."

"I'm not whispering, I'm hoarse. That happens when I go without a good night's sleep. I had a real scare last night. I thought someone followed me back to the house after I left you."

"Shit."

"It was a tree, Kyle."

"Why do I believe that?" he asked. "But you do realize we had guys working that area all night? Sure it wasn't one of them?"

"He would have had to have been on his way to a black-masked ball, Kyle."

"What?"

"Look, it was dark and it had started to rain. It felt like someone was behind me, so I turned around and saw this guy on the path a few yards back."

"I thought you said it was a tree."

My mind tripped. I had seen the figure twice. Right before I fell. Another burned-out stump? Possibly.

"Phoebe, are you there?"

"I'm here, I was just thinking." I pushed the possibilities from my mind. "Anyway, my imagination gave wings to my feet and I took off running and dropped this stone fish that—"

"What stone fish?"

"This thing I found. It's on a silver chain. The chain looks new."

"Phoebe, meet me at McDonald's on Grand at noon. I might be a few minutes late, but wait."

"Sure you can afford it?"

"Don't bring the fish. Put it away somewhere. Let's keep that between us for now—"

"This cloak and dagger routine is wearing thin."

"Come on, Phoebe. The Queen of Cloak complaining? Noon, okay? And put those other two items with it."

"Kyle—" The line went dead.

McDonald's on Grand Avenue at noon is an agoraphobic's nightmare. I sat in the westbound lane and waited for ten minutes before I could make a left and pull into the parking lot. Kyle's Blazer wasn't among the Chevy Luvs or Datsun trucks that sat on oversized tires five feet off the ground. I pulled in between a white one with smiley face running lights and a black-and-red job that boasted a couple of hundred empty Rainier cans in the back. My 1949 Chevy truck was dwarfed and stood out like a bag lady on Rodeo Drive.

I walked toward the doors. A group of guys, obviously in rut, were standing in front of them, shoving, elbowing, and flexing for a couple of long-legged, short-skirted girls nearby. It's not that I don't like kids, but some men march to the tune of a different drummer, and some women don't hear the tick of their biological clocks. I'm one of them. I spotted the kid who would be trouble as I neared the door: a dark-haired guy with burnished skin, either Mexican or Indian, with spiked hair and a tail down the back.

"Hey, babe . . . Buy a guy a burger?" His hand reached out and barred the door at the same time I reached to push it open.

I stared him straight in the eyes and smiled. He did the same and puckered a little kiss my way. Laugher rolled through the group. It's hard to pin down what's so damn intimidating about kids that age. Maybe it's because they're so uninhibited. Anything goes and usually does. I felt my face flush.

"Louis, chill out." A high, nubile voice whined somewhere behind me.

"Good advice, Louis. You're just the man I was looking for. Maybe you'd like to buy a lady a burger." I turned and looked up at Kyle.

Louis visibly shrank.

Kyle grabbed one of the belt loops of Louis's jeans and led him toward the door. "Open the door and show her how polite you can be."

"Fuck," Louis mumbled as he pushed the door open. Kyle was pulling the loop up just enough that the kid had to walk on the tips of his toes. The group laughed again, but this time it was controlled, quieter, and coated with ill-at-ease respect.

I followed them as Kyle walked through another door that led outside to an area enclosed with a wrought-iron fence beside a big red caboose. He motioned to a still grumbling Louis to sit down at a white, laminated table. Louis sat.

"I love seeing law enforcement at work, and that snuggie hold is nothing short of brilliant. Glad to see you guys have been trained in testicle tactics," I whispered in Kyle's ear as he swung one leg over the opposite bench and sat down. He didn't respond.

"Where were you last night, Louis?" Kyle asked.

"Hanging out at home," Louis answered. The macho had returned. He glowered at Kyle.

"That's not what I hear, Louis. Have you heard from your buddy James? The way I got it, you were with him last night."

"James? No way, man."

"You've got about five seconds, Louis, and then I'm taking you down to the station and making a call."

"Shit!" Louis turned away disgustedly, shook his head, and then turned back to Kyle. "Maybe I saw him. Why?"

"Where?"

"Around."

"Around where, Louis?"

"A party. On the street. In my dreams, man. Why the hell are you shaking me down about James?"

"James was swimming in the river late last night."

"That's a real fuckin' crime. You personally bust him, or was it a sting operation?" Louis leaned across the table and smiled at Kyle.

Kyle's hand slammed down on the table so fast and so hard that both Louis and I came a foot off the bench.

"The crime, Louis . . ." Kyle began, his voice low. He drew out each word as he braced himself on the table and leaned down over the cowering kid and continued, "was that someone tied his hands behind his back, put the muzzle of a twenty-two at the back of his head, and scrambled his goddamned brains. That's how James went swimming. Now where and when did you see him?"

I watched the bluff and the tough seep out of Louis. His eyes filled with tears as he lowered himself to the bench and looked away from us. With a quick swipe of his hand, Louis wiped the tears from his cheeks and stared off into the distance.

"Come on, Louis. Help me on this one. I liked James."

"Sure, man." Louis looked toward Kyle, pain running down his face. He sniffed. "You like all of us. Right?"

"Cut the shit and just tell me where you saw him."

Louis glanced at me, noticeably embarrassed over the tears. "At a party. Up at Pryor. I'd gone up there with Genevieve. She had some people to see, and I told her I'd get a ride back to town. James was there, and I hitched a ride in with him."

"What time did you come back to town?"

"Before midnight. A couple of other guys rode down with us. One was a guy from Crow I've seen around. The other one I didn't know. We let them off on Montana. James dropped me off at home."

"What did James have to say? Did he talk about meeting anyone later? Was he working any deals?"

"Man, you know James. He always had something going. He'd been real down about Matthew Wolf. He said he knew something, something maybe that would help."

"Did he say what it was?" Kyle's voice softened.

"No. He'd been drinking. I figured he was just bullshitting me. He—"Louis stopped. You could see his mind working behind his eyes. He shook his head, trying to dislodge the thought, and looked away.

"What?" Kyle coaxed.

"Nothing, just some weird shit."

"Look, I *did* like James, and I don't give a damn whether you buy that or not. If you've got anything, give it to me." Kyle reached over and grasped Louis's arm. Louis shook it off. Something flashed through his eyes and disappeared behind a deep brown sadness.

"He had some things. Old things."

"Like what?" Kyle asked.

"Stuff. Relics. I don't know what you'd call them. He showed them to me when we got to the house. Said he knew who wanted them, wanted them bad enough to do Monday, and that Matthew would be able to get out of jail. He just kept grinning at me like some fool."

"I need to know what those things were. He may have been right. It might help Matthew."

"It was crap. Probably fakes. Nothing worth shit."

"Let me decide that."

"Beadwork. That kind of stuff. A couple of pipes in bags and . . ." Louis paused. "I don't remember all of it. Wait. A fish. Yeah. A stone fish."

"Fish?" I asked. Kyle shot me a keep-the-hell-out-of-this look.

"It was about this big and had a hole in its eye." Louis held up his thumb and index finger and spread them apart. "It was made out of soapstone. I tried to buy it off him, and he laughed. Said it was a fetish and worth a bundle."

"What was he going to do with them?"

"I don't know. But he wouldn't sell it. You know Genevieve loves that stuff. I thought I'd give it to her. Does she know about James?"

"I just left her. She knows."

"I gotta get back to school, man. We've got three days left and I don't want to blow it." Louis looked through the fence at the honking Chevy Luv and stood up.

Kyle nodded toward the truck. Louis left without saying anything else.

"You could have dropped that bomb on him a little easier," I said.

"He didn't have any preparation this way. Two or three hours to think about it and he wouldn't have told me a damn thing. Let's get out of here. I've got someone for you to meet."

5

Berman Towers rises twenty-six stories above the Yellowstone Valley and lays claim to a prime chunk of real estate in the middle of Homestead Park. On certain days, bronze-tinted windows create a sepia-toned parallel universe when cumulus clouds sail like puffs of cauliflower across the summer sky. It was one of those days and one of those skies.

Never one for heights, I felt my stomach knot up and my head start to spin as we stepped into the elevator that runs up the outside of the building. It rose swiftly, cutting through the bronze clouds that sailed all around us. Kyle took one look at me pressed up against one of the glass walls and laughed.

"You won't think this is so funny when I puke on your shoes," I said as my mouth filled with saliva.

"You're right. I won't," he answered just as the elevator stopped.

The stainless steel door slid silently open. We stepped out into a wide hallway with carpet so plush you could lose your shoes in it. Kyle reached out and guided me to the inside of the hallway. The air was clean. Too clean. The kind of air that you know is used and filtered over and over again just to get someone else's breath out of it. It just didn't smell like real air.

"Don't look out the windows and you'll never know how high we are," Kyle said.

"Right," I answered as I took a deep breath and wondered who had breathed that air last.

"Here we are." Kyle stopped in front of two heavily carved doors, turned the knob on one of them, opened the door, and ushered me in.

There was a brass plaque on the door. Genevieve Cramer, Ph.D. Class stuff. The reception area was impressive and smelled faintly of vanilla. The walls were off-white and covered with exquisite prints by some of the best Native American artists. I recognized a couple: Kevin Red Star, a local talent and a Crow who'd achieved international fame, and Rabbit, a Cherokee from Oklahoma. Money lived here. Who the hell was Genevieve Cramer, Ph.D.?

Kyle walked to another set of double doors and knocked. They opened almost immediately. I'm seldom taken by surprise, but I found myself staring. She was tall, at least five foot nine or ten, and had hair as black as coal that hung down almost to the scarf that encircled her waist. A long, floral-printed skirt, a simple pair of leather sandals, and a white cotton shirt were all she wore. Silver earrings dangled from each ear, still not reaching far enough down her swanlike neck to touch her shoulder. What caught me most were her eyes and her smile. Both sparkled as she reached her hand toward me.

"I'm Genevieve. I've heard so much about you from Kyle that I feel like we're already friends." She shook my hand and turned toward Kyle. "Did you find Louis?"

"Sure did. He was right where you said he'd be. I need to use your phone and let dispatch know where I am."

"Go on in. I'll grab us all a cup of coffee. My secretary took the afternoon off, so I didn't schedule any appointments. We won't be interrupted. Do you take it black?" she asked as she smiled at me.

"Fine. You're Louis's sister?"

"No. I'm not. I'm more like his watchdog. That's probably nicer than Louis would put it. He had a few problems in school in Pryor, so we worked out a deal with his parents and he's not doing too bad down here. What'd he have to say for himself?"

"Not much. It started out a little rough."

"Louis give you a bad time? Don't take him seriously," she said as she handed me a mug of hot coffee. "He's really one of the good guys. He graduates this year. Steady three-point-eight on his grades. Smart kid."

My mouth dropped open. She laughed and nodded in the affirmative. "He's interested in medicine. There's Indian money out there that can do a lot for him. That's how I went through school. It took me a while to decide what I wanted to be when I grew up." She waved her hand around the room. "I haven't done too bad. I did a couple of years in Indian Health Services, but I loved it. It pays off in the end."

She was right. It had paid off. I couldn't remember when I had been in classier surroundings. I knew Kyle wasn't married, never had been, and I hadn't noticed a ring on her left hand. I wondered if they were lovers and hated the twinge of jealousy I felt. It surprised me. I looked around the room and asked a couple of mundane questions concerning the artwork, which she politely answered. When I turned I saw a light smile on her face, and an intense curiosity in her eyes. We stood there for a moment and said nothing.

Finally, with great forethought, I surpassed even my own intellectual savvy and asked, "What do you do?" I raised the mug to my lips and missed. Coffee ran down my chin and soaked into my shirt. She tried not to smile and handed me a Kleenex.

"I'm a psychologist. Like I told you, it took me some time to make up my mind. I originally wanted to become an archaeologist. Those were three of my best years. Then I got interested in law and thought I'd be a prosecutor and stick a lot of white-collar criminals behind bars."

"What changed your mind?"

"It was soooo boring." She laughed again and flashed her white smile. I wondered if she used that oxygen toothpaste crap you could buy at Kmart.

"You like what you're doing?"

"Usually. Now I deal exclusively with white-collar dysfunction. Most of my patients are yuppie women. They wear the latest fashions from Santa Fe and ski Taos in the winter. They like coming to me. Their reasoning may be wrong in the beginning, but I think in the end I do something for them. At least that's what they tell me."

I followed her as she walked back toward the office. Kyle was just hanging up the phone. "I gave them this number. Okay?"

She handed him the extra mug of coffee she was holding and gave him a you-know-better-than-to-ask look. "Sit down, both of you. I'm anxious to hear what Louis had to say."

Kyle relayed the conversation to her as she sat behind her desk watching him intently.

"He was telling you the truth. I did take him to Pryor last night, and he did get home before me." She furrowed her brow and looked at me. "You might be interested, Phoebe, that I was in Pryor to talk with Matthew Wolf's family. They told me they had retained you."

"I'm still not convinced that they need a private investigator." I turned toward Kyle. "What I do need is the name of the public defender they gave Matthew."

"Randall Brigham III."

"Luck of the draw," I answered. "Eager. Very eager, but new. I've met him."

"What she's trying to say is that he doesn't even shave yet. Right?" Kyle laughed.

"Something like that. So, Monday's missing. James Eagle is dead. And everyone, including this German, seems to have an interest in a bunch of artifacts—"

Genevieve interrupted. "There's more to this than a bunch of artifacts, as you call them. I told you that I considered going into archaeology. Well, those three years led me into a lot of situations. I met a lot of people and saw a lot of scams."

"Really? How so?"

"There's so little left of our culture. Every tribe in North America has been ripped off for three centuries. There are more Indian artifacts in Germany than almost anyplace else in the world, and what isn't there is spread out in museums and private collections. We're hot stuff. Now more than ever."

"Why do I get the feeling this is going to tie in with Monday Brown?"

"It does," Kyle answered.

"I've been doing a little research on Monday myself. He was as much a part of the reservation as I was. He married a Crow woman and built a house on her land, raised his kid on the res, and sent them to school in Pryor," Genevieve said.

Kyle nodded. "I think the general consensus was that everyone looked at him like just another white man who loved to wear buckskins, fringed leather jackets, wide-brimmed hats, and beaded headbands. He was quite a character. The ultimate wanna-be. Hell, the tourists used to take pictures of him."

"But people heard things. Maybe people always heard them and sloughed them off," Genevieve said and looked sullen.

"What she's trying to say is that he was an asshole." Kyle grinned.

"He hung on to the bar his dad had run down on Montana Avenue. It's been closed for years, but it would have made the Arcade look like the country club." Genevieve shook her head in disgust. "He sold booze over the bar and out the back door. Sometimes he just gave it away. But he always called in his chips."

"How?" I leaned forward in my chair.

"They, the Indians that frequented his place, brought him things. Family things. Just like they did for his daddy. Things that were worth a small fortune to the right buyer. He stockpiled, again, like his daddy. Sold some off. Traded for other items, and made a bundle. But he got greedy."

Kyle turned toward me. "Monday started robbing graves. I doubt that he missed a reservation in the state. What he couldn't con, or buy, or booze away from somebody, he dug up."

"Shit." I sat back in my chair. "Do you guys know what you're saying? You've fingered someone Indian. The motive would be there. Someone had a stomach full of Monday and took him out."

"That someone was probably *not* Matthew Wolf. I'd bet my life on it." Genevieve picked up a pencil from the desk, tapped it a few times, and threw it down. "Two days a week I still work for Indian Health. I spread it out over the state. I fly up north to Rocky Boy, Flathead, Fort Peck, wherever. There were rumblings."

"Rumblings about what?"

"About Monday. He'd been bragging that he had the *mother lode* of all *mother lodes*. He got his hands on something—"

"Or," Kyle said, "he had it all along and just decided to go public with it."

"What the hell would be worth killing him over? Beadwork? Scalp-lock bags and finger-bone necklaces?" They both looked at me at the same time with the same look. It made me feel very, very white. I moved around in my chair. Genevieve looked horrified. "Maybe I'm missing the point here."

Kyle recovered first. "Phoebe, let's start with the monetary value and work our way up. The German guy that's in town has been waving a receipt around for almost half a mil. What does that tell you? You could double that price."

"Or triple it," Genevieve added.

"We could speculate all day. The point I'm making is that both sides of the fence are pretty attractive."

"What's on the other side?"

"The Indian side. Let her tell you."

"Phoebe, I've got some buttons that are pushed real easy. I apologize for overreacting."

"No apologies necessary. I just don't see where any of this is going. I agreed to look into things for John Wolf. I like the guy. But hour by hour this gets heavier. No one knows whether Monday is dead or what, and now we've got a real corpse. I've got a finger-bone necklace, and"—I tried not to shudder—"a scalp-lock bag that could or could not be stolen property."

"Kyle told me you lost a couple of brothers and your dad." She leaned forward and watched for a reaction.

Again I squirmed in my chair. I don't do death well. I never have. I looked at Kyle and back at Genevieve.

"Are they buried here?"

"I don't see what this—" My body tensed.

"Are they?" she asked.

"Yes. They are."

"Let me set up a little scenario for you. Say you decide to pay some respects at the grave site. Flowers and all that. When you get there, it's been dug up. The body, or what's left of it, has been stripped. No clothes. And no skull."

"Jesus Christ. This is ridiculous." I turned sideways in my chair, crossed my legs, and looked at Kyle.

"Did any of your family put anything into the coffin? Just a little something, a rosary maybe? How about a police shield? Wasn't one of them a cop?"

"Both my brother and my dad, but what the hell—"

"Picture this. The rosary is gone, the shields, rings, everything, except for the torso, and that's been pretty ravaged by the elements," Genevieve said as she leaned back in her chair and watched me.

My thoat constricted. The point she was driving home was damn ugly. Repulsive.

"Phoebe, take what you're feeling right now and multiply it by about three hundred years and several thousand people and you might, just might, come close to what Indian people feel."

Kyle reached across the short distance between us and gently touched my arm. I put the cup of coffee to my lips and took a drink to keep down the lump that was forming in my throat. It swallowed hard.

"But we're talking about finger bones and scalps for Christ's sake.

I don't see those hanging on jewelry racks at Target. I gotta tell you they seem damn barbaric."

"Are you Catholic?" Genevieve asked.

"Recovering."

"Did you ever take communion?" she continued.

"Sure, but—"

"Body of Christ? Blood of Christ? That didn't strike you as a little cannibalistic?"

"Symbolism. Simple symbolism."

"But, Phoebe"—Genevieve's eyes sparkled—"one of the mysteries of the Mass is that mystically, magically those wafers and that wine really do turn into the body and the blood. Natives in New Guinea ate their enemies so that their enemies' courage and power could live in them. It all ties in."

I shook my head. She was right.

"When I did my archaeology stint, I saw box upon box of skulls and remains in basements of museums all over the country. They took measurements and tossed them aside when they were through. I even saw one made into an ashtray in the study of one of my professors."

"Shit," I said.

"Last year, the Smithsonian agreed to return all remains they had to the Tribes if the Tribes could identify them and prove they belonged to them."

"It doesn't take much to figure out what those odds are." Kyle laughed snidely.

I unfolded my body and straightened up in my chair. "So, where does all this go from here?" I asked.

"The rumblings I heard hinted that Monday had more than your everyday artifacts. I've been trying to pin it down. It's hard. But I'll find out. Eventually." Genevieve also relaxed. "In the meantime, if we don't find out where Monday is, dead or alive, there could be a bloodbath."

"How so?"

"Monday loved to pit people—traders, collectors, and particularly Indian people—against each other. He'd been doing that between the Crow and the Cheyenne for the last year. He loved to brag himself up and say that he caused and won more pissin' wars than anyone else."

"Great term."

"Pissin' wars are what the traders and collectors get into when

they're dealing. It can get down and dirty. Believe me. I've witnessed
it."

"Where does the bloodbath come in?" I asked.

"Monday was stringing a lot of people along. He gave little hints
about what this mother lode was. He loved hinting that people out of
the country were interested, which drove the Indians and American
traders crazy. Those days of Indian people sitting back and letting
this shit happen are over. We've already got the German in the picture. One Crow kid is dead, and another one is in jail. If what I heard
is true, it could get ugly."

"Let's nail down just what you heard."

"There was a Cheyenne chief named Rain in the Face. There is
no known picture of him in existence. Thomas Flying was another
Cheyenne chief. He was at the Little Bighorn the day Custer got his.
Thomas Flying there are pictures of. I've got a book with one of him
in full regalia." Her eyes lit up. "Incredible warbonnet, war shirt,
leggins with weasel tails trailing down them. Powerful, heavy medicine, and priceless. There are other things. Medicine bundles. Important medicine bundles."

"Word has it that Monday said he not only had the only picture
of Rain in the Face but everything Thomas Flying was wearing the
day they captured him on film." Kyle was watching Genevieve as he
spoke.

"The Cheyenne have already gotten wind of Monday disappearing, and about Matthew being a prime suspect. If they figure the
Crows have Monday's mother lode, they are going to want it back,
any way they can get it."

"Ancient enemies and all that crap," Kyle said. "It's always been
damn strained. We've got two tribes that look for reasons to kick the
shit out of each other, a German buyer in town, and God only knows
how many traders out there wondering how they can get their hands
on the stash."

My head was swimming. "I'm on overload. I have to get home.
Roger is probably doing some work out at the house as we speak. I
agreed to an afternoon jog," I said, grinned uncomfortably, and
looked at my watch. Roger was right. I should have stayed out of
this. All I wanted was to get out of there, with or without Kyle.

"I can't give you answers, but I can open some doors for you."
Genevieve leaned forward and smiled at me. "If you can spare some

time within the next couple of days, I'd like to come over and talk. I guess what I'm saying is that I'd like to help. You'll need someone who knows their way around the Indian people. Would you mind?"

"Why not?" I shrugged. "I'll give you a call."

The phone rang. Genevieve answered it and handed it to Kyle. "It's for you."

It was a short conversation. Nothing showed on his face. Only a long string of uh huh's came out of his mouth. He handed the phone back to Genevieve. She looked at him quizzically.

"Trouble?"

He turned toward me. Only then did I see the look in his eyes. That little voice inside my head told me I didn't want him to say anything.

"Phoebe, John Wolf called nine one one from your house. Someone ransacked the place."

I stiffened.

"They took Roger to St. Vincent's."

"St. Vincent's? Is he okay?"

"Roughed up. That's all I know."

"Jesus." Genevieve's voice floated in from somewhere, vague and distant. "Here we go."

"There was another person. A guy."

"Who?" I asked. My voice was trembling.

"They don't know. Or at least they didn't say. He was hanging from a cottonwood in your backyard," Kyle said and shook his head.

"You've got to be kidding."

Kyle took a deep breath. "Phoebe?"

"Goddamnit, spit it out." I knew I was rising out of my chair.

"His face was painted black."

6

A girl never forgets her first time, and this was definitely one of those *first times:* a body hanging from the cottonwood in my backyard. I watched the distant image appear and disappear through windows in the tangle of wild rosebushes and gnarled trees that flanked the road.

I could smell the heat of the day, taste the dust from the road as gray plumes rose behind Kyle's patrol car, and feel the spit in my mouth dry up. Death was no stranger in my life, but now it had invaded my space, my sanctuary. The tree and the body disappeared from sight as we turned into the drive.

Two uniformed deputies stood stiffly just past the open gate. Lengths of yellow plastic crime-scene tape had already been stretched around the perimeter of my yard. Several men were fanning out, walking slowly, looking down at the ground. Probing, searching each square inch of the outlying grounds. Kyle pulled up behind a blue and white and parked. We got out.

"We're not supposed to let anyone back there, Wolf. The women will have to wait outside the line. No newspaper people . . ." The younger of the two deputies stepped forward as we approached. "We've got to maintain the integrity of the crime scene."

Nothing is stiffer than new Levi's or a rookie cop.

"She lives here." Kyle placed his hand in the middle of my back and ushered me past the deputy. "And she's with me." He nodded toward Genevieve.

We followed the brick walk that led toward the rear of the house. A slight breeze carried the richness of the forest and the fishy scent of the Yellowstone on its back. It was picture-book perfect, normal looking, but it felt like death and I felt invaded.

No less than five patrol cars and a van I knew belonged to the coroner's office were parked wherever the hell they felt like parking. Roger's BMW hugged the curve by the front porch. The door on the driver's side was wide open. I could see his briefcase and topcoat thrown on the far seat.

"Unbelievable," I said as we rounded the back of the house. "I paid the paperboy and haven't insulted anyone for weeks. This isn't your idea of some joke housewarming, is it, Kyle? You can get in a lot of trouble for diverting city money for this crap."

He didn't answer.

"Innovative bird feeder. Wonder what they were trying to call in?"

The disembodied voice came from a group assembled around the grotesque male body suspended a foot above the ground. Nervous laughter rolled through the men and waned. This wasn't my idea of a night at the Improv, but I did understand far too well the necessity of gallows humor. A flash from a camera splashed cold off the dead man's clay-colored skin in the noon heat. The weighted body swayed and turned toward me.

"Christ. Someone grab hold and steady him, will ya?" Doc's voice.

Only then did the crowd move back from the base of the cottonwood. I've always entertained a theory that the majority of people think death is catching. I edged closer and watched as Clint Beemer reached over and held the lifeless legs. The stark white of the surgical gloves he wore stood out in sharp contrast as his hands curled around the lean muscles of the corpse's calves.

"I've got it," he said in a flat monotone.

The flash spilled up the body this time, bathing it quickly and efficiently as Doc Joss, the county coroner, casually called orders out to the police photographer.

"All right, all right. One more. Anterior, full length. That's it," he said as a slight Scottish brogue rolled his r's. "Now, let's take this kid down. Spread that sheet out below him."

Kid? I looked up. It was hard to tell. A raccoonish black mask ran from ear to ear halfway up his forehead and followed the contour of his high cheekbones. Even with the macabre mask there was an odd sense of serenity. I'd found someone hanging once, a woman, and the expression was anything but serene. Doc was right. It was a kid, or at least a very young adult. He couldn't have been much past eighteen. Twenty at the outside.

I jumped when Kyle placed his hand on my shoulder. "Recognize him?" he asked.

"No."

I glanced at Genevieve. She moved closer as they lowered the body to the ground. Her expression was steel. Small muscles twitched on the side of her face as they responded to her clenched teeth.

"Christ," I muttered under my breath. "Let's find out what they've come up with."

Doc Joss was on the ground, kneeling beside the body. He had rolled the corpse up on his side and was sliding his hand over his back. I could see the plastic sterile sheet that would in moments become a shroud glisten in the sun. Kyle knelt beside Doc just as he eased the body back down.

"Hell, Doc. We should be fishing."

"You got that right," Doc answered absentmindedly as he stood and stripped off his gloves.

"Any guesses? Kid looks like he was big enough to put up a fight. Seems a little odd he'd end up hanged. Not the usual scenario for a homicide." Kyle rose beside the gray-haired coroner.

"Usually never. But this one definitely isn't a suicide. And as for his size, it's tough to defend yourself when someone comes at you from behind."

"What do you mean, Doc?"

"He's got about five nasty-looking puncture wounds underneath his left clavicle. Thought at first they might be small caliber. I can't rule that out yet, but they're a little smoother than I'd expect. One looks torn, more like—" Doc lifted his hand, clenched his fist, and made long slashing motions into the air in front of Kyle—"stabbing. Looks deep too. Had some powerful thrust behind them. I might be able to determine the height of the person who decided to ventilate this guy. It depends on the angle." He talked more to himself than to Kyle.

"He didn't die from hanging? Is that what you're saying?"

"At this point? Nope. I don't think so. I'd put my money on those holes. Could be wrong. But," he said as he turned and smiled at Kyle, "I'm rarely, if ever wrong. We all know that, don't we?"

Kyle nodded in agreement.

"Let's get him in the van and out of here," Doc said.

We all stepped back as two attendants brought in a stretcher. I probably stepped back the farthest. There are two sounds that drive me up the wall. The first is the sound of fingernails scraping across a blackboard. The second is the zipper on a body bag after it receives the dead.

Kyle steered Doc Joss toward the side of the house. Genevieve had been so silent I almost forgot she was there. I looked for her and didn't see her. I couldn't blame her for disappearing.

"Are you going to be involved on this one, Wolf?" Doc asked.

"More than likely. How the hell do you think he ended up in that tree?"

"Beats me. That's up to you boys. Get in touch tomorrow. I should have something then," he said as he stood and wiped the sweat from his brow. "Can't take this heat."

No wonder. He worked in the morgue. We all stepped back as they rolled the stretcher past us. Doc Joss fell in line behind the clicking wheels as they wobbled over the brick walk. I followed for a ways and stopped when I heard voices coming from inside the house. I bolted toward the front door and entered. Where the hell had my mind been? Of course they'd be in the house. Home sweet home had become a crime scene.

John Wolf was sitting on the couch in the living room cradling his head in his hands. A plainclothes detective looked up as I entered.

"If you don't have any business in here, you'll have to leave." He was clipped and insolent.

Calmly I said, "I live here."

John Wolf looked up. "Hell, I'm sorry about this, Miss Siegel. I was bringing your cat home, and the front door was open. I was going to just scoot him in and close the door, but I saw this guy on the floor and—"

"Right." The detective said cynically and then looked toward me. "Did you expect this guy?"

"Yes. I did. What happened, John?"

"Just like I said. The door was open. I could see feet as I walked in. I thought he was dead. I dialed nine one one. It's that simple."

"Uh huh." The detective wrote in a black leather spiral notebook. "He's got a kid in jail. Murder suspect. How simple can it be?"

"I told you I was expecting Mr. Wolf." As soon as I said it I realized that he never gave me a specific time. It unnerved me a little. All the dreaded what-ifs ran through my mind. But I let my gut make the decision.

"You're sure about that?"

"I said it, didn't I?"

"Wolf, you want to talk to him?" The detective's face stiffened. "Hey," he said, as he looked between John and Kyle. "Wolf. You two related?"

I turned and saw Kyle standing near the doorway. Genevieve was beside him.

"Fact is, we are." Kyle pulled a toothpick from his shirt pocket and placed it at the corner of his mouth. "You've probably got everything. Go on out and see if they've come up with something around the yard." Kyle stepped aside and motioned him out of the house.

"Where were you?" Kyle looked toward Genevieve.

"I couldn't take it out there, so I went in search of some water to splash on my face," she answered. "Hope you don't mind, Phoebe." Genevieve smiled toward me.

"No problem," I said.

She went to John Wolf and sat down on the couch beside him. "Rough times, John. Did you hear about James Eagle?"

"This morning. Bad. Real bad. I was thankful Matthew was in jail or they'd have him on that too."

"This might just pop him loose." Kyle leaned against the wall and maneuvered the toothpick from the left side of his mouth to the right.

"Any chance of that?" I asked.

"Maybe. Monday is missing, and we've got two dead kids. Seems to me that Matthew could be in more danger than trouble. I'll talk to the county attorney and see what he thinks. Then again, it might be wiser to keep him where he is."

"Kyle," I said, "didn't Louis mention a guy that was with James Eagle when they came down from Pryor the other night?"

"He sure as hell did." He tapped his temple with his index finger. "I was thinking the same thing. He said he'd seen him around but didn't know his name." Kyle straightened up. "Phoebe, if you could give Genevieve a ride to her office in Roger's car, I think I'd like to go down and see if Matthew can ID this guy. They'll probably want to talk with you before you take off."

"Kyle?" Genevieve looked up, her arm protectively around John's back. "Does John need to stick around here?"

"I don't think so, but let me check." Kyle walked out of the house.

"John, I feel like I owe you an apology or something. It's usually so damn quiet around here I just sit and listen to myself breathe."

He brought his long, lanky body up from the couch and shrugged. "I hope that . . . what was his name? The guy on the floor?"

"Roger."

"I sure hope he's all right."

"He's an attorney. He's got a hard head. I'm sure he'll be fine." But I wasn't sure of anything.

7

For the next two hours I answered an unending barrage of questions from the cops. No, I hadn't noticed anything strange when I left that morning. No, I did not notice a body hanging in my tree. That one really pissed me off. Like I wouldn't notice? No, I had no idea of who, what, where, or when. And no, I didn't mention the night before, the items that John Wolf had given me, the ghostly shape illuminated by the slash of lightning that had reached for me, or the black mask it wore.

I did blame the empty white bags from Kentucky Fried Chicken that Roger and I had eaten out of the night before on the perp or perps. What would it have served admitting to being a lousy housekeeper? They did insist that I cover the house and see if anything was missing. It wasn't. Begging off to use the bathroom, I hurried upstairs, put the toilet lid down, and climbed up on the toilet. The joy of antiquated plumbing had given me the perfect place to stash the items: in the oak water tank anchored above the toilet. I stretched and reached my hand down into the cold water. I could feel the Ziploc bag floating near the top. Not even Roger had known where I had hidden them.

You go through a crazy process when you've been invaded. Whether they take anything or not, they leave a lousy feeling, a slug trail of vulnerability behind.

Neither Genevieve nor I had a lot to say on our trip back into town. I dropped her off at her office with a vague and slightly insincere promise to call her later that evening and declined her offer to sleep over at her place. She intrigued me, I just wasn't sure why. Of course it had nothing to do with the fact that she was tall, imperious as hell, and gorgeous on top of it. Nor did it have anything to do with my vague assumption, tinged with an irrational jealousy, that she was probably sleeping with Kyle.

Even so, life is simple in Montana. If stress is your game, you have to work hard to create your own. There's a pace here, set by some internal clock that slows things down and keeps the simplicity at an appreciable level. There is, however, one exception. The dreaded Medical Corridor, a sprawling hospital complex made up of blocks of buildings and luxurious sky bridges known as the Deaconess. Its voracious appetite had consumed streets and homes and in their place laid down asphalt parking lots to rival Wal-Mart, all of which was done "to better serve the needs of the community." One would assume that to serve these needs there would have been one fucking parking spot within a two-block area.

By the time I stepped into the stainless steel elevator, punched a button, and leaned back against the wall as it surged upward, my mood was anything but good. I stepped out onto the medical floor and found out that I had not only taken the wrong elevator but couldn't find anyone to direct me toward my destination. It took another ten minutes before I found Roger on the edge of the bed, reading a copy of *The Wall Street Journal*.

Physically, he seemed fine. His mood left a lot to be desired. The doctor had insisted that he stay in for at least one night, possibly two, for observation. At least he was alive. My stomach knotted, realizing the scales could have tipped the other direction.

He remembered walking though the front door. That was it. The next thing he knew he was being loaded into the back of an ambulance. Roger does a lot of body language. Most of it is done with his forehead. When he raises his right eyebrow, he's skeptical. His left means he agrees or yes. When a furrow as deep as the Grand Canyon forms above the bridge of his nose it's flat out disapproval. But the one I hate the most is when he arches both eyebrows. It's his I-told-you-so declaration, and he relishes it. A smooth forehead and a penetrating stare I interpret as his try-to-convince-me-if-you-can statement.

"Are you okay?"

His left eyebrow raised.

"Good. Have you given a statement to the cops?"

Left eyebrow again.

"Look, Roger, you've got every reason to be pissed off, but not at me."

Smooth forehead, penetrating stare.

I don't do innocent well, but I gave it my best shot. With my index finger appropriately pointed into my chest, eyes wide, and a barely discernible gasp, I said, "How could you possibly think I had anything to do with this, Roger? I'm as much a victim as you are."

Nothing prepared me for the spasms that played leapfrog on his forehead. I swear to God it was the most garbled conversation, silent though it may have been, I had ever had with him. For a moment I thought it was some weird seizure caused from the blow to his head. I reached for the call button. Roger grabbed my hand. For a good forty-five seconds he made me squirm with his smooth forehead and penetrating stare. At least he was calming down.

"Last night," he said slowly, enunciating each word, "I begged you to call the cops, to turn that stuff over to them. Knowing you like I do, I would bet a year's salary that you still haven't told the police that you have received possible stolen property and have it at your house. Am I right?"

I have a technique that I use when Roger attempts to compromise my position or foolishly tries to intimidate me. It comes from the days when we were intimate. I visualize him at his most vulnerable, in the throes of passion. The high throes. The peak of, when he would utter those memorable words of climactic proportion: "Oh God, oh God, ooh, ooh, ooh, oh God, fuck." What can I say, it works.

I suppressed a smile and said nothing.

"Let me approach this a different way. If you had walked in that house instead of me, chances are you would be"—his voice quivered—"dead. Look, I know things have changed between us, and, believe it or not, I'm okay with the changes. But the relationship is still important to me, Phoebe. I care about you. I can't imagine life without you."

All of my guilt files, of which I have many, popped open. I tried the "Oh God, ooh, ooh" again. This time it didn't work. Roger had been through a really rough time with me about a year ago and almost didn't come out alive. Now here he was, hospitalized. Injured. I hated it.

I got out of the chair I was sitting in, walked over to the bed, and kissed him on his forehead.

"I've got to go. There were still cops all over the place when I left. Get some rest, and I'll give you a call later."

"You're not staying at the house, are you?"

"Where else? No one would be dumb enough to come back around tonight," I said without much conviction and turned to leave.

There were still two cop cars parked in the drive when I pulled in. I didn't like the idea of strangers free-roaming my property. I also didn't like the idea of spending the night alone. But my options were limited. My mother's place was out of the question. She'd hear about this soon enough or already had, and God only knew it would mean an increase in her Verelan dosage or her blood pressure would hit new heights. More guilt I didn't need. That left the couch at my sister's place, which was equally unappealing.

I got out of the car and walked toward the porch just as Clint Beemer and his partner rounded the edge of the house.

"Hey, Siegel. You just missed Wolf, he brought your truck back. Said to tell you he'd be back by later. I hear you haven't been in this place that long."

"True, Clint. Quite a housewarming, isn't it?"

"Me? I would have gotten you a door knocker. You got any ideas on this yet?"

"Not one. But I'm glad you're still here. Could I talk to you a minute?" I reached out, touched his arm, and ushered him toward the porch.

He sat down in one of the oversized wicker chairs, took his hat off, and placed it on his lap.

"What's on your mind?" he asked as he ran his hands through his hair.

I sat down on the chaise across from him and listened internally to the snapping in my neck as I rolled my head in a full circle.

"I heard you and the Eagle kid had a run-in down at the Arcade."

"Depends on what you call a run-in. They were pretty drunked up. Monday had worked those boys over pretty good. I just wanted to get them the hell out of the vicinity before anything real tough happened. The Eagle kid decided to push his luck, and I used what force was necessary to bring him under control. End of story. Don't buy into that bullshit story that's circulating about me pulling a modified Rodney King on those kids. It just didn't happen like that."

"Had you seen them hanging around down there before?"

Clint didn't answer right away but gazed past me.

"Come to think of it, no. Not before that night. At least not on my shift."

The Arcade Bar almost always guaranteed a Saturday night shooting or knife fight. Frequented by only the meanest, toughest clientele, the Arcade was to Billings what the Sun Dance was to the Sioux, with a couple of modern twists. Visions came at two dollars a shot, and death was always a possibility.

"Want me to check it out?"

"No thanks," I said. I didn't want to owe any favors to Beemer. "Are you guys through?"

"Just wrapping it up." Clint stood, waved his partner on, and started down the stairs toward his car. "Are you staying out here tonight?"

I was getting a little tired of the question. "Yeah. I am."

"I'd lock up tight then. Some of the guys followed a trail down through that underbrush. Lots of fresh breaks. Had some activity in there of some kind. The rain washed out any prints we could have gotten." He got to his car, opened the door, looked back toward me, and said, "Watch yourself."

"Thanks." I watched them both back down the drive.

Just as Beemer's car disappeared into the distance, something rustled in the bushes beside the house. I stood perfectly still, listening. It came again. From the corner of the porch I could see the leaves on the bushes tremble. I backed up wondering whether the front door or Roger's car was my best bet. My hand reached out blindly seeking the porch rail and struck an empty brass planter. It crashed to the floor just as Stud leaped up from the bushes and strutted onto the porch. He did a figure eight through my legs, his engine running. It was going to be a very long night.

8

*I*t took forty-five minutes to take what was usually a fifteen-minute shower. Under the circumstances, who wouldn't have imagined a certain Hitchcock character with an Oedipus complex standing outside the shower curtain in drag, wielding a megapiece of fine German cutlery just waiting for me to get soap in my eyes? I was smarter than that. I soaped and rinsed with my eyes open. The trick was to keep the pulsating shower massage from pounding my retinas to the back of my brain. Retinas weren't the only thing I was trying to keep off my mind.

I dried off and pulled on a pair of Levi's cutoffs and a T-shirt with IT'S GOOD TO BE QUEEN emblazoned across the front. With a pair of Birkenstocks adorning my queenly feet and a handle on my paranoia, I headed downstairs. Within minutes I had a tall glass of lemonade in my hand, a bad case of mental fatigue, and a week's worth of newspapers under my arm.

What a day. I'd taken care of the obligatory calls to my family during which I vainly attempted to quell their fears. It did nothing to minimize my own misgivings about the Wolf case. My brother Michael, a local priest, said he would pray for me. Great comfort. And my mother was right behind him. Between her committing herself to an overkill of novenas and demanding that I move home, I slipped in enough blocks of silence to get the message across that I was staying put. My sister, Kehly, was a different story altogether.

"I'm not surprised, Fee," she chided. "Just don't involve me in any way, shape, or form. Understood?"

Jeez. Some people just can't let go of the past. Granted, her fears were somewhat founded. I'd been involved in a case last year, and

Kehly had been kidnapped, drugged, and come damn close to being recycled. Bottom line? She survived. But by God, she was going to get as much mileage out of it as she could.

The phone rang off the hook with calls from the curious and the misguided, which included the local paper and one soulful condemnation from a man, billing himself as God's Messenger in Montana, ranting that I had called the devil to my home. After that one, I took the phone off the hook.

There were several newspaper articles relating to the disappearance of Monday, most of them speculative. The most intriguing was the first: the body that had fallen across the hood of the car. The disappearance of Monday made the front page, twice. Subsequent articles became smaller and ended up a paragraph or two at the back of *The Gazette*. That is, until Matthew Wolf's arrest.

Sharon Mills, a barmaid at the Outlaw, was stopped at the light on the corner of Twenty-seventh Street South and Montana Avenue around 2:30 A.M. when a man stumbled from the shadows and crawled across her hood, anchoring himself by clutching a windshield wiper. It amazed me that witnesses to crimes lost their anonymity to the ignorance of well-meaning reporters. She wouldn't be hard to find. By anyone.

I clipped what I needed and headed for the porch. The glass of lemonade, the wicker chair I settled into, and the summer evening became a meditation. I hadn't felt brave enough to go into the backyard yet. It would be a while before I could envision the cottonwood tree without the swinging body, so I purposefully positioned myself on the porch on the opposite side of the house.

My mind went back to the night before and the dark specter that had reached toward me. I knew now that haunting figure had been reaching out for help. The fine hairs on my arms stood at attention. Something cold and slimy trailed up my spine in the muggy summer heat. Could I have made a difference? Who knew?

I felt as if I had stepped into someone else's shadow. Two young Native American men, both of whom had been born too late to die in the glory of battle, were dead. And they were both too close to home for comfort. The situation had taken on a new face, a murderous one. For a moment, I was tempted to retrieve the artifacts that John Wolf had left me the day before, jump in my car, and return them. Something wouldn't let me do it. A deal was a deal, and I liked

John Wolf and his family. Even the insolent Steven had a certain cockiness about him that I admired.

There was also the potential for some real tangled law enforcement problems. The city PD was dealing with the body falling across the hood, and the county Sheriff's Department would be handling the guy in my tree and James Eagle. As far as I knew, nothing had happened on the reservation, yet, and on the res, the FBI had total jurisdiction.

That left me with a curious question: If nothing had occurred on the res, why were the Feds escorting the German to a cozy one-on-one with Matthew Wolf? And if the so-called mother lode was missing, why were pieces showing up by a body pulled out of the Yellowstone and under a car seat in Pryor?

I was born with an overactive recessive curiosity gene that bore the dreaded cross-shaped serve-or-suffer tag. The whats and the whys were all in place, and the hook was set. I am, admittedly, a curiosity junkie, and the guy in my tree had rendered the missing Monday Brown my fix.

The sun was setting, and shadows deepened as they crept closer to the porch. I stretched, thankful some of the tension was leaving my body, until I heard a car turn up the driveway, approach the house. I stood, expecting to do battle with God's Little Messenger, or at least a reporter from *The Gazette*.

Kyle, his hand poised to knock on the door, turned toward me as I rounded the corner of the porch.

"Tell me this visit is friendly. I'm on overload," I said and frowned. "Lemonade? Oh, thanks for getting my truck back here."

"No problem. Beer?"

"Lemonade."

"Why not?" he answered and followed me into the house.

I pulled the pitcher from the fridge, grabbed a glass, and filled it to the brim. "Let's take this outside; this place gets a little hot this time of day."

Kyle was in an intense, dark mood that followed me silently back to the front porch. I glanced at him sideways. No one broods better than he does. His already dark brown eyes deepen to near black, and his shoulders draw up around his neck. He sat down, stretched his legs out in front of him, and rolled the glass of lemonade between his hands as he stared at some distant place inside his mind. I knew exactly what he was doing, looking for that one elusive piece of information that was just out of reach. I'd done it a million times myself.

"Tough day?"

He turned toward me, his expression intense but curious. "What?"

"Tough day?" I repeated.

He stared at me, through me, a storm played out in his eyes. It was his turn.

"Tough day?" he asked. "You're asking me if this has been a tough day?"

"We're getting redundant here."

He lasted less than a minute. A cynical smile broke out on his face. "Do you believe this shit?"

"Could you be more specific?"

Kyle took a long, deep drink. No sooner had the glass touched his lips than a great spray of liquid flew from his mouth as he lurched forward and stood.

"What the hell is this?" he asked as he brushed off the front of his shirt.

"Lemonade," I said defensively.

"Last year's?" He set the glass on the rail of the porch. "What do you make this shit out of?"

"I buy those little yellow plastic lemons and add a little water. No one's complained so far."

He mumbled something and sat back down, leaned his head against the wall behind him, and started laughing. Both of his hands covered his face.

"Phoebe, I've been thinking that, uh . . . maybe you should back off this whole mess."

"Where the hell is that coming from?"

"Just giving you an out." He shrugged.

"Sounds like more than that to me."

"This German's name is Jurgen Mueller. His brother is some big shot with the German embassy in San Francisco and conveniently has little brother on the payroll as a courier or some goddamned thing."

"Heavy stuff. I'm scared." I faked a shiver and grinned. "Can't you do better than that?"

"He likes hookers, two at a time. Preferably one black and one white, and he plays rough. He's in and out of the country six, seven times a year, and he's funded up the ass. Unlimited assets. He buys artifacts, mostly Plains Indian, for some of the biggest collectors in Germany. It's a hobby, just like roughing up hookers. One arrogant son of a bitch."

"You've talked to him?"

"Yeah. I did."

"And?"

"Cooperative. Smiles too much. Underneath? Real iceman. Cold as a January wind. This guy's trouble, Phoebe."

"What about Matthew?"

"They'll probably hang on to him another twenty-four hours and after that turn him loose."

"You don't sound particularly elated."

"Mueller is convinced that Matthew knows where those artifacts are."

"Why do I get the feeling you think the same thing?"

"I never said that." He turned toward me. "But I do think his ass is on the line. Besides"—he stretched again—"I'm more worried about what Mueller *thinks* Matthew knows."

"Christ, Kyle. Iceman or not, he wouldn't be crazy enough to—"

"Crazy? Like a fox. We're talking some real money involved here. What's one more kid from the res compared to some high-rolling backers that are going to be pissed off as hell?"

"One more? You think this guy could take someone out?"

"In a heartbeat."

"Shit."

"Look." Kyle leaned forward, rested his elbows on his knees, and cradled his chin in his hands. "Mueller isn't playing all by himself. It wouldn't make sense. There's got to be a wild card, someone on the fringe. Someone from around here."

"Mueller has receipts, right? Showing that he paid Monday for this deal?"

"Yeah. Two different payments. Monday refused to deal in German currency, so the payoff was in good old American dollars, none of which has shown up in Monday's accounts."

"At least not in the accounts you know about."

"We're checking on it."

"I was going to talk to Matthew tonight, but I'm beat. Am I going to have a problem getting in to see him?"

"I'll take care of it."

"Will he level with me?"

"Probably not."

"Great."

"Phoebe," he said and then became silent.

"What?"

"There could be a communication problem."

"With who?"

"With Matthew. You've met Steven. Right?"

"Oh yeah. Cocky little SOB. But you have to hand it to him; you know right off where you stand."

"Well, modify that just a little and you've got Matthew. They're tight. Think alike. It won't be easy. You're going to have to work for it."

"Let's define work. Schmooze? Suck up to? Placate? One of the above? Some of the above? Which is it?"

"Just don't expect too much right away."

"Hey, he's the one in jail. It's his ass they're trying to hang a murder rap on. So I'm supposed to handle him with kid gloves or something? And where the hell does Steven fit in?"

"What one knows, you can bet the other one knows also. Forget I said anything." He stood to leave.

I reached out and grabbed his arm. "Oh no you don't. You started this. What am I up against?"

"Cultural differences," he said and sat back down.

"And . . ."

"Those differences can lead to, uh . . . misunderstandings."

"Cut to it, Kyle. What the hell are you saying?"

"Matthew has no reason to trust you, Phoebe."

"Me? He doesn't even know me. He doesn't have any reason *not* to trust me."

He hesitated and looked away. "It's not just you. All of you."

"As in all of us white people? I don't believe this shit. This is a joke, right?"

"This is no joke."

"So what the hell am I doing? I'm no mind reader, and if I'm going to help this kid he's got to cooperate."

"I'm not saying he won't."

"This is why you told me there was time to back out. Right?

You're pulling your punches with me, and I don't like it. So, fuck it. They can find themselves someone else."

I stood, glared down at him, and started to walk in front of where he was sitting. He stretched both legs out in front of him and rested the heels of his Tony Lamas on the porch rail, effectively blocking my way.

"Sit down." He smiled at me.

"No, I mean it. I don't need this shit."

"Sit down, Phoebe. And *I* mean it."

I sat down on the porch rail. "Well . . . ?"

"The Wolfs are traditional. Both boys are heavy into it."

"Ya know, Kyle, I heard this 'traditional' thing from your buddy Genevieve this morning. It's starting to leave a bad taste in my mouth. If all of you are so damn traditional, then why the hell don't you talk with Matthew and the both of you can have a traditional conversation?"

"He's not going to talk to me any quicker than he's going to talk to you. He doesn't trust me much either."

"You're a cop, you're a Crow, and you're a relative. This is making more sense all the time. I'll bite. Why doesn't he trust you?"

"I sold out, left the res, and got an education. Now I work in the white man's world, and if I work there I've compromised myself."

"Have you?"

"Maybe a little. Doesn't everybody? But that's neither here nor there. You're going to have to be patient."

"The *P* word? Come on . . ."

"You're going to have to find some way to get through to him."

"Now we're back to the question of Matthew's involvement."

"He knows something. Maybe not about Monday, but he sure as hell knows something."

"I gotta tell ya, I'm not going to *prove* myself to anybody, and I don't give a shit who it is."

"It's your call. See how it goes."

"If you think Mueller is your boy, Kyle, what the hell am I supposed to do for Matthew?"

"A case could be built on the items found in Matthew's car. You're going to have to find out how Matthew, if he did, connected with that stuff. Backtrack Monday. He has to have left a trail."

"Other than an obvious slug trail? Who knows about the necklace and the—"

"Don't."

"Don't what?"

"Whatever came down between you and the Wolfs has to stay between you and them."

"Hell, Kyle . . ."

"If I don't keep some professional distance, I could fuck this up for Matthew *and* for myself. Let me deal with Mueller."

"Don't leave me hanging out here."

"Hell, Phoebe, we don't even know if Monday is dead or took off for Cancún. If I were a betting man, I'd say odds are Monday isn't with us anymore. Which brings up the nasty fact that the missing artifacts have cost two lives already and probably a third."

"Now that you've all but told me I'm up against a brick wall, would you like to give a little advice to a friend? Where the hell do I start?"

Kyle tapped his temple with his index finger. "Up here. Be open to whatever comes up. Life on the reservation isn't life how you know it, Phoebe, and some of the answers you're going to have to come up with are going to be on that reservation."

"Great."

"You need some clout. Althea Wolf came up with an idea that might connect you with some people who can influence things for you."

"Which is . . ."

"She does a sweat a couple of times a month with some women from Pryor. She's already gotten permission from them to invite you."

"Things can't be that bad up there if they have access to saunas."

Kyle leaned his head back and laughed. "Christ. I'm not talking cushy white towels at the racket club. Like I said, just be open. Althea will get you through it."

"When is this Margaret Mead affair?"

"In a couple of days. She'll call you. And one other thing, make sure you talk to Matthew's great-grandmother Anna. No one is closer to him than she is. She's special, Phoebe, and according to John, she liked you."

"She's something else. Does she speak English?"

"Some, and that's only when she chooses to."

"God, this just keeps getting better as it goes along."

"She's got some powerful medicine."

"Heart trouble?"

"Medicine, Phoebe. Individual medicine, *power* if that makes it easier to understand. She communicates with the Little People . . ."

"I can identify. I haven't moved the pencil mark up on the doorjamb since I was fifteen years old."

Kyle smiled and shook his head. "Jesus. Maybe you *are* in over your head. I'm not talking about a throwback in the Siegel clan, I'm talking about the Achillea, a race of dwarfs, with great spiritual powers, that live up around the Castle Rocks."

"Uh huh . . ." I couldn't quite get that look of disbelief off my face, so I turned away from Kyle and looked into the distance.

"They're spirit helpers, Phoebe. If you can take their abuse, they give you their powers. Anna's had those powers since she was a girl."

"You believe this?" Kyle had been my touchstone for years. Now I was beginning to wonder how touched he was.

"Yes," he stated simply. "The point I'm trying to make is that you're going to have to accept the fact that these people have different beliefs than you do."

"Like I'm loaded with beliefs?" I turned back toward him.

"They believe that chickadees bring them messages and that owls are messengers of death."

"Makes sense to me." I laughed, grabbed the toe of his boot, and wrenched it. "You're putting me on, right?"

"They don't wear clothes with holes in them because it's bad medicine, and they pull their shades at night to keep bad spirits from entering their homes."

"Kyle . . ."

"There are some words so sacred in the Crow language that they are only spoken in private or thought of inside their heads."

I finally caught on that he was dead serious. "So . . . ?"

"You're going to be entering a third world country compared to down here. Their ways are different. Most of which is going to be way outside your reality."

"Is all of this outside *your* reality, Kyle?"

He answered without hesitation. "Probably not. If you run into any trouble, John will steer you right. He's a good man. I'm out of here."

And he was. He walked down the stairs, got into his vehicle, and was gone. I sat on the porch rail and looked up at the sky. It had darkened, and only a thin line of yellow and magenta marked the horizon far beyond me to the west. Thunder, muted and distant, rumbled in the north. A gentle rain started to fall from the ashen sky. For a moment I thought about powerful medicine and little people, owls and holes in clothes, and wondered briefly if it was raining on Monday Brown.

9

I waited until midnight and drove down to the Outlaw Bar. If there was a witching hour for barkeeps, it was definitely midnight. The Outlaw was a large, sprawling building with wagon wheels edging the sidewalk leading to the front door. There were a few cars in the parking lot, but too many to be accounted for by the scant number of patrons inside. Most had probably been left from the night before, abandoned instead of ending up twisted around a telephone pole or part of a deadly head-on collision. Maybe people were wising up.

A low, bluish gray haze of cigarette smoke stretched from one end of the bar to the other and over a darker area where people at tables huddled, talking in hushed voices. The bar stools were saddles. The leather, polished from years of use, gleamed in the soft light. I walked toward one that looked closest to the floor and debated whether I should put my foot in the stirrup or just sidle on up and climb on. I chose the latter. Surprisingly, it was comfortable as hell.

Behind the bar, a bleached blond with trailer park hair and chipped nail polish was talking with a guy two saddles over. A slim brown cigarette held precariously between her fingers punctuated each statement as she stabbed it this way and that. I guessed her to be in her early fifties, with one of those histrionic personalities that allowed her to wear skintight Levi's, a low-cut white satin shirt, and a gauzy little red scarf tied at the side of her neck, the kind you would have seen in the fifties that gave the wearer a sense of real tack.

She looked my way, took a drag off her cigarette, mumbled something to the guy she was talking to, walked over, and stood in front of me.

"What'll you have, darlin'?" She smiled broadly, revealing a black hole on the side where a tooth was missing.

"How about an O'Doul's?"

She looked puzzled. "A what? Is that one of them new imported beers?"

Glancing at the guy down the bar, I watched as he slammed a shot down his throat and followed it with a Silver Bullet chaser. I shifted in my saddle and leaned forward.

Whispering, I said, "It's a nonalcoholic—"

"It's one of them near-beers for Christ's sake, Sharon." I turned again toward the man who had downed the shot. "It's what them alkies drink!" he shouted in an obnoxious slur as he swung his head toward me and smiled. "Put it on my tab."

She waved her hand at him, frowned enough to shut him up, and turned back to me.

"Sorry 'bout that. He's having trouble with his old lady." She leaned close and whispered. "He don't mean nothing."

She turned away, searched the cooler for an O'Doul's, came up with one, popped the top, and sat it in front of me.

"Tah dah! Can't keep up with all the labels anymore. Just too many of 'em."

She took another, longer drag off her cigarette, extended her bottom lip, and exhaled straight up her face. Her eyes, fringed with lashes so thick with mascara they could have deflected a baseball bat, didn't blink in the smoky veil. She didn't stop staring, so I confronted it.

"I'm looking for someone," I said and took a sip.

"We all are, honey. I've even found a few, sons of bitches that they were. That's how I ended up here. Let some sweet-talking guy convince me he was a rancher. I loved him too. But what do I get?" She flicked her ashes into an ashtray and took another drag. This time she blew perfect circles into the air between us. "I get a trailer out on the flats with no phone, no television, and an ex-wife kicking in the door every two days wanting child support for their five kids."

"Tough break. Where'd you come from?"

"Vegas. Sold everything to drop a new engine in his seventy-six Ranchero. Had me a good job at the Grab It and Growl steak joint and a few bucks saved up. What have I got now? An achy breaky heart." She threw her head back and laughed at her own cleverness.

"You're not Sharon Mills by any chance."

The smile left.

"Are you one of them subpoena servers?" She placed both hands on the padded edge of the bar and glared at me.

It was my turn to wave my hand. "No. Not me."

"You a cop?"

"Nope." I watched her mind search for another title.

"Then who are you exactly?"

"My name is Phoebe Siege—"

"You're one of those goddamned reporters. Damn! I told you all that I wasn't giving any more interviews."

"I'm not a reporter." This time I waved both hands in the air. "God. They can really be a pain in the ass, can't they?"

"You got that right, darlin'. They about drove me to drink. Hanging around down here, out at my place, and one even followed me into the powder room."

"Assholes."

"You got that right." She softened. "So just what is it you want?"

"Information. I won't bullshit you. I'd like to ask a few questions about *that* night. It must have been horrible for you. How are you doing with it?" I spoke in a lower tone and as sympathetic as I could.

"Well, I'll tell ya . . ." She covered her heart with her hand. "I darn near died of fright. Damnedest thing that's ever happened to me. You want another one?"

"No, I'm fine. God, I don't know how I would have handled it."

"Well, I didn't have time to think about it. There I was sitting at that light. No traffic. Just me, a woman alone on my way home."

"It was raining, right?"

"Had been. Real downpour. But it quit by the time I came over South Bridge. I took the Central Overpass down to Montana Avenue and turned up Twenty-seventh Street when I hit the light. There I was sitting there, and that damn train light starts flashing behind me. So I look up into the mirror, and I'm watching that arm come down?"

"Right." If you let someone talk long enough, you'll find out everything you want to know.

"Anyway, I was watching this arm come down, and all of a sudden I feel the car rock and something hits in front of me. And there he was. Whole damn face smeared across my window. And his hand," she said and grimaced as she flailed her own hand, palm open, in front of her. "That hand just kept winging around, and then he grabbed my wiper blade and did he hold on."

"What did you do?"

"I stared right back at him, right into those dead-looking eyes. It was like he was blind or something, fighting to live. He pulled himself up toward the window, and that's when his lips just kind of spread out over the glass. I could see his teeth and his tongue"—her mouth was stretching. She was the mime reliving a terrifying tale—"and all that blood just oozing down the window." She shivered.

"Is that when he fell off the car?"

"No," she answered and became serious. "Y'know how things come back to you?"

"I sure do. Has something come back?"

"I'm not sure, but I've been thinking about this. The cops keep asking me over and over, 'What do you remember, Sharon?' " Her voice, a singsong tenor, mimicked the cops. "As soon as I tell them something, I get this funny thing about something else."

"What?"

"Wait a minute." She stepped back from the bar, folded her arms in front of her, and watched me. "Who did you say you was with?"

"I didn't say. For the record, I'm with myself. The gentleman"—I almost choked on the word—"that is missing is a friend of mine. I'm concerned. It's that simple."

She was immediately back to the edge of the bar. Her hand reached out and patted mine. "Oh, darlin', I'm so sorry. I've had losses and grief in my life. Ya know what they say? This too shall pass."

"What did you remember?" I was pushing, but what choice did I have? I tipped my head sideways, acknowledging her sympathy and words of wisdom.

"I told them he fell off the car, and now I'm just not sure. That damn crossing bell was dinging like crazy behind me and that train was rumbling by and that face just suckin' up against my window. I wasn't thinking right and I couldn't take my eyes off that face. But he was fightin'. I believe he was fightin', holding on to that wiper for dear life. And I saw an arm."

"The man's arm . . ."

"No, it couldn't have been. It came from an odd direction. There was something going on, on the right side of my car. Something . . ." She paused and placed her hands by her temples and shook her head, trying to jar the memory loose. "Somebody maybe was pulling him. The light from the blinker on the crossing disappeared, like someone was behind the car, and then it came back again. That's when he fell. Maybe he was pulled from the hood. He took that wiper clean off."

"What did you do next?"

"I forgot my car was even running and started turning the key in the ignition. That thing was whining and grinding." Her voice rose to a nerve-grating crescendo and then dropped. "Then I just tromped the gas pedal and flew out of there. There was blood on my windshield and it started raining and it was running, that blood I mean, just like a bunch of . . . uh, of squirmy red things. And I only had one wiper."

She sounded exhausted.

"So you think you saw a hand other than the man's hand?"

"Uh huh. I think I did. Maybe more than one extra. There was this activity, like I said, at the right side of the car. Like a bunch of blackbirds swarming around. Real spooky night. Y' know"—she leaned down close, looked up and down the bar, and then whispered in a raspy voice—"they been wanting me to be hypnotized, put to sleep, to see what I can remember."

"They who?" I whispered back.

"Them cops!" She bristled. "But I know all about that mind control bullshit. No sir. Not this woman. No way. No time. No place."

"Don't reject the idea right away. You'd be surprised what can come out under hypnosis."

"You think I want all my personal life spread out in front of those *men*?" She spit the word rather than pronounce it. "We women have a right to privacy and what if they pulled stuff out of me that was embarrassing and talked it up all over town."

"That wouldn't happen. I can guarantee it," I said as I watched her adjust the gauze scarf at her neck. "You identified a picture in the paper as the man that fell across your car. Are you sure they are one and the same?"

"You think I'd forget that face? Only that windshield was between him and me. You bet I'm sure. It was him all right." There was an arrogance in her statement that convinced me she was convinced.

"Thanks. Can we talk again? Say within the next couple of days. Maybe you'll remember something else."

"Really don't want to. Been too much attention paid me already. He was a lucky man to have so many friends."

"So many friends?"

"Yeah! One guy has been in a few times. Keeps offering to buy me dinner, but I ain't at too good a place with men right now. He's a looker, that one."

"Did you get his name?"

"Sure, but it's one of those foreign names. Hard to remember."

"I understand that." Jurgen Mueller.

"Want to meet him? He's been sitting over in that corner most of the night. Not very . . ."

I tried to spin around on the saddle and nearly decrotched myself. I dismounted clumsily. My eyes scanned the darkened room.

"Guess he took off while we was talking. He came in right after you did. Didn't you see him outside?"

I tried to expand my constricting throat. "No, I didn't. Where's your phone?"

"Right over there by the pool table. Costs twenty-five cents. Used to cost a dime."

"Thanks. I'll be in touch."

I walked to the phone, dropped a quarter in, and dialed. On the ninth ring, someone picked up the other end.

"Mama?"

"Who is this?" she answered sleepily.

"Your daughter. Phoebe. Are you up?"

"Of course, Phoebe. It's one-thirty in the morning by my watch, and I'm just starting my laundry."

"Can I come stay over tonight?"

"Of course. What's the matter, Phoebe? Did something else happen?"

"No, nothing more."

"Well come on. I'll wait up. Lord, is it storming out. And drive carefully. It's a killer out there."

Little did she know.

10

A phone was ringing in some distant space beyond what I was capable of comprehending. I rolled over and tried to open my eyes. Squinting, I surveyed my surroundings and tried to make sense of the parfait yellow walls and white lace curtains. I rolled onto my back, pulled the covers over my head, and tried to block out the persistent screaming of the phone. It stopped. I breathed deeply, filling my nostrils and lungs with an overkill scent of Downy. Christ. I was home.

I threw the covers off my head and looked around. Sure enough, I was floating in a four-poster boat in the lemon meringue room I had grown up in. The sights and sounds were all there. Only one thing was missing. As though the thought cued the deed, *the missing one thing* materialized.

"Phoebe!" The shriek wound through the house and wrapped itself around me. "Kyle Wolf is on the phone."

I snuggled the blankets up under my nose and took one last deep sniff. There's a lot to be said for childhood memories, even when you despise the color yellow and always found the smell of fabric softener nauseating.

"Tell him to hold on. I'll be there in a minute."

With great effort I crawled out of bed still wearing my GOOD TO BE QUEEN shirt, pulled on my Nikes and a red flannel robe that my mother had thoughtfully placed on a chair by the side of the bed, and headed downstairs. I wake up hard. It takes me an hour just to find my lips and pour some coffee down my throat. Only then am I able to speak, and that's only in early Neanderthal.

Mama was standing at the sink, and my sister, Kehly, was sitting at the table reading the paper, a steaming cup of coffee poised in midair in her hand.

"Très chic." Kehly grinned.

I glared at her, grunted something, and reached for the telephone receiver that was dangling from the wall phone.

"Coffee?" Mama asked.

I nodded yes. "Hello?"

"When you weren't home, I figured you'd be there."

"There where?"

"There. Where you are."

"Where are you?"

"Is this that 'Who's on first' routine?"

"Hold on a minute." I reached for the cup of coffee Mama was handing me, took a drink, and tried to clear my head. "Let's start over. What time is it?"

"Six-thirty."

"Six-thirty? Shit!" I turned, leaned against the wall, and slid down to squat on the floor. Kehly and Mama both frowned with disapproval.

"This can't wait. John Wolf called about an hour ago. Matthew took off."

"He broke out of jail?"

"No. They released him last night. John came down and picked him up."

"Mueller called Wolf's shortly after they had gotten home and talked to Matthew for thirty minutes or so. An hour later, Matthew was gone."

"He didn't tell anyone about the conversation?"

"Nope."

"Then how do you know it was Mueller?"

"John answered the phone and said the guy had a heavy accent."

"And John didn't ask Matthew what was going on or what the guy wanted? I find that hard to believe."

"That's not how it works, Phoebe."

I glanced at Mama and remembered how she unabashedly listened in on our phone calls any chance she got. That was how it worked for us.

"There's no type of bond on him, is there?"

"No, but he was supposed to be available for questioning. I think

I can cover his ass for a day or two and that's about all. He's not off the hook."

"Kyle." I stood and tried to stretch the phone cord around the corner and into the bathroom, lowering my voice. "I had a talk with Sharon Mills last night."

"Yeah?"

"I think—no . . . I *know* Mueller was following me."

"You saw him?"

"No," I said feeling edgy. "I was getting ready to leave and she offered to introduce me. Thought I knew him already. She said he had come in right after me and was sitting at a table in the corner. Mystically, magically, when I turned around he was gone."

"Shit."

"My thoughts exactly. Listen, I'm going to get off here. Touch base with me tonight."

"No problem. Your mother invited me over for dinner."

"Really? Dinner?" I turned and faced my smiling mother.

"Can't turn down an offer like that. Hey, I forgot something."

"Yeah?"

"Genevieve has been trying to get ahold of you. Give her a call when you get a chance."

"I'll do that. I thought I'd take a run up to Pryor. Maybe talk with Monday's wife."

"I don't know what new information she can give you, but it's worth a try. She helps the priest out up there. Stop in the church first."

"You've been talking with my mother, haven't you?"

Kyle laughed, and I hung up.

"Now don't you get upset with me, Phoebe. I haven't seen Kyle for a long time, and Lord knows he'd probably be grateful for a home-cooked meal."

"Couldn't you have checked with me first, for Christ's sake? Would that be too much to ask?"

"Don't go ballistic, Phoebe." Kehly looked up from her paper. "This is a special occasion."

"What?" I shrugged and caught myself bobbing my head in her direction.

"Michael's birthday."

"I thought we did Michael and Jesus on the twenty-fifth of December." My pious brother Michael was the perfect one, the priest.

"That kind of talk isn't necessary, Phoebe. Now, sit down and I'll get you some breakfast," Mama commanded.

"I don't have time . . ."

"For your morning Pop-Tart?" Kehly needled.

"Do I need this shit?" I walked to the stove and poured myself another cup of coffee, took a drink, and eyed my sister over the cup. "What are you doing here this early?"

"I have a step-up class at six, and it was canceled, so I thought I'd spend some time with Mama before I had to go to work."

"Well, I'm glad to see she has at least one dutiful daughter."

"Oh, stop it, you two. You'll put me in an early grave." Mama pulled a plate of scrambled eggs and bacon from the oven and placed it on the table.

Kehly said, "My sentiments exactly. None of us need an early grave. Did Phoebe tell you she's working on another case?"

Mama's gasp echoed throughout the room. "Does it have anything to do with that man someone chopped up in your yard?"

"Chopped up? Chopped up? Where the hell did that come from? He was hanging." I turned toward Kehly. "Did you tell her that?"

Kehly grinned and shook her head no.

"Mrs. Davidson told me, and she heard it from a friend whose cousin's son heard it from a police officer. She said they only said hanging on the television because it was so gory they didn't dare tell the truth."

I sat down at the table and pushed the plate toward Kehly. "I'm not hungry. You eat it."

"I don't do fat." She pushed it back.

It was obvious that she didn't. In spite of an insatiable urge to wring her neck, I loved her and was proud of her. She was beautiful. More important, she had kicked one helluva drug problem. She was clean, and other than the fact that she tried to twelve-step me, as she called it, every damn chance she got, we had a good relationship. Tenuous sometimes, but good.

"It shows. How's work and the boyfriend?"

"Both fine. How are things with you?"

"Hectic. Mama told you about Roger?"

"Yeah. I went up and saw him last night. He doesn't seem any worse for wear. I'm sure the back rub he was getting definitely helped the knot on his head. Damn. When I had my appendix out, I didn't get the hot lotion-thirty-minute-hands-on rubdown. She's quite a babe, Phoebe."

"What are you really saying, Kehly?"

"I'm not really saying anything. Just that I offered him a ride home this morning if they released him and he said that he had it covered."

"Of course he has. I have every intention of picking him up. He knows that."

"I don't think so, Fee. I think good old Roger and Florence Nightingale are working at becoming an item."

"Bullshit."

"Nope. You didn't see the—"

"He who hesitates loses. That's what I've always said." Mama threw in her two cents.

"What is this? He's a grown man capable of making choices in his life. You think this bothers me? Well . . . it . . . doesn't. I've got enough on my plate as it is."

"I like Roger. Don't you, Mama?"

"Yes, yes I do." She wiped her hands on the cobbler apron that had become her uniform over the years. "I always hoped that—"

"Enough. Could we change the subject?"

"So . . ." Kehly leaned forward and rested her elbows on the table and her chin on her hands. Her voice was barely above a whisper as she glanced over my shoulder at Mama. "What's the deal with the guy in the tree? This isn't going to be a repeat of the Mary Kuntz thing, is it?"

"No, Kehly."

"I mean, I don't want Mother in any kind of jeopardy. Please, Phoebe."

"Jesus. Do you really think I'd do that?"

"Not intentionally. But somehow, you always manage to—"

"Don't sweat it."

"Then tell me what the deal is with the guy in your tree."

"I can't. In fact, it's real close to being an open and shut case. A couple of days from now it will hit the paper, and the following day it will be old news and some tacky little scandal at City Hall will make headlines." I held my cup up as Mama approached the table with the coffeepot.

"Are you in any danger?" Kehly asked.

"Danger? Who's in danger?"

"No one is in danger, Mama. Christ, Kehly, let it rest."

"You know, Phoebe, I felt better with your father working the streets than I do with you and this private investigation thing. Nothing is out in the open."

"And law enforcement is?" I asked incredulously.

"Of course. Your father shared everything with me."

Kehly and I just looked at each other and suppressed our smiles.

"Will you be seeing Rudy today, Kehly?"

"Uh huh."

"Make sure you invite him to dinner this evening."

"I will, Mama." Kehly leaned toward me again as Mama walked to the sink and turned the water on. "She still won't acknowledge the fact that we live together," she whispered. "Later, you two. I'm outta here." Kehly stood, walked over to Mama, and kissed her on the cheek.

"We'll do lunch one of these times, little sister."

"I'd definitely check out the hospital, Phoebe," she said in an irritating singsong voice on her way out the back door.

"I'm going to take a shower and get dressed, Mama."

"And I'm going to mass, so I probably won't be here when you come down. Don't forget tonight. We'll eat about six."

"Gotcha," I said and kissed her on the cheek. "I'll call if I'm going to be late."

"Oh no you won't. You won't be late."

11

Roger was sitting on the edge of the bed, reading a copy of *The Wall Street Journal*. "I tried to call you all night, and this morning. Where the hell have you been?" He said as I walked into the room. "Christ, I was worried."

"Really? Worried enough to call Mama's? Did you give a shit enough to try and find me?"

"Hey. Hold on here a minute. I'm the one in the damned hospital. Where the hell is this coming from?"

"From what I hear you've required some special handling, so . . . I find it a little incredible that you even had time to worry about me, Roger."

He reached out, took hold of my hand, and pulled me down onto the bed to sit beside him. I've always held okra, mosquitoes, and hysterical women in contempt. I was sounding like the last.

"What's really going on here, Phoebe?"

"Nothing."

"The buzzword was *really*."

Roger and I had called it quits over a year ago. Why? Because he knew me, knew my inability to commit, and I had no choice but to concur with his observations. But he remained my best friend and confidant. Emotionally, I just wasn't prepared to deal with the thought of losing whatever it was we had left.

"Are they treating you all right?" I asked.

"Fine. What's up, Phoebe?"

"I'm worried about you. Are you getting out today?"

"Maybe. The doctor hasn't been in yet."

"Need a ride? I'm driving up to Pryor today and thought you might want to come along."

"Pryor? What the hell is up there?"

"Business."

"Business. Great. This wasn't enough?" He pointed toward his head.

"Now it's personal. I don't have a choice." I reached up and placed my hand at the back of his head. "Still hurt?"

He winced. "Hell, it could have been me hanging in that tree. Or you, for Christ's sake. If that guy hadn't shown up, I could easily be dead."

"But you're not—"

"Too close. Twice now. And each time it's had something to do with *business*. Turn the items, which we can already surmise are stolen property, over to the cops. Let the authorities take care of it. But, then again, you don't know the definition of the word *authority*."

"You used to have a sense of adventure, Roger." I smiled and squeezed his hand. "What happened to it?"

"My sense of survival is what happened to it. Do this, for me," he pleaded. "Please."

"I can't."

"Listen to me. I've done some pro bono work for the tribe. You don't stand a chance. They—"

"They who?"

"Those people . . ."

"Funny how you think you know someone, isn't it?"

"What?"

"Those people. I never thought I'd hear you talk about anyone like that."

"What the hell do you want me to call them?"

"There you go again."

"Forget it. It's not going to work, Phoebe." He raised both hands in the air. "Far be it from me to try and talk any sense into you. Have it your way. That's how it always has to be, isn't it?"

I looked at my watch. "I think I've spent enough time cheering you up. Do you want a ride home or not?"

"I've got it covered."

"So I hear."

"What the hell does that mean?"

"Are they still teaching the nurses how to make the patient without disturbing the bed?"

"What?" Roger shot up off the side of the bed, groaned, grabbed the back of his head, and sat back down.

"Never mind. Forget I said it."

"Like hell I will. What did you mean, Phoebe? Damn, you can be nasty."

"Excuse me. Is there a problem in here, Roger?"

I looked toward the voice.

"No problem. Just a slight irritation." He looked sideways at me, eyes wide and pleading.

"We can hear you down the hall." She turned toward me. "I'll have to ask you to keep it down or leave, uh . . . Miss . . . ?"

"Phoebe, this is January."

"No, Roger. It's the end of August."

"I'm January," the nurse said.

"You're both in good shape."

"January, this is a friend of mine, Phoebe Siegel. I was at her home when I was assaulted."

Her chin tilted down toward her chest as she eyed me. I had to give it to him. She was beautiful, in a big sort of way. She even had big hairs, big blond hairs, that were woven into a single rope-thick braid that hung over one shoulder and halfway down her big chest. Maybe it was the flawless, freckle-free, fair skin, or the big, blue eyes that were better fringed, naturally, than Tammy Faye's, that made me immediately dislike her. Or, it could have been the *fuck me* signals that torpedoed back and forth between Roger and Florence Nightingale.

She walked toward him, reached out, and touched his shoulder. His hand went up and covered hers.

"How's the head?" she asked.

Roger slips into a fix-me, heal-me mode quicker than most. "I'm hanging in there," he replied and looked up at her with cocker spaniel eyes.

"When the doctor comes in, be sure and tell him you're still having some pain. He might want to keep you one more night."

"Shit."

"I'm off tonight and"—she glanced toward me—"I have no intention of leaving you up here by your lonesome."

Who the hell did she think she was fooling? She saw attorney, unattached, dollar signs, and gullibility. Now the big blues were riveted on me. She said nothing. It was so transparently for effect, I had to keep myself from laughing.

"Well, *Phyllis,* have you and Roger known each other long?"

"Yes *June* . . . " I answered.

"January."

"Phoebe."

The torpedoes turned from *fuck me* to *fuck you.* I have a standard, and that's never to waste my time doing mental battle with an unarmed opponent. After slipping the chart back into its holder at the foot of his bed, I walked over to Roger, and, much to his amazement and mine, I planted a big kiss on his lips, turned, and walked out. Life was getting weirder by the minute: Monday was missing, January had moved in, and coupled with the fact that the month of March had always been the albatross circling my ship of life, a quiet gnawing in my gut told me I had to be prepared for anything.

My house loomed in front of me. I sat in the truck for a good five minutes before I got out and walked onto the porch, unlocked the door, and went inside. The silence was ominous. Walking from the foyer into the main living room, I immediately reached for the tatted shade pull and tugged lightly. The shade flew up and clattered as the force of the spring wound the shade and the pull around the wooden dowel. This was my home, my refuge, and I fought to quell the rising feelings of some unseen presence.

"Here, kitty, kitty . . ." I called for Stud. "Come on out, boy, breakfast is coming."

Something crashed behind me. I spun around and saw my umbrella plant spilled onto the floor in front of a walnut table at the foot of the stairs. Stud stood on top of the table, his tail puffed out and switching sharply. He paced back and forth, meowing a deep, throaty disapproval of my absence. God only knew what would be next in his reign of terror. I checked for shredded curtains, clawed furniture, or further evidence of dumped plants, his favorite act of terrorism.

"Goddamnit, Stud. I had a choice here. I could have left you foodless until tonight." I walked over, picked him up, and carried him to the kitchen.

He sat silently at my feet as I opened a can of Sheba and placed it on the floor in front of him. I jumped back as he took a temperamental swipe at my leg and growled.

"Look, you hair ball. Behavior like that might make me think you're rabid. You know what they do to rabid cats? They take them to Bozeman to the state lab and they cut off their heads for analysis. So watch it. Do we understand each other?"

He stopped eating for a minute and growled without even looking up.

"Your choice, big boy."

I turned and prepared for one of my legendary Frisbee throws with the cat food lid that, with any luck at all, would sail smoothly into the garbage can that sat by the back door. The lid never left my hand. The back door stood wide open, framing the yard and the woods beyond. On the floor, a few feet inside the porch, was a legal size manila envelope with a baseball size river rock resting in the middle of it.

I did a drumroll on the countertop with my fingertips and inadvertently dropped the tin lid to the floor. Stepping toward the door, I didn't feel Stud's tail under my foot until he screamed and turned to claw my leg. My hand swept the counter and sent a glass crashing to the tiles. Between us cacophony echoed throughout the house.

When I'd quit doing a foot-stomping dance of pain, I walked over to the door, leaned out, and looked in all directions. The river rock had caught the morning sun and felt warm to my touch, which led me to believe it had been there for some time. I picked up the rock and the envelope, walked back into the kitchen, set them both on the table, and stared at them for a long time.

I opened the envelope and pulled out the contents. A small Post-it note, neatly typed, was stuck to the front page.

EVERYTHING YOU NEED TO KNOW
IS ENCLOSED.

Everything I needed to know about what? I removed the note and started to read.

COYOTE—THE TRICKSTER

It was a time of no shadows. The small child held the gnarled brown hand in hers and gently led the old man through the woods. The full moon slid in and out behind the broken layers of clouds that had rolled in from the west. It had rained just enough to release the scent of fertile loam and mix it with the richness of the pine and cedar and mountain lupine. The air was ripe with the fragrance of the mountains.

They walked without speaking. Their steps were silent, carefully placed on the ancient path. The breeze coming down from the peaks teased strands of the child's long, mahogany hair and carried them across her face. She casually brushed them away, as unaware of them as most five-year-old girls would be. The sound of water cascading down from the sandstone cliff finally came within her range of hearing.

"I told you I knew my way, Grandfather," she said softly to show respect for her surroundings. "I didn't forget."

The old man said nothing. He gripped her hand, stared with milk white, unseeing eyes, and continued to follow her lead. A smile formed on his lips.

"Be careful here, Grandfather. The rocks are slippery."

She turned, grasped both his hands, and maneuvered him to a rock beside the pool. The cool vapor of the falls misted them in the darkness as she backed him up and helped him to sit. He released only one of her hands as she knelt before him.

"We're here. You did not forget, Granddaughter." His hand combed the air in front of him until it found her face and rested against her cheek. Her free hand, small in comparison with his, grasped his wrist and held on.

"Why did you want to come here tonight, Grandfather?" she asked as she looked into his blind, moist eyes.

"To speak to you of things you need to hear. You're leaving this place. Your father—" His words choked with emotion.

"I know, Grandfather. He's dead. Grandmother told me we'd never see him again." Her voice was sheathed in sad acceptance. "You were his Grandfather too, weren't you?"

The nod of his head was barely perceptible. "Be still. Your father is here." His English was broken and further hindered by his increasing lack of breath.

"But—" She started.

He raised his hand to silence her. "Listen to my words. They are the same that your father would have spoken to you. He was a warrior, and he died a warrior's death. We will celebrate him. His people are proud."

"Then how can he be here, Grandfather?" She stood and looked expectantly into the ink black night that surrounded them. "If he's here I want to see him."

"He's here. These are his words. I gave them to him when he was your age. Now I give them to you, for him."

"To keep?"

He smiled a toothless smile and laughed. The laughter brought on great spasms of coughing. When they subsided, he gently touched her face and said, "To keep."

The moonlight danced on the mercurial surface of the pool. The old man pulled her to him. She snuggled between his legs and leaned back into the frail chest that fought so hard for breath. She could feel the erratic beat of his heart against her back. As he wrapped his arms around her, she sighed and snuggled even closer.

"You're leaving us. You are going to live with your mother's people. But this," he said as he waved an arm in a semicircle in front of her, "this is where you will find the truth. This is where your people have lived from the beginning of time. It belongs to the people, as you belong to the people."

She said nothing. Sadness filled her. A knowing coursed through her child's mind. This was the last time she would see him. In her heart she felt the sadness grow.

"When you leave us, you must take the people with you in here."

He covered her heart with his hand. Her hand reached up and covered his.

"The people are your legs. They will lead you on a path you must follow. Your father will be your arms, and you must hold him close to you as I do. And here?" He covered her forehead with his hand. "Here, there will always be Eagle, your namesake. This will be your power, your strength. Like Eagle you will always learn more through

your ears and eyes than from your tongue. I have taught
you the songs of the people, and you must sing them."

"But how can an eagle be in my head, Grandfather?
Why will he be there?"

"Eagle will be your eyes. Eagle will see beyond what the
whites can see. Eagle will make you fly higher than the
whites can fly. Eagle will teach you. Eagle will teach you to
hunt fearlessly."

His breathing became more labored. He fell silent. The
knife-edged wheezing rattled and whistled from his lungs
and soon grew faint. He struggled to continue.

"You will be living in the white man's world. You will
live in his house and you will learn his ways. But you must
never think like the white man. Trust Eagle. Learn Eagle's
ways. Sing the songs of the people that I have taught you.
Akbaatadía, the One Who Has Made Everything, has given
you all these things."

There was a stirring of heaviness deep within her. She
tried to pull away from him. "Grandfather, are you going
with my daddy?"

He pulled her back into the comfort of his chest. Her
small hands tried to encircle his thin arms.

"Yes," he answered. "But look in your heart and you
will always find me. I will walk the clouds above your head
and whisper to you from the shadows. I will touch you
through the wind and dry your tears. But you must never
forget who you are."

Tears rolled down her cheeks. "I won't, Grandfather."

"Your father wanted away from here, away from his
people. Now he has come home. Coyote led him away.
One day Coyote will come to you. Be careful of him. He is
a great teacher, but he is also a trickster."

"Grandfather?"

He ignored her as he pushed her from the cradle of his
lap and turned her toward him. "Now, I want you to return to your mother. She is waiting. Who are you, child?"
His voice strained through the wheeze.

She giggled and said her name. "You know who I am,"
she answered softly as her hands reached out and held his

face. "But I don't want you to—" Her voice broke and she fell into him and wrapped her arms around him. She could feel the soft flannel of his shirt against her face, could smell the vague residue of soap in the material.

His arms encircled her only for an instant, and then he held her at arm's length. Turning his face toward the heavens, he felt the rain starting to fall gently. "Now, go. And as you go I want you to tell the trees and the stars and the rain who you are."

"Grandfather, please—" she pleaded. "Don't you want to wave good-bye to me?"

"There is no good-bye between us. I told you where I'd be and how I'd come to you. Now, who are you?"

Again, she repeated her name. Her voice was barely above a whisper as she hung her head and looked toward him through her lashes. A pout formed on her lips.

"Go," he said, and he turned her toward the path. "Go quickly."

She held his face in her tiny hands and kissed him lightly on his dry, thin lips. Turning, she looked back only once before she started running on the path toward her grandmother's house. Her hand trailed the rough bark on the pines as her small feet flew over the soft dirt. A death song rode the breeze behind her.

She said her name quietly at first. Her heart beat wildly in her chest as she tried to make her voice swell with confidence.

She broke from the trees and turned to look down the path she had just traveled. The moonlight spilled onto her as she stood staring into the obsidian darkness that was the edge of the woods. Sobs tore from her throat. Emotions she could not understand built in her. The wind whipped her hair and lifted the tears from her cheeks.

Something fluttered high above her. Her face turned heavenward, letting her eyes track the sound. And it was there. The eagle's great, white head gleamed, iridescent in the silvery light. Its piercing eyes stared down at her as it stretched its wings and screamed, shattering the night around her.

For one single second, terror seized her and then was gone. Her small hands raised toward the heavens.

"I love you, Grandfather. I won't ever forget who I am!" She screamed. "I won't ever forget."

She screamed her name to the heavens. The words echoed around her, and her small voice started to chant as she ran for the lights of the house.

I set the pages down on the table. The hair stood up on the back of my neck, and a lump formed in my throat. If in fact everything I needed to know was in those words, all I needed to do was figure out what the hell it all meant.

12

Billings was built on the iron back of the railroad as it clawed its way across the Great Plains. The houses and the streets are no nonsense. People still stop you and ask after your family, and strangers will share a smile and a wave. Billings missed out on the visionaries who built grand Victorian mansions in the gold towns to the west as testaments to the fortunes they had gouged from the earth.

Instead, the Yellowstone Valley made the practical dreams of hardscrabble farmers, predominantly German, come true along the banks of the Yellowstone River and its tributaries. But there's another history here. One most of us, conveniently, ignore. For the native people, the dreams, the visions, became a nightmare, and I was headed toward the result: the reservation.

As I drove through Billings and wound my way onto South Billings Boulevard, I crossed streets with names like Lewis, Custer, and Clark Avenue: a couple of explorers and an early pillager who contributed to near genocide. I started feeling very white. And why? Because some asshole by the name of Monday Brown, whose family had made it a generational tradition to rip off Native Americans, was missing and presumed dead. Tough break for Monday. For me? Some work on a house where I wasn't even sure I could get the stench of death out.

By nine I had crossed the Yellowstone River and was parked in the parking lot of the Blue Basket Travel Shop with a Conoco road map stretched across the inside of my '49 Chevy truck. The truck is built like a tank and in mint condition but short on room. It took five minutes to find out I was on the right road and another fifteen minutes to fold the damn map back up. I filled the gas tank, bought some Hostess Twinkies, and started off for Pryor.

The two-lane highway wound through a scattered housing area

known as Blue Creek. The canyon narrows through what the locals call South Hills, a rolling series of foothills that rise from the valley floor and join sandstone ruins to form the southern wall of the Yellowstone Valley. It fans out conveniently like it knew the posh Briar Wood Golf Course would someday be built in its lap of sandstone and sage.

As the houses thinned out and the road climbed and the canyon narrowed again, I reached over, rolled down the passenger-side window, and filled the cab with pure Big Sky air. Soon I was on a camelback stretch of highway that awakened all those carsick memories from my childhood and filled my mouth with saliva.

The convoluted plains stretched as far as I could see on either side of the road. Coulees, bathed in purple-gray shadows, offered scrub pine and juniper a protected place to nurse coveted water in pools deep below the surface of the land. Irregular-shaped saline seeps, white and stark, were nothing more than fringed pools, long dried with no memory of spring rains. The ground within was parched and cracked. A far cry from the pristine forest described in the cryptic pages I had received.

I glanced in the rearview mirror and saw the Yellowstone Valley and Billings disappear behind me. In front of me as I crested the hill stretched shimmering waves of golden summer wheat swaying slowly under the seductive hand of the late-summer breeze. In the distance a deep azure silhouette of a mountain range rose from the plains and the sky stretched beyond forever.

I dropped down onto Pryor Creek Road, hung a right, and followed the highway as it cut through the great stands of cottonwood trees that canopied the road. There were no signs heralding my crossing from the county onto the reservation, but I knew. Two-story Monopoly board houses, different only in color and the number of abandoned cars in the yard, peppered the land in faded pastels. Clothes pinned neatly to lines hung limp and lifeless in the early-morning sun. Television antennas, broken and bent, teetered atop the roofs.

The distance between the houses grew shorter, and without warning I rounded a curve and was on the outskirts of the small, tired reservation community of Pryor. The main street was nothing more than a wide spot in the road with a sign that said 25 MPH. A small, yellow cinder-block building with Old Glory swaying in the breeze passed as the post office. I slowed down, giving a slower-moving black-and-white dog the opportunity to cross the street up ahead. Head hung low, tongue lolling out the side of his mouth, he ignored me completely as I neared, intent only on making it to the other side.

I drove past twelve buildings and saw that only four were in commercial operation: the post office, the BIA Tribal Cop Shop, the Pryor Trading Post, and the Quik Stop gas station, which was housed in yet another cinder-block building at the far end of the street. I flipped a U-turn at the Quik Stop and decided to take one more cruise through town looking for some semblance of a Catholic church. Two Jurassic gas pumps stood smothered in the high plains heat attesting gas at fifty-nine cents a gallon. Nothing else seemed much newer.

Narrow dirt roads spoked off the main street and mustered lazy flumes of dust into the air behind the truck. Weeds grew window high in front of an abandoned house, in sharp contrast to blossoming rows of yellow marigolds that framed the walk in front of a well-kept but small trailer behind a chain-link fence. There was a pattern here; the weeds were winning about fifty to one.

I wound back to the main drive and slowed down as I passed the BIA Cop Shop. Genevieve Cramer was standing outside, talking to two uniformed men. I watched for a minute, waited until she headed for a burgundy Pontiac Bonneville, then pulled up beside her. She looked as I leaned out my truck window.

"Phoebe. What are you doing up here?"

"I came up to talk to Monday Brown's wife and see if I could locate the Wolfs."

"Then you've heard about Matthew?"

"Kyle told me this morning. Do you think he's run?"

"Do I think *they've* run?"

"They? What . . ."

"Louis is nowhere to be found. He got a call from Matthew late last night. He was agitated, but when I talked to him he said nothing was wrong. Then, during the night sometime, he slipped out."

"Do you think they're together?"

"Yes, I do. I have a couple of friends with the tribal cops and thought maybe they could make some discreet inquiries without alerting the powers that be in Billings."

"Have you got time to talk for a minute?"

"Sure. Park your truck and come sit in here. I have an appointment this afternoon so I've got to get back to town."

I parked, walked over to her car, and got in.

"I know I was a little rambunctious in my office the other day, Phoebe. Forgive me?"

"I have that tendency myself, so don't sweat it. I appreciated you coming with us to the house."

"I couldn't believe it. If I had someone hanging in my tree I doubt that I could ever walk back into the house again. I'd at least have the tree cut down."

"Wasn't the tree's fault. I bought that place initially because of the trees, so I don't have one to spare."

"We have a real mess on our hands, don't we?"

The *we* puzzled me. "I think Matthew has a rough road ahead. I need to talk with him, and now it looks like I'm not going to have the opportunity."

"Oh, he'll show up. They always do."

"Genevieve, did you know Monday?"

"Only slightly. I had done some work with the kids at the high school and his wife was involved. As I recall he was there a few times, and I chatted with him, once, maybe twice."

"How long ago?"

"Actually, the last time was a few days before he disappeared."

"Did his wife ever mention anything or seem out of sorts?"

"No. She's cool as a cucumber. Controlled. But you know, now that you mention it, she was different around him. Quieter."

"What did you think of him?"

"Boisterous. Probably a bully, and it wouldn't surprise me if he battered her."

"Physically?"

"Maybe. But more than likely it would be mental and emotional. He seemed like he would be too clever to leave visible signs of abuse around for people to pick up on."

"What's your take on this, Genevieve?"

"I'm not sure I have one. I'm biased."

"How so?"

"I thought he was a maggot. What he was doing was wrong. There is so little culture left, and the clown made a living off selling culture to the highest bidder. God, don't get me started on that."

"Do you have any idea where these boys would head for?"

"The mountains. Definitely the mountains." She looked toward the east. "Probably right up there, in the Pryors."

"Maybe this is just a fishing trip or something." I laughed and watched her as she silently stared into the distance. "Right?"

She didn't answer for what seemed a very long time.

"Genevieve?"

"Hmm?"

"Could they have just gone fishing?"

"Maybe. I doubt it, but we'll see. I have to get back. I'm going to be late as it is. Can I call you later?"

"Sure. How about tonight?"

"Great. Kyle tells me you're going to be doing a sweat tomorrow. Are you going through with it?"

"I'm gonna give it my best."

"Maybe we'll run into each other after it's over. You'll enjoy it, Phoebe. It's quite a challenge."

"Great." I got out of the car and leaned back in.

"Why don't you come around about nine or nine-thirty? I have to eat dinner at my mother's, but I should be home by then."

"Sounds fine to me. See you then."

I got into my truck, followed another winding dirt road down through a thicket of bushes, and finally spied the beckoning spires of a white clapboard church. The words ST. TIMOTHY'S CATHOLIC CHURCH were carved in a rough-hewn sign set in concrete on the edge of the manicured lawn.

I got out of the truck and walked up to the front doors. They were unlocked, a rarity in churches today, considering the vandalism that takes place. The door I pushed opened hard. The hinges emitted a low groan of rusting disapproval. Once I was inside, the heavy door swung closed behind me. The sound reverberated throughout the church. Lit only by a tier of votive candles whose petite flames danced under a breeze I could not feel, the entire place seemed haunting in its stillness.

I moved down the center aisle, resisting the memory that instinctively would have me reach toward the font, dip the tips of my fingers into the holy water that I had always suspected was bottled by Evian, and cross myself. I walked toward the chancel rail, my eyes fixed on the figure of Jesus nailed to the cross that hung behind the altar.

A painted statue of Mary, practically as tall as me, was tucked conveniently into a Gothic-looking alcove to the left of the rail. At her feet, the tier of votive candles cast eerie shadows across the walls. An intricate beaded shawl was draped over her arms. She stood, eyes cast downward, clothed in suffering and compassion. If such instances as spiritual enlightenment do exist, I was in the middle of one, for at that moment I knew I was in the presence of . . . guilt. It was ingrained into the walls and floors and the holes in Christ's hands.

And Mary? My father's question, jokingly to my mother, was always the same: How did a Jewish girl explain to, of all people, her Jewish mother that she was pregnant but no one had touched her? There I was, in the middle of all that enlightenment, a smile breaking on my face, when out of the corner of my eye, a great shadow was looming toward me. The black silhouette of a hand, something long and sharp was arcing down upon my own shadow. There was no sound, only the screaming pulse in my temples as a massive hand sunk its fingers deep into my right shoulder.

13

I don't recall fainting, but there was definitely a blackout of some kind. The last thing I remember was incredible pressure against the side of my neck. Coming to, I felt someone holding me up underneath my arms. So I did what comes naturally. I rammed my elbow into the figure behind me and spun around to face my attacker. My would-be assailant didn't budge under the jab, and I found myself looking into a massive chest of black cloth.

"Lord help me," a low, almost jovial voice said. "I'm so sorry I frightened you. I've been working in my garden and heard someone pull up. You must have heard me come in. Are you all right?"

"Sure," I lied. Other than the greenstick fracture that was more than likely spiraling up my arm and the lack of breath to fill my lungs, I was, in fact, all right.

Looking down at me from a height of at least six foot four was a clone of Little John. His chest and shoulders were wide and massive. His face was as light as porcelain, his eyes a deep black and wide set. The smile impressed me the most. It was wide and white and welcoming. I felt like a fool. Dressed in a black cassock, the biggest priest I had ever seen in my life stood before me.

"I'm Father Tom. And you are . . ."

"Phoebe . . . Phoebe Siegel."

"And what brings you here, Phoebe?"

"I'm looking for someone. Ardena Brown."

"I'm afraid she won't be in today. Her husband is missing, you know. Sad, sad situation." His smile vanished, and he shook his head back and forth almost violently.

I watched in amazement as his chubby cheeks quivered under the motion. A shock of jet black hair fell onto his forehead. "Do you know Monday?" I asked.

"Of course. A good man. A good, good man."

Leave it to a priest to canonize an asshole.

"Maybe you and I could talk for a minute. Do you have time, Father?"

"I have nothing but time. But call me Tom. We're a little more relaxed up here. What is it exactly that you would like to talk about, my child?"

I recoiled at the "my child" shit but bit my tongue and tried to make the best of being in the presence of a Cardiff priest holding a hoe.

"You look like you were busy." I laughed a little and tried to relax myself.

"This?" He raised the hoe. "Life is like a garden. If you don't cut the weeds down," he said and slammed the wooden handle of the hoe onto the plank floor so loudly I jumped, "they strangle and eventually kill all that's good and fruitful. Let's sit outside in the sunshine."

I followed him toward the altar, where we took a left and walked down a hallway and out a door into the light. The garden was beautiful. A stone path wound around the near end and ended at a huge rock grotto with yet another statue of Mary. He sat down in one of two redwood chairs and motioned for me to do the same. I sat.

"Now. On with it. What's on your mind?"

"Do you know the Browns well?"

He threw his head back and laughed. "Well? Probably better than they know themselves. I've worked with Ardena all the time I've been here. Their son, Shawn, was baptized right here." He patted the arm of the chair. "Monday and I have spent many a day fishing over the years."

"Then you're fully aware of the situation and the speculation around his disappearance?"

"Poor, poor Monday. Ardena has been so calm through this whole thing. She's strong in her faith, you know."

The pious attitude irked me. "What do you think happened to him?"

"Are you a police . . . person?"

"No, I'm not. I'm a private investigator. You're probably aware of the fact that Matthew Wolf was detained as a suspect in Monday's disappearance."

"Yes, I am aware of that."

"I'm looking into a few things for Matthew's family."

He gazed into the distance and didn't respond. I pushed. "Do you know the Wolfs?" Still, no response. "Father?"

"Have you ever wondered why the mountains in the distance always look so blue and then the closer you get, there's nothing blue there? Just the green of the trees and the brown of the earth and bark. Odd, isn't it?"

"Pardon me?" I caught myself shaking my own head, trying to bring him back to the conversation.

"I'm sorry. My mind wanders all over the place. Yes, I know the Wolfs. Not well, but I do know them. They're traditional people, so we don't get them in mass. There are a few of those around, you know."

"A few what?"

"Traditionalists. They hold on to the old ways. The pagan ways. The Sun Dance, that sort of thing. They're the minority, but they hold on to their beliefs with the tenacity of a bulldog."

"You believe that's wrong?"

"Wrong? I don't think you can apply right and wrong to the situation. They're just misguided. Living in the dark ages. A very dangerous place to be, I might add."

"Do you think Matthew Wolf is involved?"

"I couldn't comment on that." Now he looked directly at me, his forehead wrinkled, dark eyes snapping. "Ask me something else."

"Okay." I was uncomfortable with his reaction and couldn't see the conversation going much further. "Maybe you could just give me directions to Monday's house and I'll see if I can catch Ardena."

He reached out; his massive hand easily, with room left over, encircled my arm and exerted a slight pressure. I looked down at his grasp and then at him, my own forehead furrowing. He immediately moved his hand.

"I was sharp with you. I'm sorry. You won't find Ardena at home. She teaches a summer creative writing class, and as I recall they were going on some day trip."

"Creative writing?" My mind flashed on the pages I had found on my back porch.

"Yes, and she's very good at what she does. I think keeping busy helps her keep her mind off of things. Don't you?"

"Could be. Has she said anything about what she thinks has happened to her husband?"

"Now, I can't betray any confidences, but yes, we've talked."

"And . . . ?"

"I just told you that I can't betray any confidences."

"And I haven't asked you to. How about your opinion? Can you at least share that?"

"Opinions are only unconfirmed speculations, my child."

Now I had a philosopher on my hands. "Do you think Monday is dead?"

His eyes narrowed as he scanned my face. "He's dead."

I was so taken aback I didn't know what to say. "How do you know that?"

"Because he loved his family. He loved his wife and his son and he loved this reservation. There are more than one and a half million acres here, and everyone still knows what everyone else is doing or what is going on in their lives. No one has seen Monday. He has not contacted anyone, and if he were alive, he would do just that. He would have contacted me. Does that answer your question?"

"Yes. It does. I'm sure you're aware of the artifacts that are missing with him."

"I saw him with them one afternoon shortly before he disappeared."

"You saw the artifacts?"

"Yes, he showed them to me. He wanted me to see them because they were going out of the country and I wouldn't have a chance again to see anything like them. He was quite proud of the fact that he had amassed—"

"Stolen?"

"No, he never stole. It was his life's work. He was the best. He never went after anything. They somehow always came to him. Remarkable human being."

Remarkable was one of the last adjectives I would have used to describe Monday. *Scumbag?* Maybe. But never *remarkable*.

"Do you remember what day you saw him?"

"It was in the afternoon. As I recall, on the same day that the young woman says he fell across her car. I remember that because of how happy he was. Ardena and he were together. She seemed as excited as he did, and that amazed me."

"Why?"

"They'd had some problems. External ones actually. There were some who felt that he was wrong in sending these artifacts out of the country, and instead of confronting Monday, they exerted pressure on Ardena."

"They who? And what kind of pressure?"

"The traditional people. To be more exact, Matthew Wolf and his brother, Steven. There was a group of them."

"Did Ardena tell you this?"

"I saw it. The jeers and the minor acts of vandalism. Someone slashed all her tires right out here in front of the church one night when she was working late. Monday had to come down from his house and pick her up. He was in a rage. Minutes before, James Eagle had been hanging around on the pretense of waiting for someone. It didn't take much to figure out who did it."

I thought about the beating that James had taken from Monday at the Arcade and his ensuing murder. "Was Monday active in the church, Tom?"

"No. But the Lord had his hand on Monday's heart. He would get all wrapped up in the traditional stuff, even said he had 'strong medicine,' but the Lord knew better. It was just a matter of time before . . ." Again, he faded.

"Before what?" He didn't answer. He just gazed into the distance at the blue mountains.

"I'm going to be going now," I said and moved away from him. "We'll talk again."

"Oh no you don't." Father Tom stood and towered over me. "Are you a Catholic?"

"Recovering."

"From what?"

"Forget it. I don't do church. Any church."

"Well, today you will." He again grasped my arm and started back to the door leading to the side of the church. "No one gets out of here without my special blessing."

"Look, I told you I really don't—" His grip was so strong that when he raised the arm he was holding me with, I had to walk on my tiptoes to keep up with him.

Once inside the church, he crossed in front of the altar, stopped to kneel, pulling me down with him, and crossed himself. Only then did he let go of my arm. I took my best shot and tried to walk around him. Before I knew it he was beside me again, shepherding me into a pew. Now I was pissed off.

"I don't know what the hell is going on here, but this shit has to quit. Priest or not, this is ridiculous."

His face practically fell into his hands. Sobs racked his body as he slumped down onto the pew beside me. "I'm sorry. I'm so, so sorry."

I felt like I'd been Maced with guilt. "Look, this just isn't my scene, Father. You come on with this strong-arm stuff and it, uh . . . puts me off. My brother's a priest, and I would react the same way if he pulled this shit. Damn! I mean stuff." I reached out and patted his arm.

"It's so hard these days. No one knows how hard it really is being a priest in a godless world. I'm a far better warrior."

"What?" I asked incredulously.

"What I'm saying is, I do better . . . oh never mind. Please, let's start over."

"Some other day. I really have to get going. I'd like to try and stop by the Wolfs on my way home. You could tell Ardena that I'd like to talk to her. That is, if you see her within the next couple of days."

His entire demeanor changed from that of a repentant child to that of a take-charge kinda guy.

"The least I can do is bless your mission." By now we were both standing. "You wait here. I'll be right back."

Father Tom, cassock flagging behind him, hurried down the aisle, dropped to his knees and crossed himself again, and disappeared behind the altar. I wanted to sneak out of the church but had visions of him lifting the back of my truck off the ground in order to carry out his own mission. So I waited. In short order he returned.

"Come up here," he urged softly. "To the communion rail."

"Uh . . . I don't think . . ."

"Oh, now stop that. This will only take a minute."

I walked forward, a reluctant lamb to the slaughter. With one hand placed strategically on my shoulder, he pushed me gently down onto my knees in front of the highly polished rail. With the same gentleness, he then placed his hand on the top of my head.

"Father, bless this young woman. She is needful of your guidance. Let her accept this sacrament through me from you." His hand left my head and swiftly tilted my chin up.

The only thing that crossed my mind was how things had changed with the mother church. His eyes were tender, caring, and there was something about his cherubic face that seemed suddenly so young and innocent.

"Open your mouth, my child."

"For what?"

He said nothing, just tilted that childish face that had go-along-with-me written all over it. I went along with it. As he placed the small round wafer in my mouth I fought the urge to break into hysterical laughter. It was tasteless and different in shape and size than I remembered.

"Klaatu. Barada. Nikto." His voice thundered. "Klaatu. Barada. Nikto."

"Okay. That's enough. I'm outta here."

"You'll never know what this visit has meant to me. I hope I was of some help."

"Tremendous amount. So much so that I doubt if I'll have to bother you again." Leaving now became my quest. But Father Tom was in close pursuit.

I opened the door to my truck, looked around to make sure that nothing was blocking my escape, and turned to face him. "Thanks again."

The words flew out of his mouth as he doubled up his fist and hit me in the shoulder. I flew back against the truck. Pain shot up my neck and down my arm.

"What the hell did you do that for?"

"Blue slug bug, no slug bug back."

"What?" I was so enraged, the *t* snapped off the end of my tongue.

"There." He pointed to the road going past the church and the dust trail of a small Volkswagen. "A blue VW Beetle. Haven't you ever played Slug Bug? I play it with the kids all of the time."

"Not in this lifetime. You know, Father, you could use some help. Jesus Christ."

"You're right, my dear, that's who you have to trust in, Jesus Christ."

I said as many denigrating words as I could under my breath as I got in and drove off. My tongue wandered inside my mouth trying to get the taste of the little pillow-shaped communion wafer out of it. Jeez. No wonder I was in religious recovery; they didn't even screen these guys anymore.

14

The Pryor Trading Post seemed the best place to get directions to John Wolf's. A group of young men coming out of the store carrying brown grocery bags eyed me with brief curiosity as I stepped aside and let them pass. I grabbed the screen door just before it was ready to slam closed and just before someone touched my shoulder from behind. I turned and looked up at Steven Wolf.

He smirked. His dark eyes snapped as he looked down at me and then looked away. "Come up to see how the other half lives?"

"The other half of what?"

"Maybe you're just cruising for a little cultural enlightenment."

"I don't have time for your shit, Steven—"

"Steven," he said and looked at me again. "You people are always playing with our names."

"Listen, I came up to see your father."

"He's not around."

"When will he be around?"

"Tonight. Maybe."

There was something about him that had pissed me off the first time I met him. Things hadn't changed.

"Let's cut through some of this bullshit. Kyle called me this morning and said that Matthew had taken off. It's not the smartest thing he could have done. Kyle can cover his ass for a couple of days; after that he could be in deep shit."

Steven motioned with his free hand toward the group of young men standing beside a red Ford truck.

"Robert, put this in the truck." He held out the sack he was holding.

"Going on a picnic or just your usual weekly shopping?"

"Maybe both."

"Steven, I want to help. If you know where Matthew is . . . for Christ's sake, don't you realize how bad it looks for him if he runs?"

He said nothing, but looked off into the distance.

"What the hell is it going to take? Damn. There's one very determined German out there who isn't going to play by the rules."

"He won't come up here."

"You're sure about that? The Feds can, and will. There's more going on than you know . . ."

"No. There's more going on than *you* know."

"Then talk to me."

"What's the payoff for you, Siegel? Are you one of those liberals that needs some token Indians in their lives? Or just one of those do-gooders that gets a kick out of helping us poor, dumb savages."

"God, you're an asshole. A friend of mine was almost killed, and as I understand it, a friend of yours *was* killed. And . . ."

"There's more?"

"You betcha there's more. What about the guy that ended up hanging in my tree? This isn't some Saturday matinee, Steven. Your brother's ass is in a vise, and I'm sure as hell not going to hang around and play infantile word games with you. You got that?"

Steven turned around and walked toward the truck, jumped up into the bed, and glared at me. He hit the top of the cab with his hand once, and the tires hurled gravel and dust out behind them as I stood there with my mouth open watching them disappear down the highway.

I tasted dust and communion wafer all the way back to Billings. I pulled into town a little before two o'clock, took the Twenty-seventh Street exit and followed it up to where Minnesota Avenue intersected Twenty-seventh, pulled into the curb, and parked. This was where it had happened. The Arcade Bar was a block south but within sight. I tried to imagine a dark, rainy night, a car stopped at the light, and the horror Sharon Mills must have felt when the body, identified as that of Monday Brown, fell across her car. He had to have come from some direction, and my bet was it was the alley on the southeast corner that ran between Montana and Minnesota avenues.

The light changed, and I crossed the street, walked down half a block and then west into the alley, nothing more than a wide spot on either side of the railroad tracks. There were worn loading docks, still in use, that didn't look like they would hold a man's weight much less a semi's load. Broken bottles, cardboard boxes, and remnants of clothing were strewn over the area.

A few years back they'd found a body under one of the docks that had made headlines, a dead Indian woman, her clothing pulled conspicuously up around her thighs. The picture hit the front page of *The Gazette* in all its degrading splendor and drew the outraged cries of citizens. It was a double-edged sword. There is no dignity in murder, clothed or unclothed, and news is, after all, news.

I knew firsthand that the cops patrolled the area heavily during the night, allowing sleeping vagrants to stay within their dreams as long as they didn't cause trouble. Monday was a homeboy in this area. It was what he had known his entire life. He was brought up here, and maybe, just maybe, it was fitting he had died here. If he had in fact died.

There were several places anyone could lie in wait, park a car, or hide around the docks. It was poorly lit and offered cover to the people of the night who climbed the narrow stairs through dark hallways of apartments on top of daytime businesses. In the shadows, they found sweet, if temporary, relief from one hour to the next by sharing a bottle of cheap wine or a joint, their addiction to struggle urging them on. After dark, the doorways filled with derelicts blanketed with newspapers as they tried to sleep off their pasts. This was not an uninhabited area. Someone had to have heard something, seen something.

The most likely candidate was Sammy Vargas, the proud, if not blatantly crooked, proprietor of Sammy V's Pawn Shop. Sammy and I had to talk. I covered my nose and mouth with my hand and walked back to Twenty-seventh Street, where I could breathe something other than desperation and human waste.

I walked to the truck and dropped a dime in the parking meter, tore off the ticket that some overzealous meter maid had placed on my windshield scant minutes before, and walked south one block to Sammy's shop.

Comfortably and conveniently behind the Arcade Bar and across from the state liquor store, Sammy V's was housed in a sister building to the Arcade. Both took up half the block. Both were two-story brick that had seen better days, and both preyed on those whose fate was still undetermined. People who lived a hair's breadth above poverty gathered on nice days to sit on the benches in front of Sammy's for gossip and shared complaints of misery and deprivation. Business was good on that block, even for the whores.

I'd spent my share of money in Sammy V's over the years. He was a crafty businessman who somehow ran not only the pawnshop but a small newsstand and a back room, where he always managed to stock scarce pieces of period furniture and primitives that he sold far below the going rates of local antique stores.

I stepped over outstretched legs and walked through the door. Four or five people were milling around. A young, very pregnant, disheveled woman was openly weeping at the counter. Sammy had a weird way of doing business; he was never behind the counter but always in front. A dingy white cotton carpenter's apron hung down in front and served as his office. Occasionally you could hear coins rattle or he would pull a receipt book out of a pocket. Sammy was living the American dream, and part of that dream was copping a feel at every opportunity. Just like he was doing now.

He looked toward the door as I entered.

"Hey, Siegel. Long time no see. Be with ya in a minute."

I waved acknowledgment.

Inevitably when a woman walked up to the stand, Sammy would grab his crotch, hold on for a minute as though he were adjusting some unseen weight therein, give a little shake, and grin into her face. His own was compressed, one side scarred from deep burns in his youth; he couldn't grow whiskers through the scars, but the other side was always stubbled and glistening with sweat.

He was a chubby man with sausage fingers, dirty nails, and a squat, round head that sat upon his body without benefit of a neck. He wore the same clothes daily, like a uniform. A black, flat hat with a small bill covered his scant and patchy head of hair. Pinned to his front was a button that said HONK IF YOU'RE HORNY. My bet was no one ever honked.

I watched him sideways as he pulled a wad of bills out of his apron, peeled some off, and handed them to the young woman while she gently pulled a set of wedding rings off her left ring finger. They made the exchange and she left, but not before Sammy ran his hand down her back.

Hastily writing in a receipt book, he came toward me. "You look-

ing for stuff or are you looking for"—paused as he looked at me and
grinned—"information?"

"You're too smooth for me, Sammy. Have you got information I'd
be interested in?"

"Maybe." He turned away from me and walked to a pair of boys.
He had the eyes of an eagle and could spot a potential thief before he
walked through the door. "Touch that again, you sneaky little bastards, and I'll have the cops on your ass. Get the hell out of here."

He rushed at them as they stumbled over one another trying to get
out of the shop.

"Goddamn sticky-fingered little fuckers," he said and wiped some
of the sweat off his forehead. "Come in here and think they'll steal
me blind. Well, they got another think coming. Like my foot up their
ass. Think they got the message?"

"Oh yeah. I think they got the message, Sammy."

"Now, let's get back to business. Just what brings you down here.
And how's that old '49 running? I got me some real serious buyers
when you decide to dump it."

"You'll never see the day."

"Never say never."

"Monday Brown, Sammy. Can you help me?"

"Poor son of a bitch. It was just a matter of time."

"How so?"

"He was a bad ass. Never gave anyone a fair shake in his life. Then
he comes up with this batch of stuff and puts the word out that it
goes to the highest bidder and the fool already had a done deal. Huh
uh. No good."

"The fight between Monday and some Indian boys, did you hear
about it?"

"Hear about it? I saw it. Whipped those boys. Damn near all of
'em. Then the cops came, and Beemer, there's another mean SOB,
broke the whole thing up. But not before he got his knocks in."

"What started it?"

"You expect me to know that? I don't hang out in the Arcade. You
know that as a fact, Siegel." He grinned mischievously.

"If we're talking facts, I also know that nothing goes on down
here that you don't know about."

"That's about right, I guess. I sure hate to get caught up in this
until they find out who did old Monday in."

"They had someone jailed for suspicion."

"That Indian boy? No way. Anybody with any brains would know it would take more than some young punks to pull that bull down."

"Do you think he's dead, Sammy?"

"Sure do. Dead as a nail and probably rotting away somewhere. Should be able to smell him by now." He sniffed the air, lifted one arm, and faked a sniff to his own armpit. "Hell, for a minute I thought that was Monday, and I'll be damned if it isn't me." Over the years the sweater that Sammy wore had become too small to cover the belly he had nurtured with greasy food and Danish. I watched, mesmerized, as his gales of laughter expanded his stomach and pulled the sweater higher and higher. When he was through, he took a more serious tone. "His old lady was leaving him, you know."

"No, I hadn't heard that."

"He was mean. To her and that boy of his. She's a bright gal, real educated. A teacher or something up on the reservation. Guess she just had a snootful."

"How did you hear this?"

"On the street. Seems like she had a little something of a serious nature going on the side. Hadn't heard that about her before. Monday? Now he was different story."

"That's pretty common knowledge. Were any names mentioned where she was concerned?"

"Nah. Just said she'd be taking the kid and leaving after Monday did his deal."

"Has anything come through your place that could be part of that stash that's missing?"

"Nope. Not a damn thing. And I'll tell you right now, I'd be hard-pressed not to do a deal under the counter so to speak. I'm no kid myself anymore, and I gotta think about retirement."

"Would you tell me if it had, Sammy?"

"Damn you," he roared and stomped the floor with his foot. "Now you know what I thought of your daddy. Hasn't been anything as good as him on the streets since he died. Except for your brother Ben."

"I know. Just asking. I need to get a lead one way or the other on this deal. I agree with you, I don't think Matthew Wolf was involved, but there's sure a helluva lot pointing a finger at him. Will you keep your ears open for me?"

"I'll do better than that. I've had every cop down here and even a couple of federal boys asking about the night Monday crawled up on that car. I got me some things I never told anyone."

"They are?"

"Well, there was a storm, lots of thunder and lightning. I'd had some strange dudes casing out my place, so I brought a cot down from upstairs and slept right in here. I was ready. I was even hoping someone would come through that door or a window so I could shoot their ass. I haven't shot anybody since I shot that fella in self-defense in seventy-six. Never even held me over, just let me go. They knew I was right. There's another night I remember with—"

"Sammy, what about the night it was raining?"

"I was in here on the cot, and I could see shadows through those windows out there. I could see people. Two, maybe three wrestling around. I figured it was those assholes I was expecting trying to stage a fake fight, so I stayed in here quiet as a church mouse and waited. They moved off down the street."

"That's it?"

"Hell no. A minute went by, and I thought I heard this thump against my wall. Well, I loaded up my Saturday night special and sat here. No one. No one came. So I got up and tiptoed over to the door and that damn train came through. There was only one car up at the light, the train was rumbling by, and I see these two people standing by the car."

"The ones at the light?"

"Right."

"I thought it was some punks hassling someone, so I yelled down there and waved my gun. One of them looked at me and waved me back. And then they seemed like they were helping the guy in the middle that looked drunk. He was stumbling and almost fell to his knees once."

"Why didn't you say something to the cops?"

"Well, there's a couple of new girls on the street. Off the Minnesota strip? Good-looking girls. I couldn't see if it was them or not. I thought maybe they had some trick they were getting ready to bed down."

"Are you saying they were women? The people by the car?"

"Couldn't tell. But they were tall, just like Gin and Tonic."

"What?"

"The new girls? The ones I just told you about?"

I shook my head and started laughing. "Is that what their names are? Gin and Tonic?"

"Yup. They don't do singles. They just do doubles. Nice girls, too. I wouldn't want to get them into any more trouble than they bring on themselves."

"Anything else?"

"Do you understand why I didn't say anything? It would have been my ass if I fingered someone. I play by the rules. You know that."

"Where could I find Gin and Tonic? Are they working for someone?"

"Nah. They're independents. At least for now. Doubt as if they'd talk to you, and like I said, I don't know if that was them or not. One was sure as hell tall. Tonic is like that. Damn near six feet."

"Sammy, if you hear about anything, or remember anything, will you give me a call?"

"I will. If you keep me first on your list when you dump that fortynine."

"Will do."

"Where do these girls work?"

"Up on the corner around Studio One. Sometimes up on First Avenue if they don't think they'll pull in an undercover cop."

"When?"

"Ten on."

"Thanks, Sammy. You're first on my list."

"How's that brother of yours doing? The priest?"

"Still priesting."

"Is he one of them liberals?"

"Michael? Hell no. Why do you ask?"

"That gal he dated in high school is back in town."

"Cara Menendez? I thought she was living in New York."

"Not now. Heard she was asking about him too."

"She'd be barking up the wrong priest, Sammy. Trust me. How the hell do you hear all this shit?"

"I keep my ear to the pavement. Never know what could bring in a few more bucks."

"Is that a hint? You want me to pay you?"

"No way. Not you, Siegel. We go back. Right?"

"Right, Sammy. We sure do."

"Siegel?"

"Yeah."

"Take it easy and slow on this one. Seems to me like there are some strange ones hovering around this whole Monday thing. Could get messy. Know what I mean?"

"Why don't you spell it out for me, Sammy?"

He leaned close and whispered. "Everybody was looking to get in on Monday's big deal. Since he disappeared, everyone's just keeping their mouth closed. You'd think somebody would be beating them hills for that kind of money."

"You'd think so. Are you sure they're not?"

"Hell yes, I'm sure. This big dude, some foreigner, put the word out on the street that *he* was looking for information on those missing items."

"That's understandable. He paid money for them. No big deal."

"No big deal, huh? Let me tell you something. Tonic told me that some fool heard he could make some money by maybe shaking this guy down. Well, word has it that he met with this fella and things got ugly. Real ugly. He put this guy's—"

"Which guy?"

"The foreigner put this guy's arm through the bumper of his car and kneeled on it. Broke it right at the elbow."

"You're sure about this?"

"Sure as I can be. Can't imagine Tonic pulling my leg. I guess the guy went to the emergency room, got a cast on the damn thing, and hopped a freight that night headed for Chicago."

"How'd Tonic know about this?"

"Her and Gin are fucking this foreigner. Sometimes twice a night."

"I love it when you're tactful, Sammy."

"Oops." He covered his mouth with his hand in a childlike way and blushed through his glistening sweat. "Sorry, Siegel. You're just one of the guys to me. I forget you're—"

"Well, Sammy now that you've lowered my self-esteem about thirty pegs . . ."

He immediately looked hurt.

"No problem. I want you to take this, and if something comes up, anything, call me, and if I'm not there, leave a message on my machine." I handed him my card and left.

15

No sooner had I parked in front of Mama's than a horn blared behind me. I looked in the rearview mirror and saw Kyle pull up in his Blazer.

"I've been trying to find you all day," he said as he followed me to the sidewalk. "How did it go in Pryor?"

"I struck out. I ran into Steven Wolf, who informed me his father wasn't available. Every encounter with Steven is interesting. But Genevieve was up there talking to the tribal cops. From what she says, Louis is with Matthew, or so she thinks."

"She told me. That's the least of our problems."

"Let's take a walk over to the park. We won't get a chance to talk once everyone gets here."

We walked in silence until we reached Terry Park and sat down on the grass. Kyle's long legs stretched out in front of him. In the last few years I had seldom seen Kyle out of uniform. But today he was sensually casual. I'd known Kyle since my days at Eastern Montana College. We'd taken criminology classes together. We were unsure of our futures in law enforcement but knew we were headed in the right direction.

I watched him as he watched some kids playing on a rope suspension ladder between two jungle gyms. I caught the twitch of a muscle in his jaw. For as well as I thought I knew him, I really didn't know any of the personal stuff like what he did in his off time or if he had a lover. I'd be lying if I said I didn't have a few lustful feelings about him now and again. I was sure I wasn't alone in those rambling thoughts. He was gorgeous. Tall, lanky, finely chiseled features, and a complexion the color of coffee laced with cream.

He had a reputation in the Sheriff's Department of being a guy who played by the rules, and those rules included meting out his form of street justice when the situation called for it. Kids were his soft spot. That didn't mean he applied the usual trout stream rules of catch and release that some cops did when they caught a kid smoking a joint. One joint to Kyle was a big deal, and hard as he was in the beginning, he never failed to stick to the kid like Velcro, lead him into rehab programs, and offer unlimited off-time support.

We'd never talked about it. Most of the personal information about Kyle was secondhand. And now, sitting with him on the grass, watching him watch the kids play, made me want to know more about him. Only this wasn't the time.

"So what's up?"

"We've got a major problem."

"I think we've had major problems from the beginning. Is this something new and wonderful?"

"Jimmy O'Donnell wants to give this over to a grand jury. We've got forty-eight hours, max, before they bring Matthew back in."

I said nothing. Jimmy O'Donnell was, among other things, a very hungry assistant U.S. attorney who pursued his cases like a shark that smells blood in the water. It was rumored that Jimmy had no heart and ran on the venom that was pumped through his veins by some steely mechanical device that dwelled inside his sunken chest.

He bragged openly that his salary had increased by $8,000 increments every five years since he had graduated from law school. He'd climbed the ladder into the U.S. attorney's office on the backs of anyone he could sink his cloven hooves into. The last person Matthew Wolf needed on his ass right now was Jimmy O'Donnell.

"You're kidding, right?"

Kyle looked at me, his deep-set eyes brooding and dark.

"Kyle, they don't even know if a crime has been committed, for Christ's sake."

"What do you think, Phoebe? Has a crime been committed? What do you feel in here?" He pushed his fist into his stomach.

"Hell."

"They just convicted that guy in Bozeman on a piece of microscopic brain tissue they found in his pickup camper, for God's sake. What the hell do you think is going to happen to an Indian kid from Pryor who, for some damned reason, had some of Monday's missing property stuffed under the front seat of his car?"

"How the hell do you know about that, Kyle? You told me you didn't want to even discuss it with me."

"Well, we're a little past that. John told me the whole goddamned thing this morning. He couldn't find you at home so he found me. Do you still have those things?"

"Do you want me to lie to you or tell you the truth?"

"Do you have them?"

"Yes."

"Where?"

"In my toilet."

"What?"

"They're in a waterproof Ziploc bag in that oak tank up on the wall above the toilet."

"Who else knows about them?"

"Roger."

"Great."

"You think Roger would sell me out?"

"Would Roger throw his entire career down the tube by lying to a grand jury?"

"They'd call Roger?"

"O'Donnell would put his mother on the stand and ask for the death penalty if he thought she'd perjured herself."

"Wait a minute here. How would he even know Roger, or for that matter I, was involved?"

"Clint Beemer."

"Clint?"

"You talked to him. Right?"

"Right, but—"

"No but's, Phoebe."

"I talked to him about the fight down at the Arcade. Nothing more."

"That's all it took."

"Where is this coming from? Why the federal interest?"

"I told you that Mueller has diplomatic connections, and no one wants this to turn into some national headline maker. Look at the rap Miami is taking. The Germans are warning their people to stay the hell out of Florida, Miami in particular."

"This isn't exactly Miami, Kyle."

"No. It isn't. And the government and the state want to keep it

like that. One Indian kid? In fact, let's go further. One Indian kid that
was heard in public threatening to kill Brown and the small matter of
the items under his damned car seat. Open and shut?"

"Circumstantial at best."

"O'Donnell can take circumstantial and turn it into something the
size of the Scopes trial. There it is," he said and waved his hand wide
out in front of him, "for all the world to see. Matthew goes down,
Mueller gets off, and any hint of an international incident is soon
forgotten."

"And O'Donnell climbs one more rung up the ladder."

"You got it."

"What do we do?"

"We hit this thing with a sledgehammer, *before* they call a grand
jury."

"Any suggestions?"

"Steven. He's the key."

"Well I'm no fucking locksmith, and he hates me. I tried talking
to him and ended up with a mouthful of dirt."

"What?"

"Never mind, Kyle. What about Genevieve? What about you, for
that matter? I can't walk the rope between professional and personal.
If I got pulled in front of a grand jury, I could not justify lying. Could
you? Let's get back to the house. Mama will see the cars and wonder
where the hell we are."

"Tell her we were playing footsie in the park."

"Have we got time?"

Kyle reached out and placed his hand on my shoulder. "I might
have to make time and hold you to it one of these days."

There was a God.

Birthday dinners at Mama's have three sections. The first is Mama
acting harried as she prepares the favorite food of whatever person is
being honored. This time it was Michael, and the pungent smell of
basil and oregano filled the kitchen as she fixed his annual spaghetti
dinner. Kehly stood over the pot, tasting again and again the rich red
sauce as it simmered. Rudy sat in my father's chair in the living room
and used the television remote like a submachine gun as he cruised
the channels, the static sound irritatingly loud. Michael spent his time
between the kitchen and Rudy, trying to get a word in edgewise be-

tween Mama and Kehly and then trying to outtalk the static coming from the television.

The second stage is dinner being served. Everyone crowded around the table, eating, laughing, and pretending we're far past missing the hell out of my brothers Ben and Sam and my father. But it's there, and somewhere in the course of the meal, silence is served up and we all get pensive, sad, and someone makes a vague reference to some small memory of one or all of them. Mama waves her hand in the air, commanding a change in topics, rises, and brings the cake to the table. But we all find room for the food, the stuffed feelings, and the birthday cake.

The cake heralds in the third stage: the reliving of Mama's pregnancy, delivery, and the ensuing birth of the honoree. In graphic detail she shares everything but the moment of conception. Then we slip into an easy conversation, shoving sad memories aside. That day was no different, with one exception. Michael was quiet and unresponsive.

"Excellent meal, Mrs. Siegel. Wish Kehly could cook like that." Rudy leaned back in his chair and patted his stomach.

"Why, thank you, Rudy. You should come by and eat more. You're welcome anytime. A young man like yourself, out on your own, needs to make sure he eats properly."

"I'm not saying Kehly doesn't cook—" Kehly shot a look at him that would have killed the average man. He caught the drift and changed lanes. "Thank you, Mrs. Siegel. Anytime you want to invite me, I'll be here."

"Kyle?" Mama asked. "Did you get enough?"

"More than. I'm going to have to run ten miles tonight to get this off."

"By the way, have they found out who chopped that man up in Phoebe's yard?"

"What?"

"For God's sake, Mama. No one chopped anyone up in my yard."

"That's not what—"

"He can't talk about it anyway. So let's change the subject." I turned toward Michael. "You're awfully quiet today, being the birthday boy and all. How's God?"

"He lives, Phoebe. God lives."

"Did you ever check out that certain subject I asked about?" I grinned, hoping to bait him.

"The one you wanted an explanation from Rome on?"

"That's it. Heard anything?"

He laughed and pretended to flip his fork toward me. "Not yet."

"What might this be about?" Mama asked.

"Phoebe wants a written explanation from the pope as to why dogs don't go to heaven."

"Phoebe," she shrieked. "You've got to quit this."

Kehly and Rudy giggled, and Kyle gently nudged my foot with his as he shook his head.

"You've got to take your faith more seriously, young lady. I can't imagine bothering your brother with that frivolous stuff."

"It's all right, Mama. I've been wondering the same thing myself lately."

Mama looked at Michael, shocked.

"Don't tell me the future bishop of Montana is questioning papal law?" I moved in swiftly for the kill and glanced at Kehly for her support.

She shook her head no, discreetly, her eyes pleading with me to stop.

"Michael's going through the seven-year itch as they call it. It's what every priest goes through, and they all come out stronger." She reached over and patted Michael's arm and smiled. "Right, honey?"

Michael patted her hand and took a sip of coffee. I glanced at Kehly and saw her raise her eyebrows. Whatever was going on, I didn't want it to go on in front of Kyle.

"I met a priest when I was up in Pryor today. Father Thomas? Do you know him, Michael?"

"Father Tom has been around as long as dirt. I guess I did hear he was still up at Pryor. How'd you meet him?"

"I was looking for someone that works at the church and ran into him instead." There was no sense giving them the whole story. "Different kind of guy."

"He's part of the old guard. As stable as they come. His entire life has been devoted to working with Native Americans."

"Stable?"

"You didn't think so?"

"Well . . . I, uh . . ."

"So what's he doing for himself these days?" Michael propped his elbows on the table under a disapproving stare from Mama.

"Uh . . . gardening and other things. You know more about what a priest does than I do, brother dear. I did mention you. One interesting thing happened. I was surprised that the church had gotten so casual."

"How so?"

"How's your Latin?"

"Intact. How has the church gotten casual?"

"Wait a minute here. I need to ask you what this one particular term means."

"Could I have some more coffee, Mrs. Siegel?" Rudy interrupted.

"Of course you can. Kehly, would you get that young man some more coffee, please?" She looked toward me. "I'm so proud of you, dear, for taking time to talk to the priest."

"There's no hope for her, Mama."

I shot Kehly a dirty look and then went back to Mama. "It was purely business. But this guy was so off the wall. Nice, but . . ."

"Get back on track, Phoebe." Michael waved his hand in my direction. "What is it you wanted to know?"

"God. Let me see if I can get it right. Okay. The words are klaatu, barada, nikto."

Michael was quiet. Thinking. "I don't have a clue. Where did you hear them?"

"I . . ."

Rudy stopped banging his spoon inside his coffee cup and looked toward me. "What were those words again?"

I repeated them.

There's laughter and then there's hysteria. Rudy was in some spasm of the latter. All our eyes were on him. Kehly slapped him on his back as he nearly choked.

"How the hell could you know what they mean?" Christ. I considered him barely literate.

"You don't know what they mean?" he asked through his laughter.

"Come on, Rudy. There's no prize on this one."

"Haven't you ever seen the movie *The Day the Earth Stood Still*?"

"Hasn't everybody?" Now he was pissing me off.

"That's what Patricia Neal has to say to the robot to keep it from destroying the earth. Klaatu, barada, nikto."

"You're right." Michael leaned around Kehly and looked at Rudy. "It's the part where he's backing her up and she's falling over all those folding chairs and just when you think she's had it, she says . . . whatever those words are."

I tried not to let my face flush, but it was so hot it was just a matter of time before my flesh started melting off.

"Where the heck did you hear that?" Michael asked, laughing as hard as Rudy.

"It was a joke, Michael. A test." I forced myself into a loud and boisterous fit of laughter.

When that subsided, Michael looked at me seriously. "How is Father Thomas? He's got to be getting up there in years."

"Looked young and fit to me."

"Young?"

"Thirty something?"

"No . . ." He looked puzzled.

"Maybe we've got our priests mixed up."

"Are you sure you didn't run into Simple Thomas?"

"Who the hell is that?"

"Oh, Phoebe, you remember," Mama said. "He's that young man, big as a house, but simple. He stayed at our parish last year when the priest went back east to see his family. Did he create quite a stir or what, Michael?"

Michael shook his head and smiled. "It wasn't that big a deal. He playacts a lot of different personalities. His favorite seems to be impersonating Father Tom. It ended up with him convincing a few people he was a priest and taking them through some silly sacrament."

"Silly?" Now I was getting nervous.

"It was the oyster crackers, Michael. And that's far from silly."

"What do you mean oyster crackers?"

"He was giving communion to people on an individual basis and giving them oyster crackers in place of communion wafers."

"No shit," I said weakly.

By the time the tidal wave of laughter died down I was half sick to my stomach.

Kehly looked at me, holding her sides. "God, that hurts. Can you imagine anyone stupid enough to fall for that?"

I said nothing.

16

Kyle left, but not before telling me that he'd get ahold of me in the morning. I was standing out in front watching Kehly and Rudy pull away from the curb and disappear down the street, into the night. Michael walked up behind me and put his arms around me. I held on to them with my hands.

"What's this sudden display of affection all about?"

"I just wanted to hug my little sister and thank her for showing up."

"Hmm. I guess I need a hug. Why so quiet tonight?"

"Tired. That's all."

"Are you sure?"

"I'm sure. You know I've always admired you, Phoebe. You've got guts. You live your life just the way you want to. That doesn't let you off the hook for being hard to get along with sometimes."

"What's this about?"

"It's not about anything. Still can't take a compliment, can you?"

"Are you going through this, uh . . . seven-year itch thing? Mama seemed a little concerned."

"Come on, you know Mama."

"You bet I do. She brushes everything aside that's critical, and that's exactly what she did when Kehly said that."

He was silent for a minute as he nuzzled his chin down into my neck.

"Michael, you know we can talk if you need to."

I waited for him to reply. He didn't.

"I was down at Sammy V's today."

"Oh yeah? You two don't have a thing going, do you?"

I pulled away and turned to face him. "You are a mean man, Michael Siegel."

"How is old Sammy? He hasn't been in mass for a few weeks."

"Sammy goes to mass?"

"There are still people in the church, Phoebe."

"He said Cara was back in town. Have you seen her?"

"Yes. I have."

I watched the muscles tense in his face. His eyes glistened under the glow of the streetlight on the corner.

"How is she?"

He hesitated while his eyes searched my face. "Beautiful as ever."

"Michael—"

"Don't, Phoebe. Hey . . ." He looked at his watch. "I've got to get home."

"You *are* home. That's just where you live."

"Be nice. Your friend the deputy seemed like a nice enough guy, but man was he quiet."

"He's got a lot on his mind. Once you get to know him, he loosens up a lot. I think you'd like each other."

"Anything going on between you and him?"

"God, is that all this family thinks about?"

"Well, now that old Roger is out of the picture . . ."

"Michael, I had a conversation similar to this one this morning with Mama and Kehly. Spare me, please."

"I left some things in the house that I have to get. Coming in to say good night to Mama?"

"I already have. Michael?"

"What?"

"If you need to talk, I'm here. You got that?"

"Thanks. But there really isn't anything to talk about. I'll see you soon."

He started to walk toward the house and then stopped. He turned around, smiling. "Phoebe, you're not the first one to partake of the sacred oyster cracker. Don't be too hard on yourself."

"How did you know?"

"Your face was as red as your hair."

"God." I didn't know what to say.

"Drop in some Sunday morning and I'll give you the real thing. It'll jar your memory and you won't get into trouble again."

I shrugged and watched him walk into the house.

The weather forecast on the radio predicted a storm moving from the north by the next evening. Temperatures were supposed to drop rapidly by late afternoon. I played with the dial until I caught the news.

> At noon today, Assistant U.S. Attorney James O'Donnell announced that he will make a decision within the next thirty-six to forty-eight hours, on whether he will call a grand jury in the disappearance of Monday Brown. Mr. Brown is reported missing and assumed to have met with foul play. Although Mr. O'Donnell would not comment further, he did state he was confident that an indictment would be handed down. And now for the latest agricultural report. . . .

I turned the dial until I found K-BEAR, the only station in town that plays real music, pure fifties and sixties R & B. Even the sultry beat of Aretha Franklin singing "A Natural Woman" couldn't take the chill out of my mind.

My headlights flashed on a car as I turned into my driveway. I pulled up behind it just as Genevieve walked into the beams. She shielded her eyes with her hands and came toward the truck.

"Am I late?" I asked as I got out and walked toward her.

"No. I got here early. I was having a moment of peace in the dark on your front porch. How was dinner?"

"No surprises. Come on in, Genevieve."

Once inside the house, I led her into the dining room, flipping lights on as I went.

"Would you like something to drink?" I motioned for her to sit at the dining room table while I walked on into the kitchen.

"Tea?"

"Coffee? I don't do tea."

"Coffee would be fine."

"I love your place. Mind if I look around?" Her voice faded as she moved toward the front of the house.

"Be my guest."

"There's such character in older homes. Have you ever wondered who lived here before you?"

"I got the history on the house before I bought it. Do you use cream and sugar?"

"Both."

I looked around the edge of the kitchen door and saw her gazing up at the brass chandelier in the living room.

"I was joking about the cream. Will two percent do it?"

"Anything is fine. This is a beautiful piece. It's good to see that some people have enough of a conscience to have left it hanging there through the years. I have a confession to make. I've been curious about you for a long time."

"Kyle must have been talking out of school."

I entered the dining room carrying two cups of coffee and balancing a carafe in the crook of my arm. Returning to the kitchen, I grabbed a five-pound bag of sugar, tore open the top, shoved a spoon into it, and took the milk from the refrigerator. By the time I got back to the dining room, she was sitting at the table.

"There's informal and then there's"—I placed the sack of sugar on the table—"this. So what's this reputation that's preceded me?"

"I followed the Mary Kuntz trial thing last year in the papers very carefully. It was a relief when they found her not guilty. How's she doing?"

"She's going to be fine, eventually. I get a letter now and then. She's down in Wyoming."

"How did *you* fare, Phoebe?"

"Is this some psychological test Kyle set up?" I smiled but felt uncomfortable with her probing. "Or have members of my family contacted you?"

"Is that how I'm coming off? I apologize. That's what a degree in psychology does for you. You stop having normal conversations. I'm not probing, Phoebe. It just struck me at the time that the entire situation must have been cathartic for your family."

"In a way, maybe. We went through the entire grief process again, but this time it was without the baggage."

"Of suicide?"

"Right."

"As I recall, your ex-husband was killed . . ."

"Genevieve, this isn't a subject that I'm comfortable talking about."

"I did it again. Damn."

Things had been going all right for me the past year. I'd lived in a bitter fog for three years since my brother Ben had been found in his car on top of the Rims with a single gunshot wound to the head. She was right, it had been cathartic. And we had gone through a cleaner grief, but the fact remained, I had shot Lanny Wilson, a man I had been married to, had loved and made love to. It was something that would sit like a pus-filled cyst at the back of my mind for the rest of my life. I didn't need a shrink to pull me into some casual conversation about it.

"I've got something I'd like you to look at if you wouldn't mind." I reached to a stack of papers on the corner of the table and pulled out the manila envelope someone had placed inside my back door.

"What is it?"

"You tell me. You're the expert. I'd like your take on it."

"Let's have a look."

She read each page carefully and without expression. When she was through she glanced briefly through it again, then set it back down on the table in front of her.

"Weird, huh?"

"I'm not sure that's the word I would use."

"What word would you use?"

"Sad. A memory. Someone possibly reaching out to be understood."

"You don't think this is a joke of some kind? A badly written piece of fiction?"

"Possibly. But I don't think so. Where did you get it?"

"It was left here sometime either last night or early this morning. Was it written by a female?"

"Could be either. The little girl thing is almost too obvious. It could be a ploy to throw you off. What was *your* reaction to it?"

"It spooked me. Mainly because someone opened my back door and placed it on the floor inside the porch. They pulled James Eagle out of the water not far from here, and yesterday . . ."

"My guess is you've heard from your killer."

"My killer? How the hell do you figure that?"

I'd gone through the FBI Academy at Conduce and had been intrigued with the forensic psychology courses I'd taken. It wasn't improbable that a killer would play catch-me-if-you-can. But, why with me?

"Bad choice of words. I think you've heard from *the* killer. Have you told Kyle about this?"

"Not yet. I bagged the envelope and thought I'd have it checked out for any latent prints."

"There won't be any prints. Whoever wrote that would take every precaution."

"If it's from the killer. What if it's some word map that's supposed to lead us to Monday?" I picked up the papers and placed them back on the corner of the table. "Anyway, have you heard from Louis?"

"No. I haven't. I really don't expect to."

"Great. Just fucking great."

"I take it you didn't accomplish what you set out to in Pryor."

"Don't ask."

"I wish I could help in some way, but I really have no more author-ity up there than you do."

"I thought Louis was your responsibility."

"When he's down here, I do what I can. Keep him in school. On the straight and narrow." She shrugged. "Louis is a special kid. I can say the same thing for Matthew. They're bright. Both of them."

"Bright? This is not bright."

"What can I do to help?"

"Tell me where I can find Matthew."

"I wish I could do that, Phoebe. I have to believe that, sooner or later, he'll show up."

"Dead or alive?"

The phone rang. I excused myself and walked into the hallway to answer it. I said hello and waited for a response. Nothing came. I could hear someone breathing on the other end.

"In one second, I hang up."

"Matthew wants to meet with you."

"Steven?"

"He'll be at the Big Ice Cave—"

"The what?"

"Don't talk. Just listen. I put the directions of how to get there in your mailbox."

"Steven, I've got this, uh . . . thing going in Pryor tomorrow late in the morning. How the hell far is it from there to where Matthew will be?"

"It's all in your mailbox. You get one shot at it. That's all. Oh, and one other thing. I wouldn't say a thing about this to whoever's at your place right now."

"Steven, wait a minute. Genevieve Cramer is here, and I can have her out in two minutes. We'll talk. Okay?"

"It's in your mailbox. If you don't come alone, it's all off."

The line went dead. I placed the phone back on the base and walked into the dining room.

"Anything wrong?"

"No. Nothing. Listen, I'm beat. Could we get together in a couple of days?"

"I was just thinking the same thing. Are you sure nothing is wrong? You look a little stressed out after that call. I hope it was nothing—"

"My, uh . . . my little sister. I had dinner over there tonight and left something she thought I might miss. No big deal."

I walked toward the front door and all but ushered her out.

"Nice that you could drop by, Genevieve. I'll be in touch."

She waved her hand, got into her car, and drove off. I stood and watched as the taillights were swallowed up by the night. Tomorrow seemed a long way away.

17

The path wound through tangles of native wild rose and choke-cherry. Virginia creeper twined snakelike up the mahogany-colored trunks of river larch and alder just a step ahead of the slower-growing wild clematis that eventually demanded death of all it strangled. Cottonwood trees dusted the air with delicate puffs of white that had exploded after an early-morning rain into a seductive scent of mildew and resin. I stopped, enthralled with how the seeds, wrapped in cotton boas, caught the shafts of sunlight as they sailed unencumbered through the air in search of fertile ground.

I've never classed myself as the granola type, but my father was. God, he loved the edge of the Yellowstone, the bottoms, as he called it. As kids, we walked while he waxed, never proselytizing, at length on the mysteries of the Cabala and the lessons to be gleaned from the *Pirke.* He was a cop and a scholar and committed to a religion that he lived quietly within himself. According to my father, Indian people knew something, some secret thing about oneness that the rest of the world was too pious to accept. For one moment, under a canopy of cottonwood trees, my fear subsided. Being there just seemed right.

"I was beginning to wonder if you were going to make it." Al-thea's voice caught me by surprise. I turned and saw her standing a few feet from me. "Beautiful out here, isn't it?"

She reached out and picked a canary yellow rose blossom from a nearby bush, brought it up under her nose, and breathed deeply. "You look white as a sheet. Relax."

"I think I'm going to throw up." I gave myself a reality check and wondered how the hell I had even been talked into this. And I thought men were chromosomally challenged. "There are other ways to get around this *trust* issue. I hate heat, and get real weird in confined spaces. And besides, I'm not in the habit of proving a damn thing to anyone. You go ahead without me and share the experience with me later." I turned to leave.

"Nonsense," she said as she reached out and caught my arm. "Relax. You're going to love this. Do you remember everything I told you?"

"Sure. Don't puke, don't die, and . . . oh yeah, the switches. Beat myself with the switches. That's real Benedictine. This is some sick shit, Althea."

"You need an attitude change." She laughed. "Follow me, and I'll introduce you to everyone." Althea rolled the stem of the rose between her fingers. I watched it twirl, the glint of the sun reflecting off the dew-covered petals. She turned and disappeared down the path. I followed and within minutes broke into a small clearing. Four women, standing beside a broad, slow-moving stream, stopped talking and turned toward me. My mind locked. They were nude. I could handle the nude, almost. The tough thing about it was they were all legs, the combined length of which would have easily spanned the distance between Billings and God.

Admittedly, I have a leg *thing*. My sister has long legs, long, gorgeous legs. The world has legs. Me? I was cursed with reptilian appendages and an inseam that would only be found at the ABC Kiddie Shops. I'd been assured over the years that as long as my legs reached the ground, I was in good shape. I accepted that with some hesitation but had learned to live with it, that is, until now.

"Phoebe, this is Karen Old Crane, Ellen Rides at Night and her daughter Susan, and Ardena Brown. I believe you've met Anna Wolf."

I turned and saw the old woman, Matthew's great-grandmother, sitting in a green lawn chair near the water. She held a stick and was scratching in the soft sand at the water's edge. Althea guided me toward the group.

"Take everything off," she said matter-of-factly, until she saw the look of horror on my face. "At least all the outer stuff and your shoes and socks."

A small, dome-shaped lodge, layered with canvas and quilts, grew out of the ground at my left. I concentrated, staring at it while I stripped. It was no more than four feet high and seven feet in diameter, large enough to accommodate four, maybe six people. There was a small door that faced toward the east. Near it a fire had burned down to bright red coals. A stack of rocks on top of the coals glowed with intense heat for inches around them. I had the sinking feeling that part of this experience was going to be me walking across the shimmering coals.

Althea Wolf said something in Crow, dropped sweet grass into what was left of the fire, and fanned the pungent gray smoke toward herself. The scent was both nauseating and intoxicating. The two younger women who had been standing nearest the stream, their arms folded over their bare breasts, stepped forward and did the same.

Althea motioned to me to come closer and said, "You might want to take that off." She looked down at the delicate silver Star of David, which had been my father's, hanging from a chain that encircled my neck.

"I don't take this off," I answered more defensively than intended. The Star of David doesn't have any religious meaning, not like a crucifix, anyway. It's just a good luck charm, an identifier. If the Jews could wear them as armbands under the Nazis, my father said he could wear this one. He told me once that, according to legend, when David was hiding from Saul, he took refuge in a cave. A spider wove a web across the front of it, and when the soldiers came looking for him, they saw the web and decided that no one was there. My Aunt Zelda just laughed about that; she said no one knows how it all came about. None of that really matters; it was my father's, and now it's mine.

Althea smiled. "It'll be okay. Clear your thoughts and think positively. Remember, take nothing negative in there with you, Phoebe. You have an opportunity to be revealed to yourself. Find out who you are."

Negative? Wasn't fear negative? Nude under these circumstances, bare-assed in the middle of the forest primeval with total strangers, who, furthermore, had legs, was about as negative as I could get. Yes. Nude was definitely negative. And as far as being revealed to myself? Hell, why not? Standing half nude in the middle of strangers was revealing enough.

I stepped forward and clumsily fanned the smoke toward my body. I closed my eyes in a vain attempt to keep them from watering.

"Ellen and Susan will be taking care of things out here," Ardena said as she stood beside the door to the lodge and motioned everyone in. "Althea will be conducting the sweat. She was given the right from Anna."

Karen and Althea ducked down and disappeared inside. I followed.

To the right of the door as I entered I saw a small pit dug into the earth. I moved away from it and positioned myself toward the rear of the lodge on a small canvas mat. Ardena joined me.

I leaned my head back and tried to play several scenarios in my mind that would get me the hell out of there and still save face. Althea reached over and patted me on my leg reassuringly.

"Thank you for joining me in this sweat." Althea's voice was low, reverent. "Last winter John went to Billings for medical tests. He was sick. I pledged to do a sweat if the tests turned out all right. They did. We have trouble of a different kind now and need strength."

I was a little disappointed. I thought there would be a flowing dissertation that would overwhelm me. It turned out to be short and to the point. Karen said something in Crow and reached for a ladle in a bucket sitting beside her. She wet her hair and her face, and spooned water down her arms and legs with her cupped hand. She drank from the ladle and handed the bucket to Ardena. When all four of us had completed the ritual, Althea leaned toward the door and placed the half-empty bucket outside. Another was handed in to her.

The rocks followed, one by one. Carried on a stout wooden fork, they were placed meticulously in the earthen pit. Althea threw sage and sweet grass onto them. The intense heat carried the bittersweet scent throughout the lodge. Althea flicked water from her fingertips onto the rocks. I was amazed as that single gesture cleared what was left of the lingering smoke.

I reached up and ran my hands through my wet hair, tilted my head back, and took another deep breath. Without warning, the lodge was plunged into an unreal blackness as Althea dropped the flap to the door from the inside and fastened it tight. I stiffened, sat straight up, and stared into the darkness.

A crack as loud as a rifle shot exploded as the first dipper of water hit the rocks. The shock of molten steam forced my head back, searing my nostrils. The hissing sound reached the pitch of a thousand attacking snakes. Panic and shock turned to terror as I covered my face with my hands. Acutely aware of the opening of each and every pore in my body, I felt the sweat gush from them, tasted it in my mouth, and tried to block the stinging release of salt that tore at my eyes.

My pores stretched, expanded until my flesh was rendered down to a pulpy mass. Another dipper hissed, and then another. I fought for breath and steeled myself to keep from tearing through the side of the lodge. My mind screamed, commanding me to escape, to dig if necessary through the dirt to freedom.

There were sounds, words, floating toward me. Floating away from me. Claustrophobia tightened its steel vise. I reached out to ward off the walls I knew were moving toward me. My hand groped for Althea in the dark. The fourth and last dipper of water hissed as it hit the rocks. My hand found the calf of her leg. I squeezed, unable to speak as the temperature of the steam rose rapidly. A hundred and thirty-five degrees, a hundred and forty, a hundred and forty-five, and beyond.

Althea pried my hand free.

"Lean forward, lean forward." Her words were nothing more than vapor in the dark. "Lie down on your side."

I was without form, without mass. Flesh no longer covered bone, bone no longer existed. I was flying, soaring somewhere beyond myself. Images danced and teased and touched the core of me. I had no doubt I was dying. I tried to draw my knees up and touch them with my forehead. Time was no more.

I floated high above myself, accepting, with no recourse, my fate. Someone was talking, chanting, but it meant nothing. The flap lifted. Light purged the darkness. Sitting up, I inhaled and filled my lungs with the life-giving cool air that rushed in as my resurrection.

The terror returned as darkness descended once more. Seven more dippers of water were spilled onto the rocks. Someone thrust a small bundle of switches into my hand. I wrestled for memory. Althea had told me what to do with them. With weakened arms I brushed the bundle over my body.

Again, the light. Again, the soothing stream of cool, fresh air. And, again, it was gone. The temperature climbed and neared a hundred and sixty degrees. Ten dippers spilled. My mind was free, at peace. I sailed through clouds and felt them as they touched my body with satin softness. Spinning, soaring to heights never imagined, I, She of No Compromise, She of Little Faith, released myself to the experience. Unaware of the flap opening a third time, I knew nothing of the endless dippers of water that drenched the rocks.

Something moved against my neck. I reached up and grasped the chain that was sliding down the slickness of my skin. I held it coiled in my hand and brought it to my chest. There was no wall, no shield, as my hand penetrated my being. My fingers stroked my heart. I could feel the smoothness, could feel the pulsating throb push against my own touch and hear the rhythm in my ears. I smiled as tears and sweat coursed down my face. It was over.

The flap lifted, and I crawled toward the opening and out into the coolness. My legs were wobbly. My eyes squinted against the brightness. An eagle high above me caught a spiraling thermal updraft and floated without effort upward and out of sight. My hand opened; the silver Star of David my father had worn his entire life gleamed in the sun, its barrel clasp still fastened. For one insane instant I believed I had flown with that eagle. I staggered toward the stream, brought my hands together, and plunged in headfirst. There was no shock, just the gossamer touch of the water and more freedom than I had ever known.

Althea Wolf approached me as I started to follow the other women down the path.

"Could you stay and talk with me for a moment?"

"Sure. I wasn't sure it would be the acceptable thing to do."

She laughed and reached out for my arm. "Come over and sit near Grandmother. She's been very concerned about you."

"Me . . . ?"

"Matthew came to her before he left the other night. She wanted you to know there was someone working bad medicine on you. On all of us."

"What exactly does that mean?"

She guided me to the edge of the water. The sunlight danced across the reflection of my face. The old woman started speaking immediately, her words accentuated with the movements of her hands.

"Grandmother says the spirits of the dead are restless. We call these Night Walkers, Phoebe. She's worried about Matthew. There is a witch that has very powerful medicine. An angry, spiritless person has brought dark and soulless eyes to the night."

The hair stood up on my arms as I watched the old woman's face.

Her eyes never left mine as she talked. Without warning her hand reached out; she grabbed my forearm and gestured with her stick to the sand at the edge of the pond. A crude stick figure of a person and a large bird above it were etched in the sand. Althea continued to interpret.

"She says this is the person you have to find. She is leaving this here beside the water. When the water carries this away"—she stabbed the stick into the center of the figure—"it will be over."

"Over how?"

Althea said something. Anna answered.

"She wouldn't answer that, Phoebe. But someone else will die. Maybe more than one. The owl has visited her and told her this."

"An owl came to her and talked to her. Look. Althea . . ."

"Owls carry bad news and warnings of death. It doesn't matter if you believe this or not, it's already happening."

I was speechless. The stick figure, the bird, the child in the story and the eagle, and again the eagle that flew above me just before I plunged into the stream, they were all connected somehow. Impossible as it seemed, I wondered if Anna had sent me the typed pages. Or someone close to her.

The old woman stood and moved on shaky legs toward me. She reached up and placed the side of her hand on my cheek. Our eyes met. She said nothing as she removed her hand and reached out for Althea.

"We have to go. She's not well, and I don't like her out for long periods of time."

"Althea, I don't understand any of this. You're nice people, but this is—"

"Don't question your experience here today. Let it be just that, an experience."

They disappeared down the path. I turned and looked at the stick figure by the edge of the water. Sweet as the old woman was, she'd never make a police artist.

18

There's a saying in Montana: If you don't like the weather, wait a minute and it'll change. Temperatures have been known to drop thirty degrees in the course of an afternoon. Depending on what our Canadian neighbors decide to send us, a balmy, sunshine-filled morning doesn't always hint of the temperatures that descend with the swiftness of a peregrine falcon by afternoon.

The pewter gray clouds that were sailing the sky above me foreshadowed the possibility of rapid change. The air had a sharp edge to it, the kind of edge that makes your nose hairs stand at attention with each breath.

I'd followed the directions that had been placed in my mailbox and had hung out at the Plenty Coups Memorial for an hour to make sure no one was following me. Watching employees from the State Department of Parks and Wildlife clean out the outhouses, empty the Dumpsters, and pick up cigarette butts from the rolling grass lawn was about as appealing as hanging out in downtown Billings and watching the parking meters run out of time. But there I was.

I reached up and once again touched the chain that encircled my neck. The Star of David lay in the hollow of my throat, the clasp firmly fastened. Althea had been insistent: I was not to question anything I had experienced in the sweat. I was to accept it as just that: an experience. That made as much sense as the sound of one hand clapping. There was no way I couldn't question. Had it slipped at all? Or had it slipped to make a believer out of me? And if so, a believer in what?

As I sat there contemplating the greater truths, I missed noticing the car that pulled up behind my truck. The sound of a car door

closing caught my attention. I was shocked and a little panicked to
see Genevieve walking toward me.

"What are you doing here? Supervising?"

"Just taking a break before I head back to Billings."

"Want some coffee?"

"I'd kill for coffee. You've got some?"

"I always carry a thermos and a Go Cup. It's that caffeine that
keeps me going all day." She smiled, reached out, and touched my
arm. "I'll be right back. Do you mind drinking out of the thermos
lid?"

"I'm so dehydrated I'd drink out of my hands."

She returned with the thermos and a quart-size Go Cup.

"That's a serious-size cup you've got there."

Genevieve unscrewed the top of the thermos and poured the
steaming coffee into it. "Are you coming down with something? Your
cheeks look a little rosy."

"No," I sipped the coffee. "I'm not coming down with anything. I
went through, uh . . . did a sweat. . . . How the hell do you say that?
Went through? Did?"

She laughed for about thirty seconds and again reached out and
placed her hand on my arm. "You guys—"

"You guys, meaning?"

"I'm sorry. I don't mean anything by that. It's just that your culture is into such perfection. The words have to be *right*. It's all so
word oriented. It doesn't matter how you say it. Did a sweat. Took a
sweat. I've always felt that it was because the white culture believes
that if the words are right, strung together right, plus with a bigger
vocabulary, they possess more credibility. It just complicates instead
of simplifies."

"We are pretty full of ourselves, aren't we?"

"No. Just busier mentally than you need to be. This is a simple
world. Don't complicate it."

"Aren't you going to ask me how it went? The sweat?"

"No. That would be rude." She took a drink of coffee and looked
up on the bluff that flanked the park.

"Am I like violating some sacred trust if I talk about it? I'd really
like some answers, Genevieve."

"Of course not. But I don't think I'll be able to give you any answers, Phoebe. The experience is yours and yours alone."

Again my hand went up and touched the Star of David. "I lost this during the sweat."

"It looks like you found it again."

"I didn't *lose* it, lose it. It slipped from my neck. I've worn this since my father died. Through showers, swimming. The fastener is not that easy for me to undo. But it came off. I was just sitting in there . . ."

"Just sitting?"

"Dying. The heat was so extreme, and the steam and the glow from those rocks . . . It was overwhelming. Then I felt the chain slipping from around my neck."

"You mentioned the glowing rocks. Our belief is that the Great Spirit—Creator, God, whatever you want to call him—created all of this"—she waved her hand across the landscape—"and that all things are living. Rocks are living. When they're used in the sweat ceremony, we talk to them and they talk right back to us. Did you listen?"

"Look, Genevieve. I am not a religious person."

"But was your father?"

"I think so. He was Jewish, and he always told me that being Jewish was a way of life. He kept the Law, observed the Holy Days. That's what being Jewish is all about, you know. Obeying the Law, being just. At the heart of it . . ." I took a deep breath, surprised at everything I remembered, at the things I knew without realizing I knew them. "At the heart of it, it comes down to what a teacher, Hillel, once said, when asked what the Torah said. It was something like, 'Treat others as you would treat yourself, the rest is commentary.' Judaism isn't about ritual, or at least it isn't supposed to be.

"He loved his family. And, God, he loved nature. I think he wore paths in the ground beside the Yellowstone River. He spent a lot of time there. A lot." I could feel an overwhelming sense of loss welling up inside me. My hand was still wrapped around the Star of David.

"And that's a symbol of his faith."

"Yes."

"And it slipped from your neck?"

"Yes, it did."

"This is against everything I believe in, but I want to throw a couple of things out to you. You just told me you weren't that religious—"

"I just can't buy into it. The Bible, church, the whole thing; it just doesn't fit somehow."

"Traditional people don't need a church. They have all of this." Again, she waved her hand across the land. "And a Bible? They have the wind, the rain, and the stars. The world is an open Bible if people could just see it. Native people have studied all of this for millions of years. I think your father must have had a sense of that. The symbol of his faith slipped from your neck, but you caught it and you put it back. Maybe the rocks brought you words from your father. Maybe, just maybe, he was telling you that your faith is not lost, that it just slipped away for a while, and that all you have to do is reach out and bring it back where it belongs. Our religion is based on natural law, not man's. And natural law is God's law. I believe the rocks spoke to you, Phoebe. But the interpretation has to be yours."

I know my mouth was open, and I was staring like the village idiot.

"Then again, you just might need a new fastener." She leaned back on the picnic table and laughed.

"Right. Go figure."

"I've got to get going. I have some business down at Crow, and I'm going to be late as it is. You heading back to Billings?"

"Right. But I think I'm going to sit here and do another few minutes of communing."

"We really have to get together and just talk. That over-a-cup-of-coffee patter that people do?"

"I'll be in touch."

"This has been good, Phoebe. I'm really glad I ran into you."

She picked up the empty lid for the thermos and screwed it back on. Collecting her Go Cup, she returned to her car and left. I watched as she disappeared down the highway.

At four 'clock I started out for my meeting with the Wolf brothers. I drove the narrow paved road past the St. Charles Mission, glancing with cautious paranoia in the rearview mirror. The pavement stopped abruptly, and there I was on a road that wasn't a road at all but six-inch ruts that held my truck tires like a slot car track.

The landmarks on the crudely drawn topographical map were clearly, majestically prominent. Crown Butte was to my left, towering up from the plains, a tiara without jewels crafted over a million years by the elements. To my right, paws of sandstone cliffs edged closer to the road, funneling me into the mouth of Pryor Gap.

The road was slow. I stiffened and fought the steering wheel as I heard rocks, lodged in the soft dirt, scrape against the oil pan. The ruts became erratic and tried to throw the wheels of the truck off-track. At fifteen miles an hour, the gap stretched forever in front of me. I rolled up the window and turned the heater on low.

There are many ways to forecast the weather in Montana, most a helluva lot more accurate then we got from the television weatherman. I particularly like the one that involves a fuzzy caterpillar whose stripes darken when a tough fall and winter are imminent. The problem is that you have to catch them crossing the road, and most become miniroadkills.

Rumor had it that a guy in the northeast corner of the state could accurately forecast the severity of the coming winter by looking at the spleens of hogs he butchered late in the fall. Without benefit of a hog spleen or a caterpillar, I relied on myself. Something was moving in. I could smell it, feel it. I just couldn't put a name on it. I should have known that the gnawing feeling in my gut was telling me this sojourn into the wilderness was a mistake.

My knuckles ached from gripping the steering wheel. A strong head wind channeling through the gap brought a generation of bugs to Nirvana against my windshield. In front of me, clouds hovered low enough to kiss the peaks of the Pryor Mountains looming up from the plains. The gap gradually widened, and I could see a sign ahead. When I reached it, it confirmed I had made my first destination: Cave Creek Road.

The road became softer, faster. Now, in yet another canyon, caves hung on the sides of the sandstone walls like gaping black yawns. Drops of rain started falling, pockmarking the soft dust of the road and spreading out against my windshield. I watched for the Forest Service cabin that Steven had told me would herald my climb up toward the ice caves and damn near missed it, had to backtrack and finally located it tucked down in among aspen and pines. The road started climbing. Again it narrowed; the loose gravel pelted the sides of the truck. I wound through towering stands of lodgepole pine and stayed to the right, wondering where the hell I would go if I met a car coming down.

The truck choked once. I shifted to a lower gear and exerted more pressure on the gas pedal. It surged forward and continued to climb. The area to my right opened up and revealed a sheer drop-off. I edged toward the left. Heights have never been my thing, and the thought of losing traction, slipping off the edge, and becoming one of God's little darts to a lower level of terra firma nauseated me. The truck choked again. I pushed in the clutch, shifted into first gear, and again stomped on the gas. I was losing steam and knew it.

"Fuck. Don't fail me now, damn you."

In the rearview mirror, the twisting switchbacks disappeared. The trees thinned out on my left. The road continued to narrow. I pushed on the gas pedal hard enough to cramp my calf. The truck lurched, crawled forward around a curve, and came to a complete, hissing stop. The needle on the temperature gauge was all the way to the right. Steam spewed from under the edges of the hood and disappeared into the cold air.

I got out of the truck and did the ceremoniously appropriate thing: kicked the shit out of the front tire. It did nothing to remedy the situation, but I sure as hell felt better.

"Okay. Don't panic. It's not like you're up here all alone. There's two guys within yelling distance. Right? Right."

The sound of my own voice was little consolation. I positioned my hands on either side of my mouth and yelled. "Steeevennn!"

My own voice came back to me, three, maybe four times. I yelled again. No answer. The stillness was like nothing I had ever *not* heard. The sign at the base of the mountain had said it was seven miles to the Big Ice Cave. I had to be damn close. I checked my watch. It was six-ten. Steven had made it clear that they would not wait past six-thirty.

I started walking and hadn't gone very far when I heard the muffled sound of a vehicle somewhere ahead. The rain picked up a little. I turned the collar up on my windbreaker, wrapped my arms around myself, and pushed forward. The sound of the vehicle became louder and then stopped altogether. Just when you think you've seen it all, there's always more; I rounded a corner and in front of me, in the middle of nowhere, was a graveled parking lot, and in the middle of the parking lot, Steven and a taller young man were standing beside a black Ford truck with a cab-over camper on the back.

"Where's your ride?" Steven asked as I approached.

"Back down the road about a half a mile. It overheated." I reached out my hand toward the tall young man standing beside him. "Matthew? I'm Phoebe Siegel. We've got to stop meeting like this."

His shake was firm, his smile quick and wide. But his coal black eyes betrayed an overwhelming sense of hypervigilance. He was well over six feet tall, with broad, well-defined features. Steven shook his head in undisguised disgust, walked off, and parked himself on top of a picnic table some thirty feet away.

"Was all this necessary?"

"Yeah. Thanks for coming."

"It would have been easier over a cup of hot coffee at the 4 B's. I'm freezing to death."

"Steven thinks I'm crazy for even talking with you. This was the best I could do. Let's go in the camper. It'll give you a chance to warm up."

I stepped up through the door, squeezing myself into the cramped booth. Matthew followed with Steven, who apparently had decided to abandon the picnic table, directly behind him. Matthew slid into the seat opposite me. Steven pushed a foot-square piece of material to the side of a small window and positioned himself so that he could watch the road I had just walked up.

"Let's cut through the shit. Why did you take off, Matthew?"

"I got a call from this guy. He'd worked a deal with Monday, and now he thinks I have Monday's stash."

"Do you?"

He looked away, took a deep breath, and looked back toward me. "You have exactly what I had."

"Shit. Does the name Jurgen Mueller ring a bell?"

"That's the name. That's the guy that came down to the jail with a couple of Feds and made me a cash offer."

"Did you tell him you had some of the missing items?"

"Hell no. It didn't take long to figure out that he didn't give a damn whether Monday was alive or not. He wanted his shit and he thought I had it. I'd like to know who put him on to me in the first place."

"You were in jail on suspicion of murder. Monday's murder. That's not that tough, Matthew. Who the hell else would he come to?"

"I sure as hell didn't *do* Monday."

"What did Mueller say when he met with you?"

"He just played with me. He said nothing would stop him from recovering the things he had paid for. Something about his investors were getting nervous and he wasn't about to ruin his credibility."

"And you said . . ."

"I told him I didn't know where Monday or the artifacts were. That didn't impress him. He just sat there with this shit-eating grin on his face. Then he went into this thing about how he respected our people, our culture—"

"Doesn't everybody?" Steven interjected.

"—and that I had forty-eight hours to come up with the artifacts or he'd snap my head off like a bottle cap."

"What did you take that to mean, Matthew?" Steven asked in a high-pitched, whiny imitation of my voice.

"Shut the fuck up, Steven. Just shut the—" Matthew stood and faced his brother.

"You were in jail, and he couldn't touch you there. You also had a court-appointed defense—"

"Randall Brigham? That's a joke. He came in to see me once. I asked him about bail, he said he'd check into it, and I never saw him again. The whole time I was with him he kept looking at his watch and writing. Back and forth between the two. I thought he was taking notes, you know? He was writing all this stuff down and I asked him if I could see it to make sure he had things right and he looks at me and tells me it's a fucking brief he has to have done by morning. Great defense."

"Wait a minute. When you were released and your dad came down and picked you up and brought you back to Pryor, why did you run? You were on the reservation."

"Mueller was on the res also."

"How do you know that?"

"When he called he told me the colors of the cars parked in front of my house. I figured he was on a cellular phone or something."

"Did he threaten you?"

"I think he covered that when he told me he'd snap my head off like a bottle cap."

"I mean did he threaten you after that?"

"On the phone?"

"Yeah."

"Not directly. He just said things like it would be unfortunate if anything happened to members of my family because I wouldn't level with him."

"Matthew, I'm working for you. Whatever you tell me stays between us. From what I know about Mueller, those *unfortunate* things could very well happen. Now, I'm going to ask you something, and I want the truth."

"Shoot."

I leaned forward and spoke slowly. "How did you get the artifacts that your folks found under the front seat of your car?"

Matthew looked over toward Steven. It was the first hint of the dependency on his brother that I had heard about. Steven shook his head and looked down at the floor.

"I got to, man. Too much is at stake."

Steven took one step, reached out, and opened the door. "We gotta talk for a minute. Outside."

Matthew followed. The door closed behind them. The wind swayed the camper. I was cold to the bone as I sat in silence inside. There I was, with two young men that, for all I knew, could be stone-cold killers. A shiver moved across my shoulders.

19

The wind caught the door as Matthew opened it and threw it against the outside back wall with such force I jumped in my seat. Nothing like appearing to be in total control. Hell, I wasn't even armed. The thought crossed my mind that I should have been. Now I had to rely on the unproven and probably never thought of before concept that it would be possible to ward off attackers by hysterically attacking them, flogging them with the sopping wet nylon jacket I was wearing.

They stepped back inside. If looks could kill, I would have been dead. Steven stood guard at the window while Matthew slid back into the booth across from me.

"Well? Where to from here?" I asked.

"We were partying, ya know? Back-roading it? We were at the campground down below. The one across from the Forest Service cabin?"

"Right. I saw it."

"The campground was empty, except for us. Nobody comes out this far at night."

"Us who?"

"Steven, me, James Eagle, and this guy from Lame Deer. I don't think anyone knew him but James. Anyway, here comes this truck up the road, not to the campground, but headed up the mountain. As soon as we saw it we knew it was Thomas."

"Thomas? The priest or the other one?"

"The other one. You know him?"

"I've met him." Why elaborate? This was his truth not mine.

"Thomas, uh . . . he's not like other people in the head. He's really like a kid. He's, what do you call it? Challenged. Ya know what I mean? That's why they call him Simple Thomas."

"Shit." Steven leaned toward the table, placed his hands on the surface, and leaned down close to me. "What he's trying to say is that Thomas is a stupid ass that runs around in a loincloth at all hours of the day or night because he thinks he's some warrior spirit that's supposed to avenge whatever the hell he thinks needs avenging." He turned toward Matthew. "We've got about ten minutes, max, and we're out of here."

"Let's get back to the truck. This guy drives?"

"All over the res. I've never seen him driving in Hardin or Billings."

"You're sure that's who it was?"

"We thought we were. We didn't think much of it, started joking around about what Thomas would do if he ran into someone else in the woods when he was doing one of his warrior things. He had a half hour start on us, but we decided to follow him and try to freak him out. Sneak up on him or something."

"What happened next?"

"We were in my car, the four of us. It'd been raining on and off all night, so the road was in bad shape and it was hard going. We stopped about a mile from where we thought he'd be and decided to walk through the woods. We wanted to take him by surprise, and we knew the sound would carry if we drove much farther."

"Where did you think he was headed?"

"Here or up on the Dry Head. It's up above, a half mile or so."

"Did you find him?"

"Oh yeah. He was here all right, but he wasn't alone. We were five or six feet off the road. The rain wasn't so bad while we were under the trees, but once we stepped out onto the road, it was raining so hard it was deafening and hard to see anything. We were behind Thomas's truck, but no Thomas. That wasn't much of a surprise. Hell, he'd been out in his getups in the middle of winter. So what would rain matter to him? We ducked back into the woods on the other side of the road so we could get closer to the picnic tables, thinking maybe he was around those or in the john."

"You said he wasn't alone. Get to that."

"There were two people. Both had slicks on and hoods, hats, something covering their heads. We moved a little closer and finally recognized Thomas. He was facing us. The other person's back was toward us. Whoever it was reached out and hit Thomas across the face. He dropped to his knees and just stayed there. There was some shouting, but the rain was so damn loud we couldn't figure out what was being said."

"You stood there and watched someone hit him? Why didn't you do something?"

"We didn't know what was going on . . ."

"It wasn't any of our business," Steven said as he looked out the camper window. "Come on, Matthew. We've got to get back down. Wind it up."

"James thought it was probably the priest, and we sure as hell didn't want any problems with him. We figured the priest had been driving the truck and that he was going up to find Thomas and bring him down off the mountain."

"So what happened next?"

"Thomas was down on his knees, and the other person just walked up the path toward the john."

"Then did you go to Thomas?"

"No. We went back to the truck. James was the one who found the bags in the back."

"What bags?"

"Steven thought we should get the hell out of there. We were drinking a little, and the priest was real good at tipping off the tribal cops if he thought anyone had booze on the res."

"Were you drunk?"

"I'd had a couple of beers, and you weren't drinking at all, were you, Steven? But James Eagle and this other guy were pretty trashed. They wanted to do something to the truck, and Steven said no way. Then the two of them and Steven and me kinda got into it. Verbal. Nothing physical. We said fuck it and headed back to the car and left them there. We weren't even in the car yet when James and this guy come running up behind us carrying these two gym bags."

"What he isn't saying is that we should have left their asses up here," Steven said. He spent more energy on disgusted facial expressions than anyone I had ever known.

"The rain had let up some, but the road was muddy as hell. We got in the car and backed down until we found a place to turn around in. We almost slipped over the edge once."

"What was in the bags?"

"We didn't know until they started pulling shit out. They were stuffed with the kind of things Monday was into. James and this guy got real crazy and started throwing some things around the car. Something hit me in the back of the head, and Steven got pissed and started yelling at this guy from Lame Deer."

"What did you do when all of this started happening?"

"I was trying to keep the car on the road. When we were a mile or so from the St. Charles Mission, I hit the brakes. Steven jumped out and pulled James and this guy out of the backseat. James was holding one of the bags. The bag he had gotten out of the back of Thomas's truck. But Steven had to crawl into the backseat and find the other bag."

"Did he find it?"

"He found it, all right. When he did, he threw it at the guy from Lame Deer. Hit him square in the face with it. The guy's nose started bleeding all over the place. James got a little crazy and was trying to start a fight with Steven. Everybody was shouting, and it was just real crazy. Steven got back in the car, and we took off."

"That was the end of it?"

"That was the beginning," Steven said as he turned and again looked out the window. "Go on, you might as well tell her the rest."

"The beginning of what, Matthew?"

"We got back to the house; it was late and everybody was asleep. We had this routine, like we cleaned out the beer cans before we went in so nobody would know we'd been drinking. My dad would have had a real problem with it if he knew. There's this yard light out back of our place by the garage, so we pulled up under it and got out. That's when I saw the blood all over Steven's hand."

"From the fight, right?"

"No. We didn't know where it was from. Steven had thrown the gym bag at the guy from Lame Deer, but he never touched him outside the car."

"What about the fight over the backseat?"

"They were just slapping at each other. No one was really throwing any punches. We're talking blood. Lots of it. Steven thought at first he had cut himself and just didn't know it. We went out to the pump and ran water all over him. There wasn't a cut or anything. Nothing."

"Any stigmata in your family?"

Steven held up the palms of his hands. "Yeah. Me. Every Columbus Day. Did you think the word would be a problem, Siegel?"

I had to give it to him; he was quick in an obnoxious sort of way.

"I kinda crawled into the backseat, on my hands and knees, and as soon as my hand touched the floor I could feel it. It was blood. All over the floor and on the seat where the guy from Lame Deer was sitting. It had come from the bags."

"The bags?"

"We got up in the front and found the things that they had been throwing around, and they were bloody. We took them to the pump and ran water over them and then shoved them under the front seat. Every time that pump handle came down, we looked at the house to make sure we hadn't woke anyone up."

"Did anyone come out?"

"My sister. Right when we had finished wiping the seats down."

"Didn't she want to know what was going on? She appears to be pretty bright."

"We told her James had gotten sick and puked all over the car. Nothing else. You got to understand, we were really freaked out. They had come down the road to the car after us, and for all we knew they had killed Thomas and whoever was with him."

"Why didn't you check it out? Go back up there?"

"We're not that fucking dumb. Go back up there? Shit." I was losing points with Steven with every question.

"We did check it out. The next day. But that night we drove down into Billings and found a car wash open and hosed out the backseat," Matthew said.

"Where in Billings?"

"The west end, uh . . . a new place on Rehberg and Grand Avenue."

"Then you went home?"

"Yeah. But we stayed up all damn night. First thing in the morning we checked to see if Simple Thomas was at the church. He was. The priest was there too."

"You went to the church and saw them?"

"No. I called. Thomas answered the phone, I asked to speak to the priest, and when he came on, I hung up."

"Then Monday turned up missing. That put a whole new spin on everything. Am I right?"

"Sort of. I don't think any of us thought it was Monday up on the mountain with Thomas. Not until the thing about the missing artifacts."

"What did you do with the artifacts?"

"We left them under the front seat. They were safe there. When I got arrested, Steven gave them to Dad."

"What about the fight at the Arcade? Why did you threaten to kill Monday?"

"Hell, that happened a couple of weeks before. Maybe a week. He was an ass. We heard he'd been digging up Indian graves all over the reservation. We figured he needed his ass kicked. James got real aggressive, and Monday beat him bad. It turned into a real brawl, and the cops came."

"That's it?"

"That's the simple truth."

"This is another simple truth. You've got one choice here, Matthew. This goes for you also, Steven. Your best bet is to come back down with me and talk to Kyle."

"No way." Steven leaned down, his face close to Matthew's. "I told you, man, that'd be the first thing out of her mouth. Don't buy into her shit or we're both looking at federal time."

"There were four of you, right?"

"Right," Matthew answered.

"As we sit here, there are now two of you. This guy is playing hardball, and the ball isn't in your court."

"No way. Matthew isn't coming down and offering himself up to your white-ass set of laws."

"Steven, I've about had it with—"

"He's right. I won't come down. This guy that did the deal with Monday? He thinks I know where those things are. I don't. When James and the other guy got in the car, they told us there were several bags under a tarp in the back of Thomas's truck. They grabbed two. Where the hell is the rest of it? If anybody finds out we stashed those things under my car seat, do you really think they're going to believe us?"

No. I didn't. But I was at a loss for words. I winged it. "This is what I want. I'm going to talk to Thomas and ask him who he was up here with."

"Right," Steven said and laughed. "Thomas doesn't remember shit from day to day. How the hell is he going to remember—"

"We've got to get back down." Matthew stood and looked at Steven. "We'll get ahold of you."

"You are both making one big mistake. What about your family? These are not veiled threats."

Steven reached out and opened the camper door. The wind whipped inside, caught the curtain across the window, and flapped it against the wall. I stood and stepped out the door into light rain. They followed.

"We got people watching our family," Matthew said.

We stood there.

"I can't talk you into coming down with me?"

"Not yet. I'll know when." Matthew smiled. "I need to know something. Can you help us?"

"I'm not going to lie to you. I don't know. I talked to your dad once and haven't seen him since. Catching up with you has been all but impossible. I need some cooperation, Matthew, not just notes in my mailbox and meetings in the middle of the woods."

They started to walk around to the front of the truck. Matthew stopped and turned toward me. "Is your truck going to start?"

"It just overheated. No problem. I'll be fine."

"Hey, Siegel." Steven leaned out the driver's side window.

"Yeah?"

"Watch out for the bears."

"Bears?"

"Big black bears. They like white meat, Siegel, and this time of year they're real hungry."

I stood with my mouth open. The little bastard laughed, hit the side of the door with his hand, and pulled out of the parking lot and onto the road that continued up. One curve and they were out of sight.

The air was a fine, chilling mist that took on form as the clouds dropped lower. I started walking down to where I had left the truck. Whatever light had been left when I stepped out of the camper was quickly disappearing.

The road was muddy and slick. I stepped up onto the low bank and walked in the tall grass at the edge of the woods. There was no way, after Steven's parting remarks, I was going to step into the forest primeval and become part of the fucking food chain. I was so cold by then, all I needed was a stick up my ass and the killer bruins would have had a frozen Phoebe-on-a-stick. It was not a pleasant thought.

My steps were cautious. I was coming to a curve in the road that I recognized and knew the truck would be a short ways beyond. I stopped abruptly. My feet slipped on the wet grass, and I crashed onto my butt, my feet hanging on the road. Unsure of what I heard, I sat perfectly still, as people usually do when they knock the wind out of themselves, and listened. The unmistakable sound of glass breaking up ahead pulled what breath I had left from my body.

20

I was moving through an ethereal world where visibility changed from one moment to the next. It changed with each footstep, each time I reached out in front of me to steady myself on a low branch. The sound of glass shattering had stopped as abruptly as it had started, followed immediately by the slamming of my truck doors. The hinge I had been having problems with moaned, as it always did, fighting closure. And then, the unbearable sound of silence.

I waited, sitting on the bank, then edged cautiously up from the road and into the concealment of the trees. The foliage was thick, the area broken only by massive boulders that rose high above the ground. It must have been fifteen minutes before I worked my way through the forest and found myself on an incline above the '49.

I've experienced emotion so raw I thought I was bleeding through my skin, but nothing prepared me for the terror and desolation I felt when I looked down at that Chevy and saw the windows shattered and knew that I was alone in the middle of nowhere.

Pieces of glass hung as ragged as shark's teeth from the top of the windshield. There was no trace of glass on either the passenger or the driver's side. The side mirror on the driver's side had been wrenched from the truck and was lying conspicuously on the hood.

I wrapped my arms around a tree to keep from sliding down the steep embankment onto the road below. I placed my face against the rough bark, felt it press on my cheek, and listened. The fog rolled in as clouds dropped lower. It was sliding, splitting as it enfolded itself around the trunks of trees, depositing its dampness on the bushes, caressing me and blurring my vision.

The image of the truck slipped in and out as the fog descended and crawled the road. The only sound was that of my heart. For all I knew

I was within a few feet of God-only-knew-who or, worse yet, some hot-breathed, crazed carnivore that probably had my picture.

We had been in the camper and would not have heard another vehicle approach. Someone could have been in the woods before we arrived. The possibilities were limitless. And at that point, Anna Wolf's stick figure could have emerged from a tree. I had taken every precaution to make sure I had not been followed. I was in trouble, and I knew it.

Something crashed through the brush on the other side of the road. The sound exploded tenfold in my ears. A white-tailed deer jumped onto the road. I stepped back from the tree I was holding, grabbing brush, anything, to balance me. My feet were slipping. Leaves stripped off slender branches as my grip slid down them.

The deer leaped and lunged up the bank in front of me. It stopped for a millisecond when it found itself a mere two feet from me, turned an incredible ninety-degree corner, and disappeared into the woods. I fell, turned on my stomach, and clawed at the earth, trying to halt the slide I was in. It didn't work. I felt my feet dangling in midair just before I fell from the bank and onto the muddy road. My mind raced as I reached into the pocket of my jeans and tried to pull my keys out. I was wet and covered with mud.

Without looking around I got into the truck, put the key in the ignition, turned, and pushed the starter button. The truck groaned. I pulled the choke out and tried again. The engine fought itself as it tried to turn over. Fog swirled and crept up the hood. I tried again, and again, and then again. The grinding of the ignition became weaker. The battery was draining down to nothing.

I stopped and leaned my head against the steering wheel. My breath was warm against my hands. I needed a plan. Ask and ye shall receive. Sitting up, I put my right foot on the brake and depressed the clutch with my left. I was determined to get off the mountain even if I had to back down. Matthew had said there was a turnaround somewhere behind me. I could coast the road to the bottom. The mud and the possibility of slipping off the edge were not even an issue at this point.

Reaching down to the left, I found the emergency brake and released it, looked into the rearview mirror, and started slowly letting out the clutch. If there had been glass in the windows, the air I sucked in at that moment would have imploded the cab. The figure was spectral in the rearview mirror. Shrouded in white vapor, it stood a ways behind the truck, in the middle of the road. The mirror framed the massive man from his waist up. His face was painted black. The haunting eyes stared straight ahead, soulless globes without expression.

I grabbed the mirror and wiped the condensation from the surface. He was real. He was there. Unmoving. The fog blocked him from view. The breath trapped in my lungs surged into my mouth and escaped as a pitiful keening. He appeared again. The light was fading as fast as my pulse raced. The whiteness of the fog turned lavender-gray and gave up to the ashen dusk.

I spun around in my seat. He wasn't there. Without thought I slammed the door locks down, not feeling the splinter of glass that slashed my hand. Only the warm flow of blood against my ice cold skin alerted me to the fact that I was bleeding. The truck offered no protection. I knew it, and whoever loomed behind the truck knew it also.

I opened the glove compartment and dug through the contents, praying something, anything would be there that I could use to defend myself. I clasped the handle of a screwdriver and pulled it out. It was better than nothing. Muscles cramped in the backs of my legs as they tried to generate heat against my sopping jeans.

I waited and watched. Nothing appeared in the mirror. Darkness descended. Sitting in the truck made me feel like a sardine waiting to be plucked from an open can. I vigorously rubbed my arms and thighs. The screwdriver felt as effective as a soda straw. The figure had looked huge and powerful. My body heat was giving up to the cold wetness of my clothes. I was in trouble. Big trouble. And that knowledge screamed out in my mind.

Minutes passed. I had to get out of the truck. My only hope was the shelter of the Forest Service outhouse in the parking area up the road. That was, if I could make it. I sat in the nerve-shattering silence and waited for an arm to reach through and snatch me from the flimsy protection of the truck. It didn't happen.

I guessed the temperature to be around fifty degrees and dropping. The rain still fell gently, blurring my vision. Again, I tried to start the truck. The low moan of the engine drained what hope I had of backing down the road. Not only could I not see behind me but I knew that something waited, crouched, perhaps behind the truck or within reach outside the door. I had to make it to the outhouse. It was now or never.

Once outside the truck, I let the door close without latching. I pressed myself against the left front fender, listened, and tried to penetrate the darkness with my eyes. It was impossible. I stood, waited for my eyesight to adjust, and could soon make out the outlines of trees and the road as it rounded the corner ahead.

I balanced myself by placing my hand on the hood of the truck and immediately grazed what had been my side mirror. Any weapon in a pinch. Armed with a screwdriver and a side mirror, motivated by desperation and terror, I forced one foot in front of the other and started for the parking area.

A thousand straight pins pierced my thighs. My feet could not feel the steps I was taking. I held the mirror and screwdriver under my jacket by wrapping my arms around myself and tucked my hands up into my armpits. Nothing fended off the insufferable cold that pushed into the core of me.

My body was losing its battle to my wet clothing and the wind and the rain. I pressed on. The ground changed under my feet, and I knew, not through feeling but through instinct, that I was on gravel. I had made it to the parking area. I stopped and looked through the darkness for the outhouse. It appeared as a shapeless box a few feet from me.

When I reached it, my hand slid over the door, looking for a handle. The screwdriver and mirror fell from under my coat. My fingers were stiff and would not respond to the commands my brain cried out. I was talking to myself, willing myself to hang on to rational thought while I groped for the handle. My fingers slid under the wood, grasped it, and pulled. It didn't budge.

Something echoed through the woods. Thwomp. The hollowness of the sound echoed and faded, followed by yet another thud. In my stupor the only thing I could liken it to was someone swinging an ax, felling a tree. My thoughts were erratic, confused, and I wondered how someone could work under such bitterly cold conditions.

Fear visited my mind only briefly, in the form of a fleeting thought that I should be afraid, that I was afraid. But the cold had urged my quest to be that of warmth, away from the rain and the wind and the night. My fingers would not function. I reached down to the ground and forced them to curl around the handle of the screwdriver. I lifted it up; both hands strained to release it. I fought the urge and heard Mama's voice yelling my name from within me.

The constant thwomp, thwomp, thwomp was closing in. I stabbed with the screwdriver and lodged it tightly in the wood. Strength waned. As hard as I tried, I could not pull it from the clutch of the door. I leaned down again and ran my hand over the wet ground, looking for the side mirror. The weight of it took what strength I had and pulled it from me. I stood and ran my hand again over the door. The cold, wet steel of a padlock sent spasms of defeat through my body.

With great effort I wedged the support of a mirror through the hasp of the lock and pushed my body weight down, again and again. The hasp broke as I sank to my knees. The lock flew against my cheekbone. There was no pain. My fingers pushed in between the door and the jamb. I crawled on hands and knees into the opening. The cold cement of the floor felt warmer than my hands. A sob clawed its way up my throat and expanded my mouth as I pulled my body forward with my elbows.

Sirens called from the darkness and urged me to sleep, to fall into the soft, warm comfort of nothingness. My lips tried to form words that slid hopelessly inside my mouth. I needed to say them: To sleep is to die, to sleep is to die. My knees bumped the cement ridge as my hand reached up in front of me and touched the icy metal rim of the toilet. It was then that the hands grabbed my ankles. The shock of the hands and the hopelessness of being pulled back out into the cold awakened any sense of survival I had left.

The grip released, and I rolled to my back. With a surge of adrenaline, I stood and pressed my body against the outside wall of the outhouse. My arms flailed out in front of me, cutting through nothing, hitting nothing. I turned and tried to throw myself back through the door. The blow exploded, splintering color within my head, and I fell into the black velvet void that my mind had sought.

21

The dark provided me with images and conversations that surrounded me and gave me solace. The excruciating pain in the
back of my head had disappeared, and in its place came a
sense of loss for the deliverance it had offered from the terror and
desperation.

I moved closer to the form next to me, waiting for arms to sur-
round me, hold me close. It didn't happen. The form was solid, its
cold combining with mine to engineer a false twilight sleep that
taunted me. I was home and not home. Awake and fast asleep. I was
a child and I was dead and that deadness held nothing but a warm
contentment.

At times I was aware of the rain hammering on the tin roof, and
the sound made me smile. I pushed closer, waiting again for arms to
enfold me. The rough-wood side of the building that my bare foot
rested against blocked my stretching. I reached up and stroked the
side of a cheek. Again I smiled and slipped away.

My own babbling, a singsong dialogue to no one, pulled me back
to a superficial awareness. I turned slightly and wrapped my arms
around the only comfort at hand. There was no response, and I had
no expectations.

"Let me sleep." I pushed the thick words off the tip of my tongue
and pushed the hand away from the side of my neck.

There was speech. I couldn't join the words to make sense of them.
I was floating, being lifted from the coldness of the floor, and the flesh
I felt seared my face with its warmth.

"Please . . ." I heard the word in my mind but not with my ear.

The other words, the jumbled other words, combined in a cacophony of sound. I was bouncing, my head hanging down. The pressure

on my stomach pushed bile up my throat. I was the puppet on a floorless stage, floating above reality and at the whim of the puppeteer. I gave it up and slipped once again into the depths of darkness.

The hand slid up my thigh and over my naked hip. I stretched my eyebrows upward, hoping the motion would open my eyes. They felt crusted and sealed shut. The chest pushed closer to my bare breasts, and the shock of knowing I was naked coursed through my body as I involuntarily shook.

"Come on," the disembodied voice urged.

The smoothness of the flesh that pressed against me was as soft as kid leather and as warm as anything I had ever known. I moved closer and sighed.

"Open your eyes," the deep voice urged. "Come on. Open your eyes."

It would disappear if I opened my eyes. The feeling, the hands moving over my leg, the comfort of my breasts against the hard-soft chest that brought rhythm to my breathing. I couldn't give it up, not willingly.

"Goddamnit, Phoebe . . . open your eyes."

The hand now slid up my side, under my arm. A palm grazed my breast. This was no dream. I was there, and there was naked all over me. I fought the stupor that wanted me and willed my eyelids to part.

"Welcome back," Kyle said. His face was inches from mine, his breath warm and sweet.

"I don't have any clothes on."

"No. You don't." He smiled. "I took them off."

"It had to have been good for you. Was it good for me?"

I could feel him chuckle against my breasts. "Not as good as it could have been."

I turned my head. Pain shot through it. "Shit."

With great effort I brought my hand from under the heavy weight that rested on both of us and touched the back of my head.

"What's wrong?" His hand rested on my hip.

"Something, somebody hit me."

"What the hell happened up here, Phoebe?"

"Where the hell did you come from, and where are we now?"

"One thing at a time. We're in the back of my Blazer."

"Kyle . . ." I could feel tears well up in my eyes as the memory of what had happened glutted my mind. "Someone is here. They tried to . . ."

"It was Monday, Phoebe."

"He's alive? My God."

Kyle paused, pulled away from me a short distance, and looked into my face.

"No. He's dead. He was with you in the—"

"No, Kyle. There was someone here. Tall. His face . . . it was black and he broke the windows out of my truck."

"Monday Brown is up in that outhouse, Phoebe, and he's dead. He's been dead. You were lying next to him when I found you."

"Jesus. Are you sure?"

"I'm sure. What the hell were you doing up here, and how the hell did you end up in the outhouse?"

"It's a long story. How did you find me?"

"When you didn't come home, I called Althea. She said you'd left, so I drove up to Pryor and checked it out. There were some guys working over at the memorial that remembered the truck. They said you headed out past the mission."

"I covered a lot of ground."

"There were two choices. You were either headed for Frannie, Wyoming, which I couldn't make sense out of, or you had something going up on the mountain. My bet is it was a meeting with Matthew. Am I right?"

"Kyle, don't ask me."

"This has gone beyond me, Phoebe. Monday's body puts this thing right into the Feds' hands."

"I feel sick."

"You came damned close to feeling dead. I saw that truck and—"

"He broke the windows out."

"Matthew?"

"No, they had left—"

"I knew it. Goddamnit, Phoebe. You've got yourself in one deep-shit mess."

"Is there the slightest chance that you'll shut up for a minute? I've got this splitting headache, and you're driving spikes into it."

He reached out and pulled me closer to him.

"I've got to radio down and have someone meet us."

"Why?" I mumbled.

"So you can get some medical attention."

"I don't need medical attention, Kyle. I just want to sleep for a minute."

"I can't let you do that. Have you ever heard of hypothermia?"

"No. I've lived in Arizona my entire life."

"Did you know what was happening to you?"

"Maybe. There was a lot going on."

"Then tell me how the truck windows got broken out. Don't spare me details."

"I can't talk about Matthew, Kyle. If I do, it'll put you in the deep-shit mess you say I'm in. Someone tried to kill me."

I related the story to Kyle, fighting the need to drift off to sleep. He wasn't about to let that happen. He urged me on and on, as I relived each terrifying moment. There were parts where I drew blanks. Others were etched in my mind. When I was through, he was silent for a moment.

"Do you believe me?"

"Yeah. Are you feeling better?"

"I think this is as good as it gets."

"I'm going to radio down and get someone to meet us in Pryor."

"No way. No sirens. No ambulances."

"You're not in much of a bargaining position. Just stay put."

He crawled out from under whatever it was that was covering us and got into the front seat.

"It smells like gasoline back here. What the hell is this thing?" I raised the heavy quilted tarp and tried to push it off.

"It's an old packing quilt. I use it to lie on when I'm working under the truck."

"Great choice. It's making my headache worse."

"It's all I've got. Here," he said as he tossed his jacket over the seat. "Wrap up in this and come up here. The wind was pushing the exhaust straight back up the tailpipe so I couldn't use the heater."

I wrapped the jacket around me and crawled over the seat to the front. Warm air rushed from the heat vents. Kyle turned the headlights on. I followed the beams with my eyes. The Blazer's bumper was only a few feet from the tailgate of the '49.

Kyle tried to reach someone on the radio. The static was snapping and breaking the signal as he repeatedly called for help.

"We've got to get out of these trees and down lower before I'm going to be able to raise anyone. Put your seat belt on."

"What about the truck?" I asked as I buckled up.

"We'll have someone come up to get it. These roads were all but washing out behind me, so hold on."

"Can I just cover my eyes instead?"

"Whatever makes it easier."

Kyle shoved the Blazer into four-wheel drive and pulled up past the truck. When we reached the parking area, the headlights caught the outhouse in its beams. The door stood open, and the dark shadow of something, someone, was visible on the floor inside. I pulled the jacket closer around me, then covered my eyes for the ride down the mountain.

22

We'd come to a compromise by the time we reached Pryor. Kyle agreed not to call an ambulance on the condition that we go to the emergency room as soon as we hit Billings, and I promised not to give the ER doctors a bad time, to do whatever they recommended, and not to use the F word in front of the medical staff.

The two-way radio in Kyle's Blazer came alive the instant he said Monday Brown's body had been found. The information brought anyone listening to attention. The airwaves were jammed until Kyle ·insisted that dispatch move to a secured channel.

By the time we pulled into the emergency room parking lot, I had accomplished the near-impossible task of pulling on my wet, frigid Levi's and my T-shirt. My hair was caked with mud, which suppressed its natural tendency to frizz into something like a Brillo pad. I had no shoes, an attitude, and a sick feeling about what was awaiting me. There were no surprises: Five law enforcement vehicles, representing the city, the county, and the Feds, were double-parked along the curb in front of St. Vincent's Hospital.

Two nurses and an orderly, with a wheelchair, met us at the door of the ER. I refused the ride and started to get out, preferring to walk in under my own steam. But as soon as my feet hit the asphalt, my legs buckled, and I felt myself sinking to the ground. The next thing I knew I was on a gurney, in a curtained room, with someone stretching my eyelid up to my forehead and an intense light beam trying to slam my pupil shut. My hand reached up and grabbed the wrist of whoever was holding the flashlight.

"At least you've got a grip. I'd say you won't have any permanent brain damage. No drooling out of the right side of your mouth." On top of everything else, I was expected to audition stand-up comics.

I felt as if a flashbulb had gone off inches from my eyes. "No drooling, huh? How about the left side of my mouth?"

"Good. Sense of humor is intact. Usually that's the first thing to go and the last thing to come back. I'm Dr. Donich. How are you feeling?"

I focused my eyes and watched her materialize. She looked young enough to smell like Noxzema and pretty enough to grace a magazine cover.

"Great. Can I get out of here now?"

"Sure you want to? There are a couple of guys out in the waiting room that have first dibs on talking to you. They say they're from the FBI. And besides, I want to take a couple of pictures of your head just to make sure you're not losing brain tissue into your inner ear."

"You're kidding, right?"

"I'm kidding. Only about the draining brain tissue. You took quite a blow to the back of your head. A little lower and you would have been in real trouble."

"The FBI is out there?"

"Yeah. Arrogant little bastards. This is one place they can't throw their weight around. God, I love the power that comes with this job. Can I get those pictures now?"

How could I refuse? She was my kind of woman.

This time I rode in the chair both to and from X ray. I laid back on the gurney and shielded my eyes from the light until a nurse walked in and flipped it off. My head was pounding, and the lump at the back of my skull had taken on a life of its own. After a while I gave up fighting the drowsiness that was overtaking me. The coughing, crying child somewhere near me became more distant as I sank into a restless twilight sleep.

I felt the pressure of someone's fingertips on my wrist and opened my eyes. A nurse stood beside me taking my pulse. Kyle was sitting in a chair next to the gurney.

"Welcome back," he said.

"I need to get your temperature." The nurse reached into her pocket and pulled out something resembling a small transistor radio. "I'm going to put this into your ear."

"The f—"

"You promised. It was part of the deal." Kyle raised his hand and smiled. "There's a ruder way than your ear, Phoebe. I'd think about it."

The nurse smiled. I let her place her probe in my ear. When she had confirmed I was alive, she left.

"The doctor tells me the Feds are hanging around the waiting room."

"You're going to have to talk to them. Mueller was up here with them for a while. I'd sure like to know where his pull comes from."

"Yeah. Me too. What about Monday? Are they going up to get him?"

"They're on their way. I wanted to talk to you before I headed out."

"What?"

"They're going to have a lot of questions for you. You're past the point of not cooperating."

"Are you going to tell them about Matthew?"

"Not if they don't ask. You didn't tell me, remember? At this point it's just supposition on my part. Let's keep it that way."

Dr. Donich pushed the curtain aside and walked in. "Your pictures look fine. You're going to feel a little light-headed for a while, probably just through the night. How's it feel?"

"Like someone hit me in the head."

"I can't give you a damn thing. Sorry. My second concern was the hypothermia. You could have been dead by now if Wyatt Earp here hadn't found you."

"I realize that. I tried to tell him he owned me, but he turned me down."

"Fool," she said and grinned at Kyle. "I have a feeling she doesn't make an offer like that to just anyone."

"Who said I turned her down?"

It had to have been from the beating my head took, but I felt myself blush.

"Are you taking her home, Wyatt?"

"I could do that if it's in the immediate future."

"That it will be. Why don't you step outside and I'll find her something très chic to wear out of here? By the way, I don't recommend she stay by herself tonight." She looked back at me and winked.

"I've got that covered. Phoebe, Genevieve is going to wait at the house. I didn't think it would serve anything to pull your mother out of a sound sleep and scare her to death."

"I don't need anyone to stay—"

"Then you stay here. Lousy food, hard beds, and no guarantee on bathroom privileges. Have you ever bonded with a cold bedpan in the middle of the night?"

"Genevieve sounds great."

"Good choice. By the way, I informed those cowboys in the waiting room that she won't be receiving visitors or questions until late tomorrow. Doctor's orders. That goes for the rest of you also. Understood?"

"Understood. I'll be out here when you're ready, Phoebe."

"Now, down to business. You came real close. I wasn't kidding when I told you your buddy arrived in the nick of time."

"I realize that."

"I'm not going to ask you what the hell you were doing out in the middle of the woods on a cold, rainy night, but I would strongly suggest that you avoid the situation again."

"This wasn't exactly preplanned."

"It never is. Now, when you get home, I want you under the covers, warm and pampered. Sleep in tomorrow. I could write a prescription for a couple of weeks on a beach in Mexico, but the hospital gets pissed off. I've tried it before."

She handed me another cotton gown and told me to pull it on like a sweater to keep my ass from blowing in the breeze. I was curious about her.

"If I'm ever in need of a good doctor, do you take patients outside of here?"

"Me? Nah. Don't have time. I'm a psychiatric washout."

"Great."

She read the startled look on my face and laughed. "I said that wrong. I was in psychiatry for five years before I came up here. I lived with the criminally insane, and it washed off on me."

"Where?"

"San Luis Obispo in California. Big institution where burnout starts the minute you walk through the door. I like this much better. See this?" She crooked her neck to reveal a large, sickle-shaped scar that curved from her ear down to the front of her throat. "This guy decided I looked like his ex-wife and tried to slit my throat with a plastic knife. He damn near did it. I got the message and got the hell out."

"So here you are in Billings, Montana, where nothing ever happens." I laughed nervously, amazed *her* sense of humor was intact.

"The worst thing that's happened to me up here is a three-year-old deciding to bite me when I was trying to remove a yo-yo string she had swallowed. Goddamned yo-yo was just hanging down her chin with half the string down her throat. Damn, that hurt."

"Thanks for getting those guys off my back, Dr. Donich."

"Call me Kitty. It keeps me humble. My mother told me I'd grow up to be a stripper or a doctor. Damn, I would have made a good stripper, hedonist that I am."

"Okay. Kitty." She passed her audition with flying colors. I figured I'd see her on Ed McMahon's "Star Search."

"Here's my card. I'm going to put my home phone on the back, just in case you get in trouble. I don't usually do this, but you're a safe exception. I noticed on your sheet your occupation was listed as private investigator. I'll have you know I cut my teeth on Nancy Drew. Christ, I loved her; she wore pants and skulked around at all hours of the night."

"Well, we've come a long way since Nancy Drew."

"Right. Now you get your brains bashed out. Call me if you have a problem. I'm out of here. We've got a heart attack coming in from Hardin whose ETA is in about"—she looked at her watch—"five minutes. Take care."

"Thanks."

Kyle was standing by the door to the emergency room. I walked out in my double cotton gown and foam slippers. He slipped his jacket around my shoulders. The automatic doors slid open. We walked out into the night. It was still raining, and it felt good against my face. Kyle left me standing on the curb while he got the Blazer. I watched his headlights winding up from the parking lot.

Out of the corner of my eye I saw a car pull out of the upper lot and turn in front of me. It drove slowly and came to a stop as a young couple, the woman very pregnant, crossed the street in front of it. I smiled as the grimacing young woman held her stomach and walked very slowly.

I looked over at the stopped vehicle. The two men in the front were not hard to miss. They were obviously the Feds who had been waiting like vultures for me to emerge. They both glanced at me briefly with stone cold expressions. I smiled.

The vehicle edged forward, and as it did I noticed a third person, in the backseat. A lighter flicked. The gold glow from the flame illuminated the face under the heavy brows. The man brought a cigarette slowly toward his lips, not once taking his eyes off me. The tip of the cigarette turned molten as the flame touched it. A smile formed slowly on his lips. The nod of his head was so imperceptible I wasn't sure at first if it was meant as an acknowledgment.

Jurgen Mueller took a long drag on his cigarette and let the smoke trail from his mouth, his eyes riveted on mine. The flame from the lighter disappeared. Mueller settled back into the darkness inside the backseat as the car pulled forward, turned left, and disappeared down Thirtieth Street. I stopped smiling.

23

Kyle's voice was little more than a whisper as I sank the side of my face into the softness of the down pillow. Sleep called to me. It came as a dark seducer while I tried and failed to hear what Kyle was saying on the phone in the hallway. I was vaguely aware of his hand as he stroked my head, the warmth of his lips pressed against my temple. The couch felt soft and supportive against my back. The covers were my shield against anything that would keep me from sleep. It was exhaustion as I had never known it.

Aware and not aware of the sound of a car in front of the house, the door opening, whispered words, and the door closing, I tried to push the massive weights from my eyelids. There was a shadow looming above me, still and watchful. My eyes closed. I didn't care.

Anna Wolf poked me with the stick she held in her gnarled hand. I pulled the covers tighter under my chin and tried to brush it away, but it prodded me, coaxed me to rise off the couch. There was no pain, just the continual pressure of the stick as she jabbed it harder and harder.

I opened my eyes. She stood beside the couch, her face a seal of ancient wisdom, staring at me. Her head was backlit in the yellow glow from the lamp in the hallway. Her hand urged me to rise, throw the covers off. Sleep competed with her and called me back. She reached down and flung the covers from my body. My legs were heavy, but I tried to swing them over the edge of the couch and sit up.

She motioned with her hand, and I stood looking down into that frail, weathered face. She smiled at me. Any anger I may have had disappeared.

"How did you get here? Where's Genevieve?" I asked.

She said something I could not understand and became frustrated when I wouldn't move from where I was standing. She reached out and clasped my hand, which instinctively curled around the bony, waxen fingers. I followed her toward the door; with each step she took the staff she was holding came down with a thud on the floor. The reverberation sounded throughout the house.

She smelled of wood smoke and moved with the silent stealth of a shadow. I reached out, grasped the doorknob, and turned. The door flew off the hinges, and I tumbled, twisting and turning through the air. The night was cold, and I fell in a spiral from the stars down to the earth, landing gently on my feet in the middle of a dirt road lined with twisted juniper. Anna Wolf was at my back.

Anna opened her mouth to speak. Words did not form. A strong wind, visible to me in the darkness, roared from her mouth and pushed me back up the road. I turned to shield my face from the intensity of the wind. To my left a giant ram, with curled, ridged horns, raised his front hooves and slammed them onto a megalith of quartz. Shards flew through the air toward me, gleaming in the moonlight. Again the hooves rose and slammed to earth, again the shards. I moved hurriedly along the road as it climbed the mountain.

Briefly I turned to seek Anna Wolf. Her mouth opened grotesquely. Wind roared forth and pushed me farther up the road. I stepped to the side in an attempt to escape the driving force of the wind. A great bear rose on its hind legs to my right and pawed the air. Its stiletto claws sliced in front of my face, its hot, moist breath, dank and sour, melting the corpse-cold frost from my cheek.

I walked quickly, veering from the road only once more, and was once more met with the downward thrust of the ram's iron-clad hooves as it shattered quartz and sent the glasslike missiles toward me. The bear paced me, its shaggy head swinging from side to side, its eyes not seeing me. Only its senses spoke of my presence and the path I must take.

When my steps slowed, the wind increased on my back and pushed me forward and upward until my view opened onto a vast, open plateau. Quartz glistened all around me and caught the light of the moon in a thousand prisms. The entire landscape was illuminated. For a moment I was alone. I turned, looked in all directions, and saw no one, nothing. At my feet the frozen body of Monday Brown lay motionless. I dropped to my knees and embraced him, resting my cheek upon his, and felt the familiar, soothing cool of the frost that covered his body.

The staff again prodded me to my feet. I reluctantly pulled away from the lifeless body. The animals appeared to my left and my right and formed a gauntlet leading toward the edge of the plateau. I walked a mindless gait until I reached an edge that dropped into forever. I turned to face Anna. She held two pointed sticks high above her head, one in either hand, and brought them down toward my chest.

They pierced my flesh. I felt nothing. Blood spurted from the wounds as she pulled them from me and plunged them again into the softness just below my shoulders. I fell to my knees, my head bent, and touched the earth just as the sticks were thrust once more into my back. The wood glanced off bone and slid down, ripping through my lungs. I braced myself against the pain I knew would follow. It did not come. My body slumped to the ground, and I lay there, feeling the lifeblood drain, to be swallowed by the earth.

I heard the earsplitting screech from high above and turned my face in the soft dirt to look skyward. The eagle circled there, high in the night sky, its eyes piercing in the force with which they looked down on me. With blinding swiftness it dove. My hand flew up to ward it off as it flipped, talons outstretched and gleaming, to settle onto my body. A scream rose in my throat as the talons neared.

My hands struck out and felt the softness of the feathered beast as it settled on my face. The scream and sound of rending flesh echoed inside my head.

"Phoebe," the voice called. "Phoebe . . ."

I crawled backward, my hands groping, clawing for support.

"It's me. Hey . . . it's me, for God's sake."

My eyes opened. Genevieve's face formed before me. My jaws ached, and I realized that they were stretched in a soundless cry, near breaking. My breath came in deep, labored gasps.

"Jesus Christ, you about scared me to death."

"What happened?" I asked.

"You tell me."

"I . . . I was dreaming. Maybe I was dreaming. I don't know. What time is it?"

"Almost five-thirty. Where the hell were you?"

"Hallucinating. Tripping somewhere. So much for peaceful sleep. I think that bump on my head knocked all the sense out of me. Shit."

"How about a cup of coffee, or do you want to go back to sleep?"

"Coffee. Definitely. If I have any choice in this, I'll never sleep again."

Genevieve brought a cup of coffee. I pulled my feet up under me and sat cross-legged on the couch. The warmth of the cup penetrated my hands, which for some reason felt uncommonly cold.

"You were really out when I got here. Kyle wanted me to reassure you that he'd get your truck down off the mountain."

"When did he leave?"

"About twelve-thirty. He thought they might be up there for a while, so I couldn't pin him down as to when he'd get back. You've got free use of my car if you need it, Phoebe, and free use of my ear if you need to talk."

"Thanks." I watched her as she drank her coffee. "Ya know, I've been really rude a few times with you, Genevieve, and I apologize. You always seem to be around at the right time, or at least available."

"No apology necessary. Life gets in the way. This whole mess has been pretty hard on you, if I know the Wolfs."

The remark struck me as odd. "You don't like them?"

"It doesn't come down to like or dislike. I just knew you'd be up against it when they hired you."

"Up against what?"

"Forget I said anything. You've got enough on your plate as it is."

"No. Go ahead. I'm curious about what your take is on all of this."

"Phoebe, did you see Matthew Wolf yesterday?"

"Look . . ."

"The only reason I'm asking is that I'd like to know if Louis is with him." Her eyes teared. "No one is more aware of client confidentiality than I am. I don't want you to breach that, but if you could tell me anything, anything at all . . ."

"I've heard nothing about Louis from any source, Genevieve. I wish I could tell you what you want to hear, but I can't."

Louis had not been on my mind when I'd met with Matthew and his brother. Now he was. Nothing, not even a vague reference to Louis, had been made by either of the Wolfs. I wondered if they were even aware that he had taken off in the middle of the night, and if they were, why his name didn't come up. There sure as hell wasn't any place for him to hide in the camper.

"I take it you haven't heard from him."

"No, I haven't. Not a thing. I've checked with most of his friends, the ones he ran around with at school, and they're as stumped as I am."

"Maybe it's time to put in a missing persons report."

"Why? Why would you say that? You know something, don't you?"

Her voice rose almost hysterically as she lifted off the chair and leaned toward where I was sitting.

"Wait a minute here." I caught myself holding the palm of my hand out toward her. "All I'm saying is if you're that concerned, call the authorities."

She settled back into the chair. "Where did that come from? I've embarrassed myself."

"Not any worse than I did when I woke up a minute ago. Don't worry about it."

"This has been rough on everyone. Louis is such a good kid, and he's made such wonderful progress living down here, I just don't want to see him get involved."

"How would he get involved?"

"Who knows how they get involved with anything? Two of those kids are dead, and I don't want Louis to become the third. I just thought that maybe they had said—"

"They?"

"Phoebe, I'm not stupid. I doubt very much that you were on a sightseeing trip up in the Pryors. I was here the other night when you got a call that left you visibly uptight, and when you got off the phone you couldn't wait to get me out of here. We're both professionals, and I'm definitely not the enemy."

"Look, this whole thing has been one brick wall after another for me. I'm hired to look into the arrest of Matthew Wolf, and I can't get anyone to talk to me. And I have to tell you, that first day I met you in your office, you intimidated the hell out of me."

She threw her head back and laughed. "I was feeling intimidated by you."

"You're kidding."

"No, I'm not. Remember I told you that I followed the Mary

Kuntz trial almost obsessively? I was even in the courtroom the day you testified."

"Now you're really putting me on."

"Not so. Of course, Kyle reinforced the whole bigger-than-life image every time I asked about you. When you walked in that day—"

"You proceeded to scare the shit out of me. Plus the fact I thought you were probably sleeping with Kyle."

Genevieve erupted with laughter. It was infectious. When we were through, she stood up, took my cup, and walked into the kitchen.

"Do you want a refill?" she yelled.

"Sure. The sun is just coming up, I guess I should, too."

She returned, handed me my cup, and sat down. "It's too bad I didn't make more of an effort to meet you before all this. I could have used a friend."

"That's a very nice thing to say, Genevieve. I'm a little short in that area myself. Friends aren't exactly a high spot in my life."

"Want to lie down on the couch and talk about it?"

"You're kidding, of course."

"I'm testing out my newfound sense of humor. Back to Kyle. What made you think I was sleeping with him?"

"Are you?"

"No. Not that I haven't thought about it. I have all these issues with men, you see, and he is quite a man. I asked him if he was involved with you during the Kuntz thing, and he told me you were living with someone."

"Well, that's old news. Actually it ended during that whole affair. Roger is one of the most decent guys I've ever known, but he wanted more than I was ready to deliver."

"A commitment."

"Right. I was totally comfortable with how it was going. There was a lot of unresolved stuff in my life at that time. After all was said and done, and the trial was over, I knew I wasn't in love with him enough to try and make another go of it. What about you? Anyone in your life?"

"No. Not for a long time. I was originally an archaeology under-grad when I met a man a lot older than I was. I was the classic case of someone looking for a father."

"You never had one?"

"Oh, I had one, all right. He was kind, and generous, and aloof. I was adopted when I was eight years old. They were a wonderful couple, the Cramers, and they gave me every opportunity. He worked for the government, and we relocated a lot. It doesn't give you much chance to put down roots or make friends."

"Adopted at eight must have been quite an adjustment."

"It was. But my memories before that are few and far between."

"Were the Cramers Crow?"

"No. They were white as white could be, and I don't mean that in a derogatory sense."

"What happened to your birth parents?"

"I never knew. It just wasn't something that my adoptive parents were willing to talk about. They weren't prejudiced people or ashamed, they just didn't see how any knowledge of my early life would benefit me. We lived in L.A. for a while, and I passed for Hispanic. When we lived on the East Coast, where there was quite a Greek community, I passed myself off as Greek. Kids adapt."

"Well, what are you?"

"What—"

"I mean, nationality. Are you Native American?"

"That I do know. There was a time when Indian children were taken from their parents without reason or thought or even a chance of finding family to intervene. I'm afraid I got caught in one of those situations. I do know that I was found sitting in the backseat of a car that was parked in front of a bar in Salt Lake City. From what I understand, someone called it in and Protective Services took over. I spent some time in a youth home, and then the Cramers showed up and I had a new home."

"Jesus. I thought records were open now, that anyone had the right to information."

"Uh uh. There are things that the government has done with Native Americans that they don't want out there as public information. Like the mandatory sterilization of Indian women on reservations. Now that's documented."

"But you weren't abused?"

"God no. They were kind and loving and would have given me anything. I often thought I got in the way of the love they felt for each other. It was total devotion. My mother died of cancer when I was twenty-four, and Dad followed two years later. He was heartbroken."

"Didn't they have an extended family?"

"None. My father had a sister that died years before—she had never married—and my mother was an only child. I waited until after they were both gone; then I decided to find my roots, so to speak."

"And have you?"

She gazed off into the distance. "Well, at least the trunk. But I'm home. I can feel it. It's the only place I've ever felt a connection with. You know I haven't talked like this with anyone in my life. I'm used to being on the listening side. Let's talk about something else or I'll go on forever."

The doorbell rang.

"Who the hell would be coming around at this time of the morning?" I asked and started to get up from the couch.

"Sit back. I'm under strict orders from the sheriff's office to keep you down. Whoever it is, I'll send them away."

Genevieve walked to the front door. I could hear voices but could not see who she was talking to or what they were saying. In a moment she walked back into the living room, a stern-looking man in a Western-cut suit at her side.

"Phoebe, I tried to tell him you weren't in any shape to see anyone, but he insisted."

He stepped forward. "Are you Phoebe Siegel?"

"Yes I am."

"I'm a federal marshal, and this is a subpoena for you to appear before the grand jury tomorrow morning at ten o'clock. in the Federal Building. Do you know where it is?"

I reached for the papers he handed me. "Yes. I do."

"If you do not appear, a warrant shall be issued for your immediate arrest."

"I think I've got the message. Now get the hell out of here."

My father's words rang in my ears. Love work, hate authority, and never get friendly with the government. No wonder the Jews are respected scholars.

24

Maggie Mason was to Billings what Perry Mason was to television. She was the founding mother of Mason, Oberbeck and Herr and proudly possessed the record for being held in contempt before Montana's judges. Her reputation as a fearless and relentless defense attorney was understated. Some said the shirt she was seen wearing as she jogged around town with AMAZON WAR BITCH FROM HELL emblazoned across the front defined her best.

She'd come out of Dublin Gulch in Butte, Montana, the daughter and granddaughter of Butte miners. Married to a hard rock miner at age sixteen, she did laundry at one of the whorehouses on Silver Street and somehow finished high school. When the Anaconda Company pulled out of Butte, her out-of-work husband didn't pull his punches on Maggie. With two kids and a high school diploma, she moved to Missoula, worked her way through the university summa cum laude, and then earned her J.D.

Maggie was a friend, or at least the closest thing I had to one. She came with a high price tag and had been my first and only choice to defend Mary Kuntz. Women revered her, men feared her. She aligned herself with many law firms across the country and loved the challenge of a high-profile case. So when I called her and asked for some legal advice, the first thing she asked was "Did you kill somebody?"

My response was "No."

Her reply was "Damn. Come on in anyway. I'm bored spitless."

She came barreling through the door of her reception area dressed in her infamous T-shirt and a pair of gray sweatpants.

"Phoebe, good to see ya. Come on in." She waved me into her

office. "Do I have any messages?" she asked her secretary. "No? Good. Don't put any calls through."

I sat across from her desk. Maggie moved around it and sat down in her chair.

"So, you didn't kill anybody. Christ, I could use something like that right now just to get the old juices flowing. What's up?"

"This is what's up." I handed her the subpoena.

She read the papers and tossed them on the desk. "This couldn't by any chance have anything to do with the Monday Brown thing, could it?"

"Everything. They've got a body now."

"I heard. I also heard you were the one that found it."

"Where the hell do you hang out? It's not even noon and the whole fucking town knows."

"This is big stuff. Jimmy O'Donnell can use this as another step on his way up the scuz-bag ladder to greatness. I also heard that there's some diplomatic shit going on. Isn't the guy who got ripped off somehow connected to the powers that be?"

"I'm not quite clear on it, but his brother is supposed to be something at the German embassy."

"Do you think he's involved with Monday's death?"

"He's involved all right. How deep? I just don't know. The problem I'm going to have going before this grand jury is client privilege. I'm working for the kid that they had in custody on suspicion."

"Did he do it?'"

"No. I'd bet my life on it. But as soon as they let him out—"

"Why'd they let him out?"

"Nothing to hold him on. He'd been in a fight with Monday at the Arcade and threatened to kill Monday in front of a bunch of people. Then Monday turns up missing."

"Where'd you and Monday, uh, meet up?"

"In the middle of the Custer National Forest."

"That's what put it into Jimmy's court. Federal land."

"Can I refuse to appear?"

"You can do anything you want. Although I wouldn't suggest it. You realize, don't you, that I can't go into a grand jury with you."

"Yeah, I know. It's going to be just me and that little prick, all by ourselves."

She laughed. "That's being a little too generous with our pal

Jimmy, but, yes, it's going to be you and him and the jury. From what I've heard, that jury has been sitting for over two months. They're probably very burned out by now."

"So what's my best approach?"

"Are you retaining me or do you just want some advice?"

"For now? Advice. I can't sell this kid out. If he gets hooked into the system, there's enough connected with this whole thing that wouldn't give him much of a chance."

"You're sure he's innocent?"

"I'm sure."

"Based on what?"

"Based on my gut feeling."

"That's good enough for me. Will he need representation?"

"Let's hope not, but just in case, I need to know you'll be there."

"I come high. Can he afford it?"

"No. But I can."

"Christ, Phoebe, that deal last year must have broke you. It's something I can't compromise myself on. I'm good, the best—"

"And humble besides. I can afford it. How do I handle O'Donnell?"

"Realize he's an arrogant little piece of fluff that, outside the courtroom, has never stood up for a damn thing except to take a piss and I even question that. Play with him. Get him riled. It may backfire, and you might find yourself being held in contempt, but if you're stalling for time, maybe I can do some of the legwork for you."

"You'd do that?"

"Hell yes. I told you I was bored spitless. Besides, I'd like to upstage the little prick. Who knows? Maybe we're bucking for the same foothold."

"Do I hear a hint of some political aspirations here?"

"You never know. I'll tell you what I can do. I'll meet you at the Federal Building around nine-thirty." She picked the papers up from the desk and read them briefly. "Yeah. Nine-thirty. I rattle his balls every time he sees me. Maybe me at your side will shake him up. I scare the shit out of him and he knows it."

"God, you're a bitch, Maggie." I laughed and stood to leave.

She stretched her T-shirt out from her chest. "Amazon War Bitch. Never minimize the reputation it has taken me years to build. I'll see you tomorrow morning. If you need me before then, you have my home phone number. Didn't I give it to you?"

"No. I got it out of a phone booth. It said, 'Want a good time? Call Maggie. 555-0019.'"

"Anytime you want to borrow my T-shirt, Siegel. . . . You can't fill it out like I do, but it fits in other ways."

I accessed the messages on my answering machine from a phone booth in the lobby of the courthouse. There were three messages from Kyle, four from my mother, and one from Ardena Brown saying she'd get back to me. I stepped out of the phone booth and saw Kyle coming off the elevator.

"Hey. Hold on."

"Where the hell have you been?"

"I had an appointment. What's up? I just called in to my machine, and you sounded harried."

"Doc Joss has some information on Monday's body. I thought you'd like to go up with me and see what the preliminary on him was."

I followed him out of the courthouse to his Blazer. "Where's my truck?"

"You're not going to like this. They impounded it."

"What?" I shrieked. "Whose fucking idea was that?"

"O'Donnell's."

"That's going to be damn hard for him to justify, the little bastard."

"Not really, Phoebe." Kyle got into the Blazer. "Do you have a ride?"

"I've got Genevieve's car. I dropped her off at her apartment. I've got to pick her up at noon and take her to her office. Shit. This really pisses me off."

"It's not drivable, for Christ's sake. There're no windows in the damn thing, and someone stripped every wire they could get hold of under the hood."

"Anything else?"

"You have no battery."

"Jesus. Anything else?"

"Your seats were slashed."

"Slashed? They fucking slashed my seats?"

"Look at it this way. If whoever did this had something to slash the seats with, they could just as easily have slashed you. You were damned lucky. Seats can be fixed."

Who could argue with that? "I'll meet you at Joss's."

"One more thing."

"There's more?"

"Someone has been trying to get ahold of me. Young. Male. He's called about ten times since last night. Says it's urgent, and he refuses to talk to anyone else."

"Matthew?"

"Couldn't be. I think he was, uh . . . elsewhere?"

"Right. Then who?"

"I don't know."

"Louis?"

"Maybe. Let's hope so. Did Genevieve say she had heard from him?"

"No. Not a word."

Kyle closed his door and pulled away from the curb. I walked around the corner to the parking lot and got into Genevieve's car. Within minutes I was walking through the door into Doc Joss's morgue.

"Phoebe, isn't it?"

"Right. How are you?"

"I'm the one that should be asking that. So I think I will. How are you, young lady, since I took that guy out of your tree? Gonna have it cut down?"

"No. It's not the tree's fault, is it?"

"No. It certainly isn't. Well, Kyle. I guess you want some answers."

"That's why I'm here, Doc. What do you have?"

"A lot of unanswered questions but a good idea of what happened."

"Let's hear it."

Without ceremony, Doc Joss threw the cover off Monday's body. I was shocked at how gray he looked. His mouth and eyes were partially open. This, according to Kyle, was what I was snuggled up to when he found me on the floor of the outhouse. I felt as if I had been slimed.

"Okay, let's take a look," Kyle said, and moved toward the body.

Doc Joss snapped on a pair of sheer plastic gloves and proceeded to shove his finger into one of four dime-size puncture wounds in Monday's chest.

"I haven't gone inside yet. Thought I'd let him warm up a little. But these are curious." His finger was deep inside the hole, up to the lowest knuckle. "There's a way to go on these. They are deeper than I can reach. I used a probe earlier, and my guess is they're at least six, maybe seven inches deep."

Doc pulled his finger from the hole. "We have two of these on either side of his chest and two more just under the clavicle, both right and left. Judging from the angle, this guy was either on his knees or someone damn near his own height did something like this." He turned, raised both his hands high above my head, and plunged them downward. His fists landed gently. I felt the blood draining from my head and flooding my stomach. The hands raised again, and Anna Wolf was in front of me, not Doc Joss. I could see, feel, the darkness of my dream as he again brought his hands down. My knees buckled. I sank to the floor.

"That's about right. That's about right," Doc Joss's voice was somewhere, hammering in my ears. "Then they brought them down on his back, met bone, slid off the bone and penetrated the lungs." After that I heard nothing.

The next thing I knew, Kyle was on the floor beside me and had broken a glass vial of ammonia under my nose. My head snapped back from the shock of the strong smell.

"What the hell happened?" Kyle asked.

"I saw it. I was there . . . I saw him being . . ."

"What are you talking about?" Doc Joss asked. "I'm real sorry about this, Kyle; I thought she was giving me a hand in my demonstration. That's exactly how I have it figured. They got in the front twice, and when he collapsed, they let him have it in the back. Won't know until I get inside, but it's my best guess at this time."

Kyle helped me to my feet and to a chair. Doc Joss brought me a glass of water. I drank and felt immediately nauseated.

"Maybe we better get out of here," Kyle said.

"No. I'm okay," I said. But I wasn't. I had seen the killing. I had *been* Monday. For that split second in a dream that made no sense, I had witnessed the killing of Monday Brown. But by Anna Wolf? Impossible.

The phone rang.

Doc Joss looked over at Kyle. "It's for you."

Kyle walked across the room and took the phone from him. "Yeah?"

He listened, thanked whoever was on the other end of the line, and hung up the receiver. He immediately dialed a number. "This is Kyle," he said. A few moments later he hung up.

"That was John Wolf. His mother died last night."

"She couldn't have."

"She wasn't feeling well after supper, went in to lie down, and they found her about an hour later."

"No, Kyle . . . that's impossible."

"What are you talking about?" He walked toward me. "For Christ's sake. She died, Phoebe. Last night."

"Forget it. Nothing. It's just a shock."

Anna Wolf may have died last night, but for some reason beyond explanation she had come for me, had stood in my living room. Anna Wolf, dead or alive, had been on that dark mountaintop with me, with a bear, a ram, an eagle, and the corpse of Monday Brown.

25

St. Pius Church was actually a converted gymnasium. Some found it offensive; I found it appropriate because I had no doubt in my mind that God keeps score. My brother Michael had been filling in at St. Pius for a priest who was on vacation. The rectory was separate from the church. I tried the rectory first and was met by a clone of every Catholic church secretary I had ever met. She was probably in her late fifties, early sixties and had that same pious look on her face that those in favor, or anointed by God, always wear.

"I'm looking for my brother, Father Siegel."

The ever-present smile of goodness left her face. "Father Siegel?"

"He's here, isn't he?"

"Yes." Her thin, rather pinched lips formed the word sharply. "He's here. He's over at the church."

"It's a big place. Where in the church will I find him?"

A smile almost, but not quite, formed on her face. "I'm not sure exactly. Try upstairs or the basement. The meeting hall should be open."

"Thanks."

I walked through the front doors of the church and into the stillness, the guilt factory as we called it when we were kids. I walked toward where I knew a small office was near the back of the pews. The door was open. The office was empty. I listened for the sound of voices or footsteps and heard neither.

Skirting the front of the church, I walked behind the last row of pews and toward a door that led down into the basement. The last time I had been in St. Pius's basement, I had, unwillingly, attended a charismatic meeting with my mother. Neither of us had been prepared for what we found: a group of near hysterics speaking in tongues.

Always the lady, my mother had insisted that we stay until the last dog had been hung or the last tongue had been tongued, or whatever it was they did. The hair had stood up on my head through the entire meeting, so my memories of the basement were not pleasant ones.

I followed the stairs down, trying to be as quiet as I could. As I came around the corner, I heard muffled voices. I stopped and listened. The soft voice of a woman, crying as she talked, came from just around the corner and down the hall. Leave it to me to break in on some heavy counseling scene. There were vacant rooms on either side of a hall that ran beside the banquet room. I headed for one to hide out in while Michael finished with business.

I walked around the corner of a room midway down the hall and stopped dead in my tracks. Depending on how you define counseling or consolation, he probably wasn't doing either. He was in fact in the middle of a passionate kiss. I recognized the long, mahogany-colored hair of the woman who was definitely not fighting the moment.

Michael saw me as I tried to back out of the room.

"Phoebe," he cried out. "Wait."

I turned and sprinted down the hall. Always able to outrun me, he caught up with me in a few strides.

"Please, wait."

I turned to face him. "Let's see, Michael. Try the it's-not-what-it-looks-like routine. That's pretty standard. Or she was having some kind of physical problem and needed CPR. Which one do you think I'm dumb enough to buy?"

He just stared down at me. Pain filled his eyes. What the hell was I doing? I hated the fact that he was a priest. Or did I?

"Phoebe?" The voice was as gentle and as soft as I remembered.

I looked toward the doorway I had entered. Cara Menendez leaned against the wall. Tears were flowing down her face. I shook my head and looked at the floor.

"Come back in, Phoebe. Please." Michael led me by the elbow back into the room.

I sat down on a long turquoise Naugahyde couch that flanked one wall and rested my face in my hands.

"Fuck," I said. "Fuck, fuck, fuck."

"Can't you even say hello to me? It's been years." Cara sat beside me and took one of my hands in hers.

"Hello, Cara. Welcome home. I heard you were in town. I just didn't know you were fu——, fooling around with my brother the priest. Long time no see."

"Please. Don't judge us so harshly."

"Oh, I don't think this is anything compared to you know who." I pointed my index finger toward the ceiling. "What the hell is going on with you two?"

Michael pulled a chair up in front of me and sat down.

"Remember that night at Mama's when you asked me if anything was going on?"

"Of course I remember, but I had no idea it was something like this. I thought it would be something really important, like your collars being too starched or some kid pilfering money out of the offering. But this? Give me a break here, Michael. This?"

"We've corresponded for years, Phoebe," Cara said. "We've tried our best to let go of our feelings. I even moved out of state. But he found me."

"Oh God. You found her?"

"Yes. I did."

"Does Mama know about this?"

"No. And I don't want her to know. Not just yet."

"We haven't decided what to do, Phoebe. We just need some time. We don't want to hurt your mother, but we don't want to deny ourselves."

"That was not a state of denial that I just walked in on. God. I can't deal with this. Jesus, oh Jesus."

"Do my ears deceive me, or are you praying, little sister?"

I couldn't help but laugh. "I really don't believe this. What the hell are you going to do? Or maybe I should ask what have you done already?"

"I'm leaving, Michael. I have an appointment for a job interview with Growth Through Art in about fifteen minutes." Cara turned to me. "I was waiting until Michael thought the time would be right and I was going to call you so we could all talk. Michael was going to tell you about our . . . our dilemma."

"This really wasn't how I wanted you to find out, Phoebe. And you can't talk to Mama. It has to come from me."

"It'll kill her. You know that."

"It won't kill her. She might kill me, but what the hell." He smiled his million-dollar smile.

Cara stood to leave. Michael reached out and touched her hand.

"I'll get hold of you later. Will you be home?"

"Yes." She turned toward me. "Phoebe. We'll talk. All right?"

"Why not? We're all going to go to hell because of this one, so it had better be soon."

She grinned and laughed. "You haven't changed one little bit. I'm glad." And she left.

"Phoebe . . ."

"Save it, Michael. I need some time to think this one over. I might warn you that the Stepford Wife you have tending the rectory wasn't real thrilled about you being over here."

"Did she say something?"

"No, it was just a feeling I got. Her dorsal fin was showing above the waterline."

He held his head in his hands for a moment and then looked up at me. "It's a mess, isn't it?"

"You're the great spiritual leader of the family. You tell me."

"It's a mess. What are you doing here in the first place?"

"I was hired by the bishop to check up on you."

"Oh God."

"Not," I said and smiled.

"Don't do that to me, Phoebe. Why are you really here?"

"Believe it or not, I came for some spiritual counseling. It's important."

"Then let's go back over to the rectory and talk."

He reached out his hand and pulled me up from the couch. The pain and embarrassment in his eyes were hard for me to look at. He didn't let go of my hand until we were in his office.

"Nicer digs than your usual ones."

"It's newer, too. Father Jacoby had an illness in his family and had to leave town. I'm just covering for him for one more night. Now, back to why you're here. What's up?"

"Not a lot. After seeing you with Cara, my problems just seem to pale."

"Come on, Phoebe. What's going on?"

"Jeez. Where to start. I was subpoenaed this morning to appear in front of a grand jury tomorrow. Last night I almost died in the parking lot up at the Big Ice Cave, where some idiot with his face painted black chased me through the woods and damn near killed me, and in the middle of the night, with a near concussion, I had a dream where a dead woman visited me and gave me, with me playing the corpse, all the gory details of a murder that was committed. Is that enough?"

"Good Lord. You're putting me on again. Right?"

"No. What I'm really here about is the dream. It was real, Michael. So real I can still see it. It means something. I just don't know what."

"Tell me about it."

He leaned back in his chair, and I started telling him the story of Anna Wolf's visit.

"Whew. Heavy stuff. When did you find out she was dead?"

"I was with Kyle up at the morgue, and his office called and told him to call John Wolf immediately. What do you think, Michael? Am I nuts or what?"

"Nuts? I don't think so, Fee. Actually, you've become part of an honored tradition. In fact, it's not even particularly original, when you get right down to it."

"What are you talking about?"

"Well, just look at the Bible—"

"No, thanks, Michael. I've had enough of that."

"Phoebe, you came asking me questions, right? So just let me talk; you're going to believe whatever you want to believe anyway."

I nodded, hoping that he wouldn't rap me across the knuckles for good measure. Mom would have been proud. "Okay, Michael. We'll look at the Bible."

"I thought so." He smiled. "The ram you dreamed about. It was a ram that appeared to Abraham, so that he wouldn't have to sacrifice his son. And Ezekiel, he had a vision of winged creatures with four faces; one of those faces was the face of an eagle. And he saw the idolaters slain, just like Monday."

"That's all fine, Michael, but it's just stories."

"To you, Fee. But they form part of the basis of life for millions of people. And it isn't just in our culture, don't forget. The Indians here have a long tradition of dreamers. I mean, their young men went out seeking visions, fasting, and even torturing themselves so that they could see something, something that would guide them."

"Yeah, but—"

"No, Phoebe, no but's. If you believe in something, it works. If you don't want to take the Bible as a source, and if you want to ignore all the other spiritual experiences that've guided people, fine. Read Jung. Or Joseph Campbell."

I looked at the door and thought of Cara walking out. "And what if something stops working, Michael?"

He was good. He knew exactly what I was thinking. "If something stops working, you find another belief. You make adjustments. As long as you keep an open mind, you can keep learning. The minute you think you know it all, you might as well quit. Even absolutes have a way of changing, Phoebe."

"Okay, okay. But Anna was dead. D-E-A-D. How could that happen?"

"It was a dream, a vision. It doesn't matter if she's dead."

"Are you telling me that you believe that people can come back after they're dead and put themselves in someone's dream?"

"Oh come on, Phoebe. You know better than that. We put them in our dreams, they don't force themselves on us, at least not in the way someone can intrude on your life. On some other level, though, who knows, really?"

He looked thoughtful for a moment, then shrugged. "Let me tell you about the dream I had about Dad after he died. He came to me as sure as if he was sitting where you are."

"Don't make something up to make me feel better."

"I'm a priest. I don't make things up." He smiled.

I raised my eyebrows.

"After Dad died I was devastated, like all of us were. I didn't know what Mom would do without him. Kehly was so damn young, and you were so hurt. I've never seen anyone take death as personally as you do. Like it's a slight, a dart thrown directly at you. It fractured me. We had so much grief in our family I just couldn't fathom why this kept being heaped on us. It challenged everything I believed."

"But you had every spiritual support around you. You were always open to that hand of God crap."

"I still am, Phoebe. It just gets tight when it gets close to home. I'm still a man."

"I think we've established that."

"Don't start taking potshots at me."

"I'm sorry. Go ahead."

"The night Dad died I had come back to the rectory, the one down at Guadalupe, and sat in one of the front pews. The whole place was dark except for the novena candles, and it was quiet. Deathly quiet. All of a sudden I had the feeling I wasn't alone. I turned, and there was Dad, sitting eight or nine pews back. He was wearing that same old Harris tweed jacket that he'd worn the elbows out of, and he was just sitting there, smiling at me."

I could feel my eyes tear. "What did you do?"

"It scared the hell out of me. But I got up and started to walk down the aisle toward him. He held his hand up, and I knew he didn't want me to come any closer, so I sat back down. Then we had this sort of wordless conversation, and when we were through talking, if you can call it that, I knew we'd all be all right. We'd get through it."

"What happened?"

"He came toward me. I just sat there. When he got in front of me, he reached and touched my cheek with the flat part of his hand. I reached up and held on to his wrist. He was as flesh and blood as you are, sitting right there. I could feel the pulse in his wrist throbbing against the tips of my fingers."

"Michael . . ." I tried to speak and couldn't. "Why didn't you ever talk to me about this?"

"You're not always that approachable. I guess the point I'm trying to make is that it was the experience that was important and real. No one will ever convince me that it didn't happen. I know that it did."

"So you think that Anna Wolf had some message for me, something to show me. How do I figure out what it is?"

"You already have part of it. She showed you how this guy was killed."

"Yes, but did she do it? And when did she die? And—"

"I took a course one time that dealt with dreams and their interpretation. I'd look for the symbolism in the animals. Did you feel threatened?"

"Come to think of it, no. I wasn't afraid of the animals. They were herding me, not really threatening me. But then again, that's not entirely true. There was the eagle, and I don't know if I was frightened of it, but I knew it would and could hurt me if it wanted to."

"I'd suggest thinking about those animals or finding someone who has a good Jungian background and see what they have to say."

"I've got to go, Michael."

"What about the grand jury deal? Want to talk about it?"

"That I think I can handle by myself. Thanks. I mean it, Michael. I appreciate you taking time out for this."

He stood, walked around the desk, and reached out for me. I walked into his arms and felt him hold me tighter than he had ever held me before.

"Anytime. You might find me on your doorstep one of these days."

"Then I'll come back at ya. Anytime. Day or night. I hope you know what you're doing."

"So do I. Don't say—"

"You don't have to say that to me, Michael. You know that."

I walked out of the rectory, got into Genevieve's car, and pulled out into traffic.

26

I sat on my front porch and watched the day disappear into dusk. Stud was curled up on my lap in one of his rare I-need-affection moods. My hand stroked his back, and I could feel him purring against my legs. I dreaded going up against Jimmy O'Donnell if for no other reason than that I had the feeling I'd end up in jail. There was no way I would blow the trust Matthew had placed in me in spite of his brother's protests.

The kid was innocent. But everything was stacked against him. My worst fear was that they would impound his car and find microscopic traces of Monday Brown's blood. That fear was about to come true. I dumped the cat off my lap and ran into the house to get the phone.

"You sound breathless."

"I am. What's up, Kyle?"

"They pulled Matthew's car down from Pryor at noon today and flew someone in from the State Crime Lab in Missoula. Monday's all over the place. They've issued a warrant for Matthew and Steven."

"Shit."

"You don't sound surprised."

"I'm not."

"Phoebe?"

"Yeah?"

"Maybe I should come out and we should have a talk. You don't want to get yourself in trouble with O'Donnell tomorrow."

"I don't think we need to talk, Kyle. What you don't know won't hurt me."

"That's my point."

"Trust me on this. You're better off not knowing. Have you talked to John?"

"I took a run up there. They're dealing with a lot. Anna is a loss for the entire tribe. There are very few elders left. She was a wonderful woman and totally devoted to Matthew."

"Should I send something up there? Food? Flowers?" My mind flashed to the dream. Matthew was who she was trying to protect, only she overestimated my powers of deduction. "I'm really not very good at this kind of thing."

"It's covered. Food was already pouring in when I got there."

"What about Monday?"

"They released him to Ardena. It's going to be a quick burial. Tomorrow at three P.M."

"Isn't that a little fast? Did Joss get through with him?"

"He did. Ardena was in town for questioning. She said she had tried to get ahold of you and would again, tonight."

"Thanks, Kyle. I tried calling her when I got home, but there wasn't any answer."

"Phoebe, they brought Thomas in."

"For what?"

"Someone saw him in his warrior mode on the reservation last night. There's a good chance he was the one who—"

"Damn near killed me?"

"It looks like it. The priest is having a fit and has been raising hell down at the station all afternoon."

"Where are they holding him?"

"Yellowstone County Detention Facility."

"Can you get me in to see him?"

"I'll see what I can do. Why do you want to see him, Phoebe?"

"Because he knows who killed Monday."

"I was in with him for two hours this afternoon. He's pretty out of it. Incoherent as hell."

"I don't care. I need to see him."

"No promises. But I'll do what I can. By the way, Joss did say that Monday was on ice a long time before he made it to the outhouse. We figure he was dumped in the Big Ice Cave and you happened to show up about the time someone decided to move him."

"I'm not known for my timing. Kyle, have you been subpoenaed?"

"No."

"Good. I might need you out there."

"Goddamnit, don't pull any grandstand plays, Phoebe."

"I gotta go. Let me know if you can get me in."

"Wait a minute here. I need to ask you something else."

"What?"

"What happened in the morgue today?"

"I can't talk about it."

"Phoebe . . ."

"I really have to get off here, Kyle."

I hung up the phone, picked it up again, looked for Ardena Brown's phone number, and dialed. After three rings she picked up.

"This is Phoebe Siegel. You've been trying to reach me."

"Yes. I have. We need to talk. I have some information for you."

"Which is?"

"Matthew Wolf did not kill Monday."

"I've pretty much figured that one out. Do you know who did?"

"No, but Anna Wolf knew. Anna knew lots of things. She knew my marriage to Monday was not that easy."

"So I've heard."

She was silent, and I wasn't sure she hadn't hung up on me.

"Ardena?"

"I'm here. Just give me a minute."

Again, a space of silence.

"This is very hard for me to talk about."

"I'm going to level with you. I heard you were getting ready to leave Monday."

"What? Who did you hear that from? I never would have considered that. He would have killed me."

"I'm only telling you what I heard."

"Did it ever cross your mind that Monday spread that around for reasons of his own?"

"What reasons, Ardena?"

"To discredit me. I knew things about him. Anna knew them also."

This time I was silent.

"I knew where he got some of those artifacts, and I threatened to turn him in to the tribal council."

"He robbed graves."

"How did you know that?"

"Matthew Wolf had a confrontation with him at the Arcade about that very thing. I'm sure you heard about it." I wondered if this woman was just covering her own ass.

"Monday told me he'd been in a fight with the boys. He wanted to know if I had said anything to any of the Wolfs. I said no, I hadn't. But that wasn't good enough for him. He always liked taking things a step further."

"Further?"

"Yes. Further. I'm glad he's dead. I was hoping they'd find him dead. I know you can't understand that, but it's how I felt."

"Why are you telling me this, Ardena?"

"I know Matthew Wolf did not kill my husband. I don't want him blamed for what I know he didn't do."

"Did you tell this to the police when they questioned you today?"

"Yes. But they're so damned convinced that Matthew did this, nothing I could say would change their minds."

"Did they ask you if you killed your husband?"

"Yes, they did."

"And your answer was no."

"Don't think I didn't think about killing him. A million times in my mind. I came so close one night I sat up and waited for him with a rifle. But I knew I couldn't do it. I couldn't do it because of my son. No, I did not kill Monday."

"Does your son know yet that they found Monday?"

"Yes. He's having a hard time. He's eleven years old. Monday was devoted to Shawn."

"Why didn't you ever get help? Or talk to someone?"

"I'm not a stupid woman. I did go into counseling."

"For the abuse?"

"Yes. My counselor suggested that I leave him, but it was my land, my mother's house. I just couldn't walk out."

"Where's all this going?"

"Matthew Wolf came to see me one time when Monday was out of town. We talked about what Monday was doing and how wrong it was. He told me he was going to turn Monday in. I begged him not to. Monday would have thought it was me and all hell would have broken loose."

"And then what happened?"

"As soon as Matthew left, Jurgen Mueller came to the house. He had flown in from San Francisco. Monday wasn't expecting him, or at least he hadn't told me he was coming. I was nervous around Jurgen. He always made me uncomfortable. I tried to explain to him that Monday wasn't home, and he just stood there and stared at me."

"Did he leave?"

"Not then. He . . . he tried to . . ." Her voice trailed off. "He said he saw a man leaving and accused me of *servicing* him. He said he always wanted to be with an Indian woman."

"What did you do?"

"I was shocked. My son was sleeping in the next room. I asked him to leave and he hit me. Said I should be used to that kind of treatment. He grabbed me and threw me down on the couch. My son heard me and came out of the bedroom. I yelled at him to go for help. As soon as I said that, Jurgen left."

"Did you tell Monday?"

"Yes. He slapped me and told me I must have been coming on to him. I wondered whether Monday set me up, if he made some sick deal with Jurgen."

"Jesus. Did you talk about this stuff to your counselor?"

"Of course. It was then I started talking about the graves and what Monday was doing. I was so bothered by what he was doing to the graves on the reservation, ashamed really. My counselor said that I shouldn't say anything right away. Sit on it for a while, go to a shelter for battered women."

"Why didn't you?"

"Right after that appointment, I decided to confront Monday and go to the shelter. That was the night he didn't come home."

"Why didn't you talk to me after the sweat, Ardena?"

"I didn't know you. I still don't. But Anna told me I could trust you, that you have a good heart. Whoever killed my husband involved Thomas."

"Did you know they were holding Thomas?"

"Yes. I tried to see him but they wouldn't let me. He's harmless if he's left alone. But easily influenced. He fixates on people and becomes whatever they expect from him."

"Do you know what happened to me last night? Up on the mountain?"

"Yes. Kyle told me. If it was Thomas, he was only doing what he was told to do. I've worked around the church for a few years and have never seen him become violent."

I put my hand up to the back of my head and felt the bump that had diminished some. "Don't bet on it. Ardena, who knew about the deal Monday had made with Mueller?"

"Everyone."

"Who knew about the graves?"

"There's been speculation for years. But Matthew and Steven followed him and saw for themselves. I knew because he had to clean the stuff up. It wasn't just here. He traveled all over the state. I'm sure he robbed wherever he went. But as far as who knew for sure? I knew and the boys knew."

"Are you sure?"

"I think Anna knew. She never said anything, but she was sure there was bad medicine on the reservation. A witch."

"And you believed that?"

"I'm a Christian. I don't throw out the old ways, but I don't buy into them either."

"Ardena, if you think of anyone else who would have known Monday was robbing graves, someone it would have bothered, a lot, will you call me?"

"Of course. Thanks for hearing me out."

I wished like hell I had someone to bounce everything in my head off of. I was no closer to finding out who'd killed Monday than the day the Wolfs had graced my front porch. Anna Wolf was dead, and with that, I had a strange sense of loss.

And on top of everything else, there was Michael. I tried to remember who the patron saint of the hopeless was. I needed all the help I could get.

27

Maggie was waiting for me in front of the Federal Building.
"Our little buddy walked in about fifteen minutes ago.
God, am I going to love seeing the look on his face when he
realizes I'm with you. I love making him squirm."

"What is this open vendetta you have against him?" I couldn't
suppress a smile.

"I've whipped his ass so many times in the lower court, when he
was slumming and before his move to this place," she said as we rode
the elevator upstairs. "These guys can lose to each other and hit the
golf course twenty minutes later and be all buddy buddy. But let them
lose to a woman and they try to make your life hell. I've got a case
coming up that he's going to take a real beating on and he knows it.
That's probably why he needs to nail these kids so bad. One more
notch. According to the gossip, he's falling from grace a little with his
higher-ups. He's going to be out for blood."

"Who else will appear before this grand jury?"

"Anyone connected with the case."

"Kyle hasn't been subpoenaed."

"Kyle Wolf? God, he's got a nice ass."

"For Christ's sake, Maggie. I'm ready to puke here."

"Uh oh. Have you got the hots for him?"

"What the hell are you talking—"

She waved her hand. "I don't blame you a bit. From what I hear
he's a nice guy. Male. But nice. They're only good for one thing, you
know?"

The man riding with us shot her a dirty look. She craned her neck
at him and grinned.

"For taking out the garbage. Do you take out your garbage?"

He blushed and looked relieved when the door slid open on his floor. We rode up another floor.

"You are incorrigible. You know that, don't you?"

"I try. That's what reputations are built on."

The door opened. We stepped out.

"I know what the Christians felt like facing those lions," I said.

Jimmy O'Donnell stood at the end of the hall talking with two federal marshals. He looked up when he heard us coming.

"Siegel. Good to see you. And Maggie," he said solicitously. "You know she can't have counsel present during a grand jury hearing. Or *did* you know that?"

"Duh . . . no, Jimmy, I didn't know. I'm here as a friend. I see you don't have any friends here. But then again, you don't *have* any friends, do you, Jimmy?"

"Do you two know each other?" I asked, all innocence.

"Intimately," Maggie answered as she stared him down. "I have a Xerox of Jimmy's ass that I'm waiting to circulate."

His mouth dropped open. "What?"

"Remember that Christmas party a few years back when you got so stinking drunk and sat on the Xerox machine and took a couple of shots? I think you wrote KISS MY on it and were going to mail it to, uh . . . let me think." Maggie put her index finger to her lips and looked toward the ceiling.

"There were only two of those, and I destroyed them both."

"You should have learned to count higher, Jimmy. There were three. Take it easy on my friend."

"Are you trying to coerce me?"

"Of course not. That would be against the law. Phoebe's fragile and I'm asking you to be kind."

He turned and strutted down the hall. Within minutes a woman came out of the courtroom and called me in.

"Go eat him up, Phoebe. It'll leave a bad taste in your mouth, but what the hell."

"I'm fragile, remember?"

"Right. As fragile as I am."

Twenty people sat in two rows. O'Donnell was seated at a table next to a law clerk.

"Will you swear in the witness, please?" he said as he busied himself with a sheaf of papers.

The law clerk approached me. "Would you raise your right hand?"

I did.

"Do you swear to tell the truth, the whole truth, and nothing but the truth, so help you God?"

"I'd rather affirm."

"What the hell is this?" O'Donnell rose from his seat, caught himself, and glanced at the jurors, whose eyes were riveted on him. "It's her choice. Affirm the witness."

"Do you hereby affirm to tell the truth, the whole truth, and nothing but the truth?"

"I do affirm."

"Will you please be seated and state your name for the jury?"

"Phoebe Siegel."

"Is that your full given name?"

"No."

"Please give us your full given name."

"Phoebe Zelda Siegel," I mumbled.

"Could you speak up, please?"

"Phoebe Zelda Siegel."

I looked at the jurors. As Maggie had predicted, they looked exhausted. Distracted. O'Donnell briefed them on the fact that I was appearing before them in the matter of Monday Brown to determine if there was sufficient evidence to indict Matthew Wolf on murder one.

"What is your occupation, Miss Siegel?"

"I'm a licensed private investigator."

"Is your license current?"

I didn't know and wondered if he knew something I didn't. "Yes. It is."

"How long have you been in this occupation?"

"Four years."

"And what did you do before you became a private investigator?" He struggled with the occupational title and tried to hide the disgust in his voice. It was going to get bumpy.

"I was attending the FBI Academy at Quantico, Virginia."

"And did you graduate?"

"No. I did not."

"How close were you to graduating?"

"I don't see what this has to do with anything."

"Just answer the question, please. The more cooperative you are, the quicker we can all get out of here. These good citizens are tired. They've been here for several weeks now." He turned and smiled at them.

Shit. He had them in the palm of his hand. "Would you repeat the question?"

"How close were you to graduating from the academy?"

"One month."

He smiled a this-is-not-a-responsible-person smile. I saw a couple of men on the jury smile back at him.

"Miss Siegel, I'm sure you are aware of the death of Monday Brown."

"Yes, I am."

"On the thirtieth day of August, nineteen ninety-three, were you in the Custer National Forest?"

"Yes."

"And on that day did you come into contact with the now deceased Monday Brown?"

Christ, he was talking like I killed him. "He was deceased then."

"Then when?"

"When I came into contact with him."

"Will you describe that encounter for us?"

"I would if I could. I didn't know it was Monday Brown until later."

"Did you know Monday Brown?"

"Not personally."

"Would you recognize him if he was, say . . . walking down the street?"

"Yes."

"And you are telling us now that you did not recognize him then?"

"I didn't know I was in contact with him."

"You just told us a minute ago that you *had* come in contact with Mr. Brown. Now you're telling us you didn't know it was Mr. Brown? Do I understand you correctly?"

"Yes."

"Could you explain?"

"I was in a rest room—"

"Is the rest room you're referring to the government facility that you broke into?" He raised his eyebrows and mugged for the jury.

The jurors could just as well have been at a tennis tournament. Their heads were swiveling between O'Donnell and me.

"It was a rest room. I wasn't really too concerned with who it belonged to."

"Was nature calling when you smashed the lock on the government facility to get in?"

"No, Mr. O'Donnell. Life was calling. I believed my life was in danger, and I was going into hypothermia. It seemed like my best bet at the time."

"What or who was endangering your life?"

"I don't know who it was."

"Did you see this person?"

"Yes."

"Will you describe him for us?"

"He was big, half nude, and had his face painted black." That perked their ears up.

"Did he threaten you in some way?"

"His presence threatened me, Mr. O'Donnell."

"Are you aware of the fact that hypothermia causes delusional perceptions?"

"I am now."

"Were you delusional the first time you saw him?"

"No. I was not."

"What you're telling us is that in inclement weather, severe enough to put you into a hypothermic state, a half-nude man, his face painted black, chased you through the woods but gave you a chance to forcefully break into a government building, where you discovered the body of Monday Brown."

"Basically. He knocked me unconscious. The next thing I knew I woke up naked in the back of a Blazer."

"Were you naked by yourself or with someone?"

As soon as he said it he knew how stupid it sounded. I looked straight at the jury and watched as the majority of them bit their lips or covered their mouths to keep from laughing.

"I was with a Yellowstone County sheriff's deputy."

He stared at me with disbelief and manically shuffled through his papers. Clearing his throat, he tried to take control back.

"That would be Deputy Kyle Old Wolf." He briefly read something and looked back at me. "He administered first aid. Is that correct?"

"Yes."

"Miss Siegel, what time of day were you at the picnic area at the Big Ice Cave?"

"It was late. After six in the evening."

"Did you at any time during the story you just told us see anyone other than the half-nude man?"

"No. I did not."

"You arrived at the parking area around six in the evening. It is stated here," he said as he looked at another paper, "that Deputy Wolf found you huddled next to the body of Monday Brown around nine o'clock. That's three hours, Miss Siegel. Did you, at any time during those three hours, see anyone else in the area?"

I said nothing.

"Miss Siegel. May I remind you that you are under oath."

"I'm aware of that, Mr. O'Donnell."

"Would you please answer the question."

"I can't do that."

"You what?"

"I can't answer that."

"Is it that you can't or that you won't?"

"I won't."

He moved closer to my chair. You could hear the jury shifting in their seats. O'Donnell leaned down close to me, his mouth next to my ear, and whispered. "Don't fuck with me, Siegel, or I'll take you in front of the judge, and I can guarantee you, he will hold you in contempt."

There was no way I was going to whisper. I'd had it and I knew it. "I don't think you should talk dirty to a witness, Mr. O'Donnell."

"That's it." He walked to the table and slapped his hand down on it. "We're adjourning." He looked toward the rattled clerk. "Please see if Judge Eaton is in his chambers, and if he is, tell him I will be bringing Miss Siegel in immediately."

"I need to use the rest room."

"Fine. I'll have you escorted."

We walked out the door, and, sure as hell, he motioned to one of the marshals. He whispered something to him. The marshal ushered me down the hallway and to the rest room. Maggie was in hot pursuit as soon as she realized I had an escort.

I walked into the rest room and straight to the sink, turned on the cold water faucet, and splashed water onto my face.

"What the hell is going on?"

"You're on retainer. As of now."

"You put yourself in contempt, right?"

"I think I'm seconds away from that very thing."

"I can't help you, Phoebe. This is going to be between you and the judge. Do you know who the judge is?"

"I think he said Eaton."

"Great," she said, nodding. "He'll give you every chance. But if you don't give him what he wants . . ."

We both turned when we heard the knock on the rest room door.

"Miss Siegel? Judge Eaton is waiting in the courtroom. Would you come out now, please?"

"Be cool. He's an old cowboy with shit on his boots, and he doesn't like smart-ass women."

"Including you?"

"Including me."

"Miss Siegel?" Judge Eaton looked down from his perch above me. He had white hair, a face like Santa Claus, and wore his glasses low on his nose.

"Yes, sir?"

"What's the problem here? Are you refusing to answer because what you might say could incriminate you? You don't have to incriminate yourself."

"I understand that, sir."

"If you have committed a crime, you don't have to testify against yourself."

"I have not committed a crime."

"You're under subpoena, Miss Siegel. You have to answer. It's the law."

"I understand that also."

"Will you answer?"

"No, sir. I won't."

He slowly removed his glasses and stared down at me. "I can jail you until you change your mind. You really don't look like jail material to me, Miss Siegel. I think you would find accommodations at the YCDF a bit uncomfortable."

"I'm sure I would. But I can't answer."

"Tell you what I'm gonna do here. I'm going to give you until tomorrow morning to think about this—"

"But wait," O'Donnell spoke up.

"Now you know better than to interrupt me, son." Eaton spoke without even looking at O'Donnell. He kept his eyes riveted on me.

"I want you back here at nine o'clock tomorrow morning. At that time, if you don't plan on answering the questions you are asked, I would suggest that you bring your toothbrush, young lady. Do I make myself clear?"

"Yes."

"I want you to know that incarcerating you is not a punishment but an enforcement of power of the court. Do you also understand that?"

"Yes, sir. I do."

"You seem like a very understanding young woman. I'll see you at nine."

With that, he rose and walked out of the courtroom.

28

I had left Maggie at her car and was crossing Third Avenue North headed for the sheriff's office when I heard Roger.

"Phoebe. Wait up." He crossed the street in the middle of the block and walked up to me. "Where have you been?"

"Coming up for air, Roger?"

"Quit it."

"I've got a phone. You've got a phone. I have an answering machine."

"I've been busy, out of town. I was going to come by later and pick up some of my things."

"How about *all* of your things?"

"Shit. Don't do this. I've been worried sick about you. How's it going?"

"Great. Just great."

"I saw you with Maggie Mason. What's that all about?"

"Business, Roger. How's Miss January?"

"Phoebe, for Christ's sake."

"No, I mean it. How is she?"

"Fine."

"Is it getting hot and heavy?"

"No. It isn't. We're taking it slow. I think something could come of this. She's a good person, Phoebe."

"I bet."

"How are things going with your Indian friends? I heard they found that guy's body."

"That's all you heard?"

"We went over to Chico for a couple of days."

"That busy, huh?"

"We just got back last night. Why? Is there more?"

"Got time for some coffee?"

"Sure. How about the cafeteria in the courthouse?"

"Let's go."

I tried to kid myself that it was like the old days, sitting across from Roger sharing a cup of coffee. Only it wasn't. It never would be again. But I trusted him, and I needed him in my corner, wherever that corner was going to end up. He listened patiently as I filled him in on what had been going on, and before I knew it an hour had passed.

"It's a damn good thing we're both so hardheaded," he said and reached across the table to hold my hand. "You must be sick about the truck."

"I'm lost. No wheels. I'm depending on the generosity of my friends."

"How about a little generosity from your best friend?"

"What do you mean?"

He reached into his jacket pocket and pulled out his car keys. "Here. You have it for as long as you need it."

"My track record lately hasn't been so hot. I can't—"

"You can."

"Won't January—?"

"She won't mind. I insist. Just try to keep it out of the mountains. It's not used to anything harsher than a few of Billings's minor potholes."

"Thanks, Roger. Maybe down the road I'll be able to look at you and really tell you I'm happy for you."

"I hope that happens, Phoebe." He looked over my shoulder. "Kyle. Think you can keep her out of trouble for a while?"

"Probably not." I felt his hand on my shoulder. "How're you doing, Roger?"

"Great. Wish I had time to sit down and come up with a plan about what we can do with her, but I've got a brief to work up that I should have done already."

"Roger has been busy, Kyle. As in really busy."

Kyle smiled and patted him on the shoulder. Roger stood to leave. "Take care, Phoebe."

"You know I will."

Kyle sat down across from me, and from the look on his face I knew he knew what had happened in court.

"You're walking a thin line here, Phoebe."

"I've had enough shit to last me a lifetime. Don't you start, too. How the hell does this crap spread so fast? I just walked out of there an hour ago."

"It's an incestuous world. What are you going to do?"

"Punt."

"What the hell does that mean?"

"I don't have the slightest idea. Isn't that what everyone says at moments like this?"

"There's no way I'm going to avoid being subpoenaed."

"Kyle, I need some time."

"From what I hear, there's a chance that as of tomorrow morning you'll have more than enough time on your hands."

"I don't have a choice here, Kyle. You know that. If I—"

"Don't tell me anything." He raised his hand to silence me. "I dropped in on Doc Joss this morning. He says he's sure that Cheyenne kid hanging in your tree and Monday were both killed by the same instruments."

"Instruments?"

"Knitting needles. Wooden knitting needles."

"That doesn't make any sense."

"He's the best. It makes sense to him. He sent some tissue to the Crime Lab for analysis. Thinks maybe he can pin down the type of wood they're made out of."

"Knitting needles? I don't believe it."

"He drew me a picture of what he thought tore those guys up, and they looked exactly like knitting needles. There was an indentation around the deepest wound. Doc feels that there was some kind of decoration on the end that hit the skin and stopped it. He'll know more tomorrow morning."

"It used to be simpler. Guns. Knives. But knitting needles? Shit. Kyle, I have to get in to talk with Thomas."

"I'm looking into it."

"That's not good enough. I've got until tomorrow morning to cut something loose here."

"You've got a choice. Tell O'Donnell what he wants to hear."

"I can't do that. Not yet. Call down there and get me in. I'll owe you."

"Damnit. Give me a minute." He got up and walked out of the cafeteria.

And that's about how long it took. He sat back down.

"You're in luck. A guy I know had to hold over on his shift. He's off in forty-five minutes. If you can be down there in ten minutes, he'll give you what time he can."

"Thanks, Kyle."

"I'll collect," he said and smiled. "I'm running up to Monday's service this afternoon. Do you want to go?"

"I hate funerals. They're pagan as hell. And then there's the disgusting tradition of saying how good the corpse looks. I mean, how the hell good can you look when you're dead?"

"They're having a graveside service, behind the house. Short and sweet. Ardena said he never wanted to be embalmed, so she's holding to that."

"That's more than I would do for the son of a bitch. Why are you going?"

"I'd like to see who's hanging around."

"Good idea. Give me a time."

The YCDF sits off I-90 on King Avenue. It's new, big, and still can't meet the need. I followed the rotund jailer as he led me into the visitors' area. I sat down in a chair in front of a glass so thick you couldn't drive a car through it.

"They'll bring him out in a minute. Make it short. He's not in good shape. Not right in the head. And you tell Wolf when you see him that he owes me a case of beer."

"I will. Thanks."

I was the only person in the room on my side of the glass. A guy in blue overalls was mopping the floor with a monotonous back and forth motion. He glanced at me once and went back to his chore. By tomorrow I could be the one down here mopping the floor.

The jailer who had escorted me into the room was now guiding Thomas through another door and into the secured area behind the glass. Thomas looked at me, turned, and tried to leave. The jailer said something to him, pointed toward me, and coaxed him to the chair.

Hesitantly, Thomas sat down. The jailer then lifted a phone off the wall and put it in Thomas's hand. I picked up the receiver on my side.

"Thomas, do you remember me?"

He nodded.

"I came to see you at the church and we had a talk, you and I."

"And on the mountain, too. I saw you on the mountain."

"Do you remember that?"

Again, he nodded.

"That's what I want to talk to you about."

"I'm waiting for my friend."

"Pardon me?"

His face had the serene innocence of a child. It threw me. Even his voice had regressed to that of young boy.

"My friend is coming to get me."

"Do you mean the priest that you live with in Pryor?"

"Oh, no. My friend."

"What's your friend's name, Thomas?"

"I can't tell you. It's a secret, and I keep secrets real good."

"I bet you do. I keep secrets myself. Was your friend with you on the mountain, Thomas?"

His mouth puckered. "I can't tell you that."

"Would your friend get mad at you if you told me?"

"Yes. Very mad."

"What happens to you when your friend gets mad at you?"

I damn near dropped the phone when he slapped himself on the side of his face with his right hand. A red, angry-looking handprint started to rise immediately and covered the area from his temple to the side of his chin.

"Jesus. What the hell did you do that for?"

He looked at me quizzically. "That's what my friend does when I'm bad."

I put the phone down and turned sideways in my chair. Thomas started to get up from his chair and hang the phone up.

"No. Wait. Thomas. Please don't do that again. God. When did your friend do that to you?"

"When I was on the mountain. It was raining and I was crying."

It had to be the scene that Matthew and his friends had witnessed the night they followed Thomas, or who they thought was Thomas, driving the truck.

"What were you doing up there?"

"Helping my friend."

"And what was your friend doing?"

"Helping Monday. He's my other friend." His face brightened. "I help Monday sometimes when he needs me. Monday says I'm strong."

"Thomas. When you saw me on the mountain, uh . . . were you trying to scare me?"

"That's part of the game. Were you scared?"

"Very. I ran away from you and you came after me. Do you remember coming after me?"

"You were good at the game."

"Why did you hit me, Thomas?"

He hung his head down and looked up at me through his eyelashes.

"I'm not mad. I just want to know why."

"You were trying to wake up my friend Monday, and he needed to sleep."

"I didn't know he was sleeping. I didn't know he was even there."

"My other friend said that if you woke up Monday you would take all of his things, and Monday didn't want anybody to have them."

"What things?"

"War things. Important things."

"Do you have them, Thomas?"

He shook his head.

"Do you know where they are?"

"On the mountain. My friend said they had to stay on the mountain where they belonged. Monday got very mad at my friend."

"When?"

"No. I don't want to talk to you anymore."

"Thomas, if you told me who your friend was, I could call and tell him you're waiting."

"No."

His face contorted. He stood as the jailer walked over to the glass, looked at me, pointed to his watch, and mouthed the words no more time. He leaned down toward the chair to tell Thomas he had to go back.

It happened fast. Thomas turned on the jailer with a force that sent him sprawling across the floor. The jailer slid into the wash bucket. Water flowed across the floor. The jailer stood and slipped just as Thomas reached him, looming over him.

The prisoner with the mop punched a large red button on the wall by the door. Within seconds three uniformed officers descended on Thomas and wrestled him down. I could hear nothing and saw only Thomas's gaping mouth as he screamed incoherently. His face was crimson, his strength, shocking.

I found myself pressed against the wall behind where I had been sitting. Thomas threw the officers from him and lunged toward the glass. His palms hit the glass with such force I flinched, expecting shards to go flying. He was screaming, soundless, forming one word over and over again.

The officers were on him a second time. I saw hands and arms jerk Thomas's arms behind him. They pulled him away from the glass and dragged him, his heels leaving a trail through the water, out of the room. I was breathless; I slid down to the floor and squatted there.

The jailer came in the door that I had entered through.

"Jesus. I'm sorry about that. If I upset him . . ."

"Strong bastard, isn't he? What the hell were you talking about?"

"Just conversation. He wasn't real with it. Just like you said. Damn."

"You better get on out of here. My relief is coming in, and I'm going to have to explain what the hell happened."

"What was he screaming? It looked like he was saying someone's name."

"Who the hell knows? It was something like . . . Jimmy, maybe. I don't know. I wasn't really paying all that much attention."

"But it sounded like 'Jimmy'?"

"Look, lady, I don't know what the hell he was saying. One minute he's this little kid, and then he's some damned priest on his knees in his cell praying. Real kook. We aren't equipped to handle these mental cases."

"Has he asked to see anyone?"

"I wouldn't know."

"Thanks for letting me in. God, I'm so sorry."

"Forget it. Comes with the territory. People go a little crazy when they first come in. Claustrophobic."

"Really." I felt the walls closing in on me already.

29

I read the printed material that had been left on my back porch several times and decided that I needed a professional opinion. I called the emergency room and left a message for Dr. Donich, telling her that I would be home late in the afternoon and would appreciate her calling me. I also specified that it was personal, not medical.

I changed into something a little more appropriate for Monday's service, a red silk blouse and a pair of black pants, feeling very much like a black widow spider. But, what the hell.

The town was dead, and I assumed that everyone and his cousin would be at the Brown house for the service. I asked for directions in the store and found that it was a mile and a half on the two-lane to Crow Agency. I still did not meet any traffic. I watched for a dirt road leading off to the right and a bright blue iron gate and turned off the highway when I got to it.

I could see a house in the distance, more modern and affluent than most on the reservation, with about fifteen cars parked out in front. I pulled up behind Kyle's Blazer and parked. I looked around the yard and knocked on the door. No one answered. There was a stone path that led to the rear of the house and through a stand of cottonwood trees. Just the other side of the trees the stone path was replaced by a dirt path. On a hill about a quarter of a mile away I could see people gathered. The wind blowing across the plains was at my back and almost carried me along the path.

By the time I reached the gathering, someone was already saying a few words over Monday Brown. I was shocked to see that the coffin was open. Satin caught the bright sunlight and gave off an ethereal glow of the brightest white. As I approached, Ardena walked to the coffin and closed it. Thank God. Dead *and* ripe weren't sitting well with my stomach.

Kyle saw me and walked over to stand beside me.

"Our friend Mueller is here. He watched you come up the path with a little more interest than I'm comfortable with."

"Which one is he?"

"Right over there in the black suit. He looks like an undertaker."

Kyle was right. The guy stood out like a sore thumb. As did the two men with him, who were wearing reflective sunglasses. Everyone else was in blue jeans and shirts.

"That must be Frick and Frack, his personal bodyguards."

"I know one of them. Mark Sutter. He's not a bad guy. I was hoping I'd get a chance to talk to him alone at some point."

"That may not be a problem. Here comes Mueller."

He was ruggedly handsome, with sandy-colored hair, longer than I would have expected. His eyes were a steel blue and cold as ice. And he was big. Probably over six feet and around two hundred pounds. He walked up beside me and said nothing, just stood there staring toward the coffin. When there were no more words to be said over Monday, people relaxed and started talking to one another.

Ardena Brown walked through the crowd and toward me before she saw Mueller standing there. A look of fear crossed her face. She glanced briefly at him and then smiled at me. "I'm glad you came, Phoebe. I hope you and Kyle plan on staying around for some food. I've got more than I could possibly do anything with."

"That would be nice. We'll see how the time goes."

"Good to see you, Kyle." She reached out and patted his arm affectionately. Then she looked back at me. "Kyle and I went to school together."

She looked stressed out, or maybe she just looked relieved. When the lid closed on that coffin, so did an abusive chapter of her life. I guessed if anything good was to come from all of this, it would be her and her son's freedom. She walked away from us and worked her way through the group. Ardena stopped at each person and thanked them, touched them in some way. This was a good woman, and, like her, I was glad Monday Brown was dead.

I looked casually to my side, not wanting Mueller to see me trying to see him. I was shocked to find him staring at me. He said nothing.

Just smiled. The same diabolical smile I had seen in the backseat of the car outside the emergency room.

"Do I know you?" I finally asked.

"We've never had the pleasure of meeting, although I do know who you are. I've been looking forward to this. I'm Jurgen Mueller, a former client of Mr. Brown's."

He held out his hand. I didn't reach back, and I said nothing.

"Your reputation seems well deserved."

That cried for a response. "My reputation is usually understated, Mr. Mueller."

He laughed, clasped his hands together as if in prayer, and pressed them to his lips. "That's wonderful. That's really wonderful. Could we talk for a moment?"

I considered telling him to fuck off, but I knew if I talked with him, Kyle would have a chance to talk with Mark Sutter. "Why not?"

I walked a few feet from the crowd. Mueller followed. I turned to face him. I wanted him in a position where he did all the talking.

"Miss Siegel, or are you one of those liberated American ladies that prefers Ms?"

"What's on your mind?"

"I know that you've been hired by the family of the young man that the police had in their custody."

He reached into his pocket and withdrew a silver cigarette case and offered me one. I shook my head no.

"Let's cut to the chase, Mueller."

"Cut to the chase? I'm afraid I don't understand."

"I think you understand perfectly."

"I like your directness, but I would suggest that you keep it under control. Would you like to walk while we have this conversation?"

"Right here is fine. Get on with it."

He lit his cigarette and did some fancy inhale that was supposed to impress me. He watched my face for a reaction.

"I think we can do business, Miss Siegel. I believe you have information that could lead me to some items that I have paid for. It would be ridiculous of me to, uh . . . expect this information without some type of gratuity, a token of my appreciation. Now are you interested?"

"About as interested as I was five minutes ago. What makes you think I know anything? Maybe I'm stumbling around in the dark like everyone else."

"From what I hear, you don't stumble for long."

"Maybe I can cut through your bullshit for you, Mr. Mueller. If I had any information, you would be the last person I would give it to. As far as I'm concerned, you're as much of a scumbag as that guy they just lowered into the ground. Ardena told me about her little run-in with you. It's called attempted rape in this country, and they can haul your ass in and charge you. If I hear of you anywhere near her, I'll do everything in my power to see that you're charged."

His cheeks flushed. He took another drag on his cigarette and blew smoke in my face. "How do you Americans say it? Don't fuck with me? That's it. Don't fuck with me, Miss Siegel. You might be biting off a piece so big you could choke on it. Slowly. Your idle threats don't carry any weight with me." His accent was thick as he articulated each word very carefully. "I could squash you like a piece of dog shit and then scrape you off my shoe into the gutter. Is that clear?"

He reached out, grabbed my wrist, and squeezed.

"There are two FBI agents standing over there and a sheriff's deputy. By the time I'm through speaking you had best have your hand off me. You're a sick asshole who gets his kicks beating up hookers."

A look of disbelief smeared across his face. He let go of my wrist.

"See?" I continued. "I know you too, you sorry piece of slime. You might get off intimidating women you catch when they're alone, but if you come near me or Ardena Brown, I will personally cut your balls off and shove them down your throat. Have you got that?"

I turned and walked over to where Kyle was talking to Mark Sutter. He took one look at my face and grabbed my arm.

"What's wrong?" He looked over my shoulder at Mueller.

"I'm leaving. I'm going to say good-bye to Ardena."

I turned and walked up toward Monday's final resting place. I stopped. An old Indian man, just barely able to walk with a cane, hobbled to the edge of the grave and spit down onto the coffin. A woman, holding on to his arm, followed suit. If anyone saw what they did, no one reacted.

Ardena was standing with her arm around her son a few feet from me. I walked over and put my arm around her shoulder.

"I've got to take off. Ardena, if you need anything, anything at all, will you call me?"

"I'll be fine, but thanks. We're all going to miss Anna so very much. I had her come and talk to my bilingual writing program at the school. They loved her. She told all of us you were very special. That's quite a compliment coming from someone like her."

"You've got my number?"

"Yes. I may just call you one of these days to do another sweat with us."

"Once was enough, thank you. I'll be in touch."

On the way down the hill, I told Kyle about my encounter with Mueller.

"I should go and bust his ass right here." He stopped and looked up the hill toward Mueller.

"You don't have any authority up here, remember?"

"I'm talking about literally busting his ass. Kicking it up and down this hill a few times."

"The hell with him. Let's get out of here." I took his arm and started walking. "Kyle, I have to ask you something. Did you ever hear of James Eagle and Thomas running around together?"

"Not really. Thomas was more of a loner. Why?"

"Would he have called James Eagle 'Jimmy'?"

"Indian people don't usually chop up names like that. I've never heard him called anything but James. How many times do I have to ask you why before you answer me?"

"It's nothing. Just something I'm rolling around in my mind. Did you find out who was calling you?"

"No. But I have an idea it's Louis. He wouldn't leave his name, but they hooked into the circuit and found out the call was coming from Browning. I think he has a sister living up there. Keep that under your hat."

"Have you told Genevieve?"

"No. Why say anything until I'm sure?"

"Your call."

By the time I got home, there were two messages from Dr. Donich. The last one said she would have an hour free between four-thirty and five-thirty. I had fifteen minutes to get there. I grabbed the manila folder and left the house and a cat that hardly knew me anymore.

* * *

She was waiting in the cafeteria. When I walked through the door,
she waved me over.

"I'm glad you called. I was wondering how your head was doing.
Any problems with it?"

"Not a one. I need to pick your brain."

"It'll be slim pickings, but go ahead."

"You said you worked at a psychiatric facility."

"It was a little heavier than that. It's California's Institute for the
Criminally Insane. Not your run-of-the-mill Valium users."

"I want you to read something and give me your opinion of it." I
handed her the folder.

"Why don't you go on over and get yourself a Coke or something?"

"Sounds like an idea."

When I returned she was bent over the papers, her hands on either
side of her head. When she finished she looked past me and out the
windows that lined one wall of the cafeteria.

"What's the story on this?"

I told her the whole story, even down to Jurgen Mueller.

"Wow. I thought working the ER was pressure."

"Is there anything to this, or could it just be a hoax? Someone
playing games."

"Without knowing a little background on the person that wrote
this, the best I can give you is a good guess."

"I'll settle for that. Do you think it's male or female?"

"Could be either. If they had really wanted to fool you they would
have kept it generic. Then again, it could be a ploy writing about a
little girl just to throw you off track. Could be a man."

"Any hidden messages?"

"Look, Phoebe, I still see animals in clouds. Are there any hidden
messages? I couldn't tell you that. But there is a theme here. As soon
as I read it, it reminded me of a case I had. This thirty-five-year-old
man was committed to San Luis. He'd killed his landlady, and that
wasn't his first one. He also got some old guy that lived down the
street. No remorse. Killed with pure entitlement. He was a sociopath.
Sad kid. He'd been bounced around from foster home to foster home
for years. When he was eleven, he ran away from some relatives that
agreed to take him. He hid out all night in an old building downtown

in Bakersfield, and I guess being alone in the dark for that long scared him more than the people he was living with."

"God."

"It gets better. He went home the next morning and they had moved out. Lock, stock, and barrel. Poor damn kid. He was right back in the system and stayed there until he was eighteen. No one heard from him until they picked him up for the landlady. When he came in to us, he was carrying this album real close to his chest. I finally talked him into a peek at it. It was full of pictures of kids playing ball with a parent, swimming, camping. All different kids in most of the pictures. He even had some photos of elderly people. I asked him if they were relatives of his and he said he thought so, that he'd found the pictures at garage sales and Goodwill stores. He said he knew they must be related or he wouldn't have wanted them so badly."

"Sad. Very, very sad. But how does it remind you of this material?"

"Here was a kid who never connected. Never had a sense of roots. Fragmented and obsessive at the same time. He fixated on people. This"—she tapped the papers with her finger—"this person is fixated on a memory. Probably the only connective memory they have to their past. Fit anyone you can think of?"

"Not really. . . . Wait a minute. There's this guy they're holding. His name is Thomas. He's, uh . . . I don't know what the clinical word would be, but he pretends he's all these people. One minute he's really gentle, jovial almost, and then he loses it and goes berserk. I saw him slip into this child thing today and then rage out."

"Could be bipolar with a little schizophrenia thrown in for good measure."

"Would he fit the bill?"

"Maybe. You're looking for a needle in a haystack on this one, but I'd sure as hell watch my back."

"Dangerous?"

"Damn betcha. People fixate on the damnedest things. Just like the kid I told you about. He killed this little old lady because he thought she was his grandmother and hated her because she'd let him go through life without benefit of a family. She was, of course, no relation. People can fixate on causes, buttons, jockstraps. You name it. Bundy liked brunettes. You go figure."

"You said causes. Would they kill for a cause?"

"In a minute, and anyone who stood in their way should give them a wide path to walk. Any ideas yet?"

"A couple. What about money? Could that be motivation?"

"Greed and avarice? That's always good. Me? I'd kill for lemon meringue pie. I'm dieting, of course, but God help the man who passes one under my nose."

I laughed and got up to leave.

"Can I keep this and give it another look tonight? I'll call you if I get any hits off it."

"I'd appreciate it. If you could call me later, or at least before nine tomorrow morning."

"Going out of town?"

"Sort of."

I should have asked her for some advice on how to handle claustrophobia.

30

The toothbrush didn't sit well with Judge Eaton. I did think he overreacted just a little as I hobbled out of the courtroom; Maggie thought the leg irons were a nice touch. If you've never been booked and searched, keep it that way. It's right up there with ingrown toenails and pap smears. They issued me the latest in jail wear, a two-piece blue number that made a hey, I'm-one-of-you fashion statement.

The women's side of YCDF was full. The cops had made a sweep downtown and busted ten or twelve ladies of the night. They were all right and made no bones about who they were or what they did. I spent the first hour sitting in the recreation room listening to the raw deals they had been dealt and complaints about how their pimps hadn't shown up to post bail. Then there were the independents, girls without pimps. Even in whoredom there is a definite caste system.

Among the other roomies was an assortment of DUI's and a woman in her late sixties waiting to be transferred to a federal prison, where she would start serving out the rest of her natural life. I wondered if they would let her out if she became unnatural. There was no black, white, Hispanic, or Indian thing. You were in there, and that cut through all the lines.

At around ten-thirty the jailer who had let me in to see Thomas walked into the rec room and yelled my name. "Hey, Siegel."

"Right here."

"Come on out. Someone wants to talk to you."

I followed him through two secured doors and past the sign that said VISITING ROOM

"I don't get to use the phone through the glass?"

"Nah. You don't look that dangerous to me. When they told me you were coming in, I thought Wolf had busted you for causing all that trouble down here yesterday."

"How's Thomas doing?"

"They transferred him to the psych ward like they should have done in the first place."

"Did he ever settle down?"

"Depends on what you call settled down. We restrained him for a couple of hours, and when we took that off he started chanting and war-whooping and dancing around in his cell. I heard this morning he kept that whole damn wing up all night."

"Who's here to see me?"

"Right through this door."

He opened a door that led into something that looked like an interrogation room. Kyle was sitting on the edge of a table that was bolted to the floor.

"Thanks, Benny. I owe ya."

"Where've I heard that before? You owe me so much already, Wolf, you won't live long enough."

"Just couldn't go an hour with seeing me, could you?"

"Actually, I told him I needed a conjugal visit. He asked me what my preference was, and I told him I wanted a short redhead, not too bright, but feisty."

"You want your way with me in here? On an iron table?"

"Look, all kidding aside . . ."

"Who's kidding?"

"Phoebe. They'll have Matthew in custody by this afternoon. They got a lead on where he's been parking that truck and camper. Mark Sutter and his buddy are on their way up there as we speak."

"God, Kyle, don't let that happen."

"There isn't a damn thing I can do. That grand jury will probably hand down an indictment sometime tomorrow."

"Shit."

"Why don't you let me call O'Donnell and let him know you're willing to talk to him?"

"No way. I can't do that, damnit, and you know it."

"You're riding a dead horse. What the hell good are you doing anyone in here?"

"They've got all these hookers in here. Sammy Vargas told me he had been hearing things on the street. Maybe some of them have heard something."

"And they're going to open up their hearts to you?"

"Maybe they will. There's a couple of black girls back there that may be the ones Sammy mentioned. They're independents . . ."

"You sure picked up on the lingo down here quick enough. You'll be so hardened by the time you get out, you'll be wearing those nylons with seams up the back and low-cut blouses."

"I do that already. You just haven't noticed."

"By the way, Roger is over at your mother's. I got a very hysterical call from her. This isn't going over well, Phoebe. She wanted to come down and bail you, and I told her there was no bail."

"Fuck. I never even thought about that."

"I don't think you've given much thought to anything. Let me call O'Donnell."

"No. God, he loved this, Kyle. Particularly when the judge said to give me the whole treatment."

"He's not through with you."

"What's left?"

"The food down here. Wait until lunch comes, and you'll know what I mean."

"That friend of yours, Benny? He told me that they took Thomas up to the psych ward."

"I heard."

"Kyle, I think, no . . . I know he was involved with Monday's murder. He's got this secret friend . . ."

"He's probably making that shit up."

"No, he isn't. He told me something that put him right up there on that mountain the night Monday disappeared. I can't tell you what it is, but, damnit, I know this secret friend is the one who did Monday. That's why I asked you who Jimmy was, if it could be James Eagle."

"James Eagle is dead. You know that."

"What was that Cheyenne kid's name?"

"It wasn't Jimmy."

"Kyle. Go up and talk to Thomas. See what he tells you."

"Phoebe . . ."

"Please."

"You know what happened down here yesterday. Hell, do you think he's going to be any more receptive to me than he was to you?"

"We won't know until you talk to him, will we?"

"Do you want me to call O'Donnell or not?"

"I said no."

"Then I'm out of here. I'll try to get back down later."

"What about our conjugal visit?"

He walked out of the room without even looking back.

When they served bilge soup and hardtack for lunch, I understood what Kyle had told me. The hookers that I suspected were Gin and Tonic, ate by themselves. I started to approach them once, and even if looks couldn't kill, I still got the message. I think it was something like "back off, bitch." I backed off.

At four in the afternoon, visiting hours were on. There was a scurry of activity as the jailer called names out, one by one, and the women hurried through the doors like they were late for the prom. I was sure it was Kyle coming down to harass me when my name was called. I followed Benny and walked right past the visitors' room and toward the room where I had met with him earlier.

"Nope. This one."

Benny opened the door leading into the telephones-and-glass area. I looked around and tried to find a familiar face, or at least a friendly one. Instead, I found Jurgen Mueller. I turned to walk back out and then decided to see what the asshole wanted. I walked over to a chair across from him and picked up the phone.

He smiled and picked up his. "We have to stop meeting like this, Miss Siegel, or people will begin to talk."

"What do you want, Mueller?"

"Oh, maybe just a look at the woman who threatened to cut my balls off and stuff them down my throat. You are like a bird whose wings have been clipped."

"Well, you've had your look. See you around." I started to hang up when he pressed his palm against the window and said something. His face had an urgency about it that piqued my curiosity.

"What?"

"I have to make my position clear to you. Then perhaps you will understand. The money which I purchased the artifacts with is not mine. A group of German industrialists who have great respect for your Native American heritage invested their money. It took many years for me to build trust—"

"If they trusted you, Mueller, then they're fools and they deserve to learn a very expensive lesson."

"Oh, they are not fools. They offered me one hundred and twenty-five thousand dollars as a finder's fee. Payment for negotiating such a priceless bundle as that is rare on this market in these times."

"What do you want from me?"

"I will give that finder's fee to you, Miss Siegel, if you will tell me where the artifacts are."

"I don't know where they are."

"You're lying. I have come to read people very well over the years, and I know that you are lying. If I do not turn over those artifacts to the investors, I may well lose my life. But I won't be alone. All I have to do is tell them that Mrs. Brown and yourself have known where they were hidden all the time. They will pursue you to the end of time."

"I can't help ya. Hey, when you get home, how about sending me a couple of pair of Birkenstocks? I hear you have more styles over there."

I stood up and walked out of the room. I could hear him banging on the glass behind me.

When I walked back to the rec room, the two black hookers who had been so cold before came strutting across toward me.

"Hey, girl. You know that dude that came to visit you?"

"Who?" I asked as they sat down across the table from me.

"That dude with the accent."

I had them. "You mean Jurgen Mueller? Sure. I know him."

"Well, we know him too, honey. He's one sick motherfucker."

"Really? Do I know either of you?"

"I don't think so, honey. My name is Tonic, and this is my sister Gin. Get it?"

"Clever. Very clever. I've heard those names before. Let me think about this for a minute. Yeah. It was from a friend of mine. Sammy Vargas?"

"That cute little fucker with the pawnshop?"

"That's him. Sammy and I go way back."

"I'll be damned. Guess you can't be too bad then, can ya?"

"What about Mueller? How do you know him?" Dumb question.

"Girl, are you serious or are you blind?"

"He's a business client of yours?"

"I like that, don't you, Gin? A business client. Don't mind Gin none. She lets me do most of the talkin'. He's a sick man, I'm telling you. Show her what he did to you, Gin."

I looked toward Gin and had no hint of what was to come. She raised her blue cotton top and revealed her bare breasts. My first instinct was to laugh hysterically as I saw the reaction of everyone else sitting in the room. The matron came running in, screaming at the top of her lungs.

"Put that damn blouse down. We do not allow that in here. You just keep your damn sexual preferences to yourself. This isn't going to look good for you either, Siegel."

"I—"

"Put it down, I said. Right now." She moved toward Gin.

"Come near me, bitch, and I'll have to slap you up alongside your head, and I won't quit at one time." Gin narrowed her eyes and all but spit the words toward the matron. "I was showing her an injury. See?"

Gin lifted one of her pendulous breasts toward the matron, who looked down at it and blushed.

"Cover up or I'll have two officers in here and you'll end up in lockdown. Do you hear me?" She turned and walked hurriedly away.

For the first time I noticed an ugly, seeping puncture wound high up on the left side of her left breast.

"Shit. What the hell happened?"

"He done it to me." Her voice was shrill and indignant. "He sure enough did."

"I'd lower that if I were you. I'd hate to see you in trouble."

"Honey, we've been in trouble since the day we was born."

"Mueller did that to you?"

"Sure enough."

"How? Why?"

"We'd been partying real hard and doing, uh . . ." She leaned down close to my ear and whispered. "We was smoking and"—she faked a sniff—"and some good shit that Tonic scored. Gooood shit! Then this guy goes crazy and says he wants to *test* me. Find out if I'm really a tough bitch."

"Why the hell didn't you get out of there?"

"Man, I had no idea of what this dude had in mind. Tonic was out. I mean really out. So I lay down on the bed and he pulls out this big nail . . ."

"He shoved a nail into your breast?" The thought made my skin crawl.

"This was not your ordinary nail. This sucker was this long." Gin held her hands about fourteen inches apart. "Then he lays out a couple of lines, real innocent like, and I do those and he lays me back on the bed and starts playing with my tit, and first thing I know it feels like he's burning me."

"Jesus Christ."

"He had one of them wooden things in his hand and stabbed my tit!"

All heads turned in the rec room, and she yelled it out.

"What the fuck are you all looking at!" Gin screamed.

"Wait a minute. What wooden thing?"

"Those fuckin' nails."

"They were wooden? Are you sure?"

"Does this look like I'm not sure?"

She again revealed her breast. It wasn't a puncture as much as a ragged tear. A puncture wound gone bad.

"Gin, did they look like wooden knitting needles?"

She thought for a moment and then answered, "Yeah. They did. They looked like my gramma's knitting needles, only they was red."

"Are you completely sure about this?"

"You think I'm some dumb bitch?" Her eyes narrowed. She was rapidly losing her congeniality, if it had ever been there.

"That isn't even on my mind, Gin. Believe me. Where did they come from?"

"How the fuck would I know? He had them in his little suitcase he carries around. One of them flat things?"

"A briefcase. Right?"

"Right. He had them in there."

"What happened after he tried to—"

"I was screaming and yelling and Tonic jumped on his back and rode that sucker around the room."

"What happened to the wooden needles, Gin?"

"How the hell would I know? We told him we would shove those up his ass."

"You left?"

"Damn right. We got the hell out of there. Haven't seen that fool since. We knew he liked it rough, but no man is going to leave a mark on my tit. It isn't good for business."

My mind was racing so fast I couldn't think. I had to get the hell out of there. Get to a phone or get to Kyle.

"Sit right where you are, Gin."

I got up and walked over to the speak hole in the glass that separated us from the matron.

"What's on your mind, Siegel?"

"I've got to get hold of Deputy Kyle Wolf. When can I make a call?"

"You got a quarter?"

"Have you got a fucking phone?"

"Watch your mouth with me." She held up her index finger and pointed it toward me. "You'd best watch your mouth."

"I'll get one."

"When you find one, make a collect call from the pay phone."

"I don't think the sheriff's office is going to accept a collect call. You're going to have to dial the number for me."

"Sorry. I can't do that."

"You can't or you won't?"

"Both. You are nothing special, Siegel. And from the company you keep, I would bet you're less than that."

My first thought was to reach in the hole, drag her through it, and offer her up to Gin. I would have slit my own throat. I walked back to Gin.

"Have you got a quarter?"

"Is that some joke? Like whores carry around a bag of quarters?"

"No. This is no joke. I think I can get all of us out of here. If you have a quarter."

"They ain't going to set our bail at no quarter, honey."

"For the phone."

Tonic looked up, reached into her pocket, and tossed a quarter across the table.

"Thanks, Tonic."

I called Genevieve's office collect and hoped to hell the secretary recognized my name. Genevieve answered. The words flew out of my mouth. She agreed to find Kyle and bring him down to the jail.

A half hour passed. An hour passed. Still no Kyle. When it hit an hour and a half and I had all but worn a groove in the floor from pacing back and forth, the jailer walked into the rec room and called my name.

As I followed him down the hall, I turned to go into the visitors' room. He steered me straight ahead.

"It'd be nice if you and Wolf could find some other place for these cozy little meetings." He grinned at me and opened the door. "He'll be in in just a minute."

By the time Kyle walked through the door, I was looking for a brown paper bag to breathe into to keep me from hyperventilating. I didn't appreciate the wide smile.

"PMS?"

"PMS, hell. Where have you been?"

"Calm down."

"We've got him, Kyle. We've really got him. There are these two hookers back there with me that—"

"We already picked him up."

"You what?"

"Genevieve called. I was out in the car when dispatch got ahold of me. She told me everything you had said, and I figured I'd better get a search warrant before Mueller got the hint something was coming down."

"And? What happened?"

"He wasn't in his room at the hotel. The manager didn't have much choice but to let us in the room, and they were right where your friend said they'd be. In his briefcase."

"Where was Mueller?"

"Are you ready for this?"

"Goddamnit, Kyle. Where was he?"

"We were bagging these pins, which by the way are piercing pins—"

"What?"

"Ever see *A Man Called Horse*?"

"No. What the hell does that have to do with anything?"

"These are pins that are used in the Sun Dance ceremony. These particular pins are very old. Made out of chokecherry wood and probably stained with some kind of plant dye that makes them even redder. Anyway, Mueller walks in in the middle of this. We've got four guys going through drawers, the closet, the whole damned room."

"Did he run?"

"Hell no. He just stood there and smiled. This is the iceman, Phoebe. You could have wiped frost from his face."

"Where were his buddies? His FBI entourage?"

"They'd left him down at the elevator, but I called Sutter and let him know what was coming down. Mueller is under diplomatic bull-shit, and the embassy was taking this very personally. Seems his brother is one of the big-time investors."

"Hot shit."

"Where is he now?"

"Sutter's having a heart-to-heart talk with him down at the station. He wants to see you."

"Me?"

"You. Are you ready to blow this joint?"

"Like I can."

"O'Donnell is on his way down. Not in the best of moods, I might add."

"Kyle, I've got to get Gin and Tonic out of here."

"They're not your responsibility, Phoebe."

"Like hell they're not. God smiled, Kyle. That's why they were in here the same time I was. It's one debt I plan on paying off. Please. Do this for me."

"Let me talk to Sutter. Maybe he can swing it."

O'Donnell walked through the door. "Well, Siegel. You may have won this hand, but the game isn't over."

"I don't think I want to play with you anymore, O'Donnell. You're just not much of a challenge."

His face turned beet red. "That mouth of yours is going to be your downfall, and I hope I'm not around to see it."

"I don't do mental battles with unarmed opponents, O'Donnell, so don't hold your breath."

31

Mueller was seated in a room similar to mine at the YCDF, one table bolted to the floor and a couple of chairs. I walked into the room and saw the same shit-eating grin that had been on his face every time I saw the asshole. It was enough to make you want to take him out right there.

"You must be feeling quite triumphant at this moment, Miss Siegel."

"That's pretty generous for a loser."

"You may gloat over my temporary situation, but in fairness I felt I should share some information with you."

"It's over, Mueller. You lost."

"Have a seat, please. You'll be interested in what I have to say."

"I'm not interested."

"You have a killer out there. I did not kill Mr. Brown."

"They tell me you're in some fucking state of denial. It doesn't wash with me."

"It doesn't particularly matter whether it does or not. I did not kill Mr. Brown."

"But you did kill those two kids. And while we're on it, how about Louis? Does that name ring a bell?"

He looked at me curiously. "Should it?"

I watched his face. The coldness was there, but so was perplexity.

"Should I know this person?" he asked again.

"He was a friend of James Eagle. He's missing."

"I'm afraid I can't help you on that one."

"So what you're saying is that you killed those two kids—"

"You're too obtuse. I certainly said nothing about killing either of those young men. But that doesn't matter, does it?"

"No, in your case it probably doesn't. They tell me that your brother is covering your ass with some trumped-up diplomatic immunity. Maybe he just wants to get his pound of flesh. I heard he was one of your major investors."

"Instead of concentrating on me, I would concentrate on Mr. Brown. Whoever did kill him also has the merchandise that I paid for. I'd be curious to know what happened to it."

I sat with my mouth open. "You amaze me, Mueller. You sit there and act like you just walked out of a bad play. Offended that you wasted your time even going. What the hell is your game?"

"I can assure you this game, as you call it, is not over. All the players have yet to show their hands."

"One more time. You're only taking responsibility—"

"I'm not taking responsibility for anything. The problem here, as I see it, is that you're not listening. I did not kill Monday Brown. That is what you should concern yourself with, Miss Siegel. Simply because I'm sitting here in the custody of this agency does not negate the fact that whoever was involved still has my merchandise and my money. That's—"

"I'm not interested in any defense you're building for—"

He raised a finger to his lips and made a soft shushing sound.

"You're a worthy adversary. I told you I respected that. Call this my farewell gift to you."

"I call this bullshit, Mueller. They should have pulled you out of the gene pool long ago. So save it."

I got up and walked to the door. The deputy who had been leaning against the wall beside the door opened it for me. I stepped out and then leaned back in. Speaking loud enough for Mueller to hear, I said, "By the way. I'd tell whoever comes in contact with this piece of work to take AIDS precautions. One of his, uh . . . contacts at the jail shared a little medical history with me. She had a positive HIV test about a month ago." I looked briefly at Mueller and smiled as the color drained from his face.

"What'd our boy have to say for himself?" Kyle asked.

"Nothing much. He's just trying to buy himself some time. What's going to happen to him?"

"They'll deport him. It's already in the works."

"There's something about that, that just pisses me off."

"It shouldn't. Sutter talked with his brother and filled him in on what was going on, and Mueller isn't out of the woods yet. They may send his ass back, but there will be people standing in line when he steps off that plane for a piece of it."

"Kyle, has he admitted to anything?"

"No. It's a two-way bluff. O'Donnell says there's enough to indict him. I mean, hell, we found about fourteen items in his goddamned bags that could only have come from Monday's stash, and those piercing pins, according to Joss, will match the wounds on the Cheyenne kid and Monday."

"What about James Eagle? He was shot."

"We found a revolver in Mueller's room. My bet is he bought it off the street right here in Billings. We're running it through ballistics."

"The stuff you found in his suitcases?"

"Yeah?"

"Was it on the list?"

"Most of it."

"Are they dropping the charges against Matthew?"

"You know O'Donnell. He's a damned grandstand player. He was tossing the idea around that Matthew was in some conspiracy with Mueller. I don't think he's gonna get far with that one."

"What if all the items showed up?"

"Depends on where they've been. Why?"

"Nothing. Just curious. What about the mystery person who's been calling?"

"Haven't heard from him."

"Do you think it's Louis?"

"Let's hope so, Phoebe. I don't think Genevieve could handle it if he shows up dead."

"Hey, Wolf. You've got a call. Where do you want to take it?"

"Who is it?"

"Monday Brown's wife. Widow. Whatever."

"Transfer it over here."

"Shit. I should have gotten hold of her. Stay put while I take this."

Kyle walked to a desk and picked up a receiver. He's usually pretty hard to read, but this time he wasn't. Shock and disbelief twisted his face.

"Did you call the BIA cops?" was all I heard him say before he turned his back toward me.

When he hung up the phone, he stood for a minute and said nothing.

"What's up, Kyle?" I asked.

"Someone dug up Monday."

"What the hell do you mean, dug him up?"

"Just what I said. He's gone. Ardena's kid was up at the grave last night. Everything was fine. He goes up there about an hour ago and there's a gaping hole in the ground, the coffin is open and empty."

"I don't believe it."

"The whole place is crawling with tribal cops. They've got some tire prints and footprints up and down the damn hill. Ardena had gone down to Crow last night after Shawn had been up at the grave. She figures it happened when they were gone."

"Who the hell would want Monday's body?"

"Beats the hell out of me. I know a Crow cop. I'll try to run him down and see what happened."

"This is some kind of sick joke, right?"

"This even unnerves me. Jesus. You think you've seen it all and then . . ."

"Fitting end for a grave robber. Wouldn't you say?"

"Yeah. A fitting end."

"I've got something I've got to do. Is Genevieve still around?"

"She said she'd wait for you down in the reception area. What is this something?"

"I'll let you in on it later. I think it might exonerate Matthew completely."

"Well, for Christ's sake tell me."

"I can't. Not yet. I could be way off, but then again . . ."

"I hate it when you do this. It spells nothing but trouble on the horizon."

"Before I go, let the deputy that was in with Mueller know that the AIDS thing is a sham."

"What AIDS thing?"

"He'll know what I'm talking about, but ask him to let Mueller sweat it out. Later."

"Wait a minute . . ."

"Don't forget about Gin and Tonic," I yelled as I got into the elevator.

"Are you two having a private party or can anybody come?" someone yelled from behind Kyle.

32

"You're early for someone who thinks I'm half out of my mind. Come on in. I was just going to take a shower."

"This is crazy, Phoebe. To go back up on that mountain just doesn't make any sense." Genevieve walked past me and into the entryway.

"I thought we settled all of this yesterday."

"Right. And if you had your way we would have been up there in the middle of the night."

"So I compromised. We didn't go last night. There's coffee in the kitchen. Help yourself."

"Have you talked with anyone this morning?"

"No. But Kyle called last night. I guess the paperwork involved with Mueller is overwhelming. The asshole. Kyle did talk to John Wolf to find out if they had heard from Matthew or Steven."

"Had they?"

"They're home. Both of them. Matthew is pretty shook up about his grandmother."

"What's their legal status?"

"I don't understand."

"The indictment?"

"Kyle doesn't think much will come of it even if O'Donnell pushes. But he wants to avoid that. That family has been through too much already. That's why I have to give this my best shot."

"I owe it to you, Phoebe, to tell you this is really a half-baked idea. Let Kyle handle it."

"I can't do that. He's got his hands full."

"That's what he gets paid for."

"Look at it this way. It beats sitting in an office all day, and if there's nothing up there, what the hell. We've had a nice ride. Right? Let me jump in the shower. I'll be down in a minute."

The only real concession to modern plumbing in my house is the shower. The showerhead pounded pulsating water against my back, massaging my muscles. I'd slept like shit the night before. Genevieve had refused to accompany me to the Pryor Mountains, making a good point that there wouldn't have been much light left once we got there. After much coaxing, she had agreed to the next day.

I was on a high. Hyper. I just knew the artifacts were where Thomas had told me they were, with Monday. My gut feeling was that he was right, that even in the dark recesses of his tortured mind there was a flickering reality.

I lathered my hair and was in the middle of rinsing when I felt the presence. I wiped the soap from my eyes and squinted. The distorted shadow moved toward the glass doors, growing as it neared. My breath caught in my throat. Water ran down my face, carrying the stinging soap into my eyes and mouth.

"Phoebe," the disembodied voice said. "You've got a phone call from Dr. Donich. She says it's important."

"Genevieve?"

"Who else?"

"Shit. You scared the hell out of me."

"Sorry. I asked her to call back and she said it couldn't wait."

"I'll take it in my bedroom. Tell her I'll be there in just a minute."

I finished rinsing, got out, and wrapped up in my Garfield beach towel. Still dripping, I headed for my bedroom and picked up the phone.

"Hello?"

"This is Kitty Donich. I wouldn't have pulled you out of the shower, but I woke up to the headlines about the German. He was arrested. Right?"

"Big time. What's up?"

"I took those papers home and have been going over them. Are they sure they have the right guy?"

"Oh they're sure, all right."

"Maybe what I'm about to tell you is moot then, but see what you think."

"Shoot."

"It's tough now that they have a guy in custody, but maybe this is some fluke. Something that isn't connected to anything. My best professional guess is that those pages were written by a woman."

"A woman? How so?"

"It's the intensity. The pain. The emotion. There's a lot more below the surface there. A fragmented personality, never fully integrated. Remember the guy with the photo album?"

"Yeah. I do."

"Well, this memory, real or imagined, is the same thing as that photo album. That one precious connection with a past. A childhood. There's a rawness about it and a couple of the lines that kept pulling my focus back to them."

"What lines are you talking about?"

"Let me give you an overall first. Remember, it's written almost from the child's point of view. An impressionable, very young child. We've all had memories that through the years take on meaning or a new interpretation, right?"

"Right."

"Well, here's this little kid, with someone she obviously loves very much, and he's dying. In her child's mind, she's aware of this. It's not just the death of the person, but the death of a way of life that she's being forced to leave. The grandfather imprints her, not intentionally, but he does it just the same, with the importance of how she needs to take the *people* with her. Nice in theory, but what about in a little kid's mind when she's yanked out of that environment, going to live in the *white man's world*. Anybody with any brains would know that it would be a real cultural meltdown. She's old enough to remember and young enough that whoever ended up being her primary caregiver wouldn't give the trauma it actually created a second thought. There've been studies done on Asian kids coming out of the Vietnam War, adopted over here and never exposed culturally again to what they were imprinted with during their most formative years."

"Slow down. You're losing me."

"Let me finish. Here comes the good part. There's a line in the middle someplace, let me find it here"—I could hear her shuffling the papers—"here it is. *Eagle will teach you. Eagle will teach you to hunt fearlessly.* Let's define hunt. Isn't a hunter a predator?"

"A killer."

"You've got it. This kid grows up, clings to this one memory, actually I believe there are more, but this one is the one that stands out. Now the kid is an adult. A cause appears."

"Like what?"

"Who knows? The chop-chop thing with the Atlanta Braves. That got a lot of press. It could be anything. But now this adult has a cause and pursues it relentlessly. God help the person that stands in her way."

"Her. Then you really think it's a woman?"

"I do. It threw me when I saw the headlines. I gotta go. I've got a screaming ten-year-old with a fishhook imbedded in his scalp. Any questions?"

I heard a soft click on the line.

"Hello?"

"I'm still here."

"I thought I heard you hang up."

"We've got a lot of extensions on this line. Someone probably pushed the wrong button."

"Thanks, Kitty. I might get back to you."

The line went dead. I held the phone for a minute and listened. Nothing. Mental health professionals can inject the most stable minds with a healthy dose of paranoia. I shoved it out of my mind, got dressed, and started to head downstairs. I stopped and remembered one more thing: the artifacts in the water tank above the toilet. If I was right and found Monday's stash on the mountain, I would have the opportunity to stick them in with the original booty.

I climbed up on the toilet, reached into the depths of the tank, and pulled the plastic bag out. The soapstone fish, scalp-lock bag, and finger-bone necklace were dry inside. After wiping off the bag with a towel, I tucked it into the pocket of my denim jacket and went downstairs. Genevieve was waiting on the porch.

"Ready?" I asked.

"As ready as you are," she said and walked to her car. "Let's go."

"Genevieve, if you're really not up to this . . ."

She turned and looked at me. "It's all right."

Something had changed.

I've never been a good rider. I've always felt that if my karma was to end up mangled in steel, it would be me who was at the wheel. Genevieve's driving on the open road gave credence to that quirk.

"Want me to spell you?" I asked.

"Am I making you nervous?"

"No. I'm one of those control freaks that prefers to take instead of being taken."

"I'll slow down."

"Have you been up before?" I asked as we turned onto Cave Creek Road.

"Why do you ask?"

"I had a helluva time. I thought I'd never get there. That gap goes on forever."

She didn't comment. As the road climbed, the trees disappeared on my side of the car, and I could look out and straight down a steep incline that must have been at least a thousand yards. A knot formed in my stomach as gravel pitched out behind the car.

There's a sensation I think everyone has experienced at one time or another. It starts as a nameless, shapeless terror that seeps in through your pores and brings with it a clarity of thought that isn't easily called forth at other times. I was having that sensation. Mueller's words crawled to the forefront of my thoughts: *All the players haven't played their hands.*

Genevieve pulled close to the edge of the road and stopped. I heard small rocks and dirt tumble from the shoulder and down the drop-off.

"I've got to stretch and get a breath of fresh air. Come on out."

Genevieve opened her door, got out of the car, and stood on the edge of the bank. She pulled the clip that held her hair firmly fastened at the back of her neck. The wind caught her hair and spread it across her face. I sat and watched, mesmerized, as she motioned for me to join her at the edge of the road. I opened my door and swung a leg out. There was no ground on which to step.

She smiled and looked off into the distance. I closed the door and leaned my head back against the headrest. I had my killer. The truth was, she had me. Everything fell into place: the stick figure beside the creek, Kitty Donich's analysis, and, most of all, poor, simple Thomas. He hadn't been mouthing the word *Jimmy* at all.

I looked at Genevieve.

And she knew I knew.

I had a couple of choices. I could step out into nothingness or maneuver myself over the console and the floor shift and make a run for it. Neither would give me an edge. And that was what I needed.

I opened the glove compartment, rummaged around, and pulled out a book. I tried to remember if I had ever heard of someone fending a person off with a car manual. I couldn't find one fucking incident. Genevieve started back toward the car and got in.

"Why didn't you get out? The view is beautiful."

"I'm not sure how much I would have seen on my way down."

Genevieve smiled and started the car. Gravel flew out behind it as she stomped the gas pedal and continued up the road.

"Genevieve?"

"What?"

"We need to talk."

"We probably do. But there's something I want you to see first."

"I'm not really in the mood for a sightseeing tour. Let's not take this cat and mouse game any further."

"Am I the cat?" she asked and looked toward me. "Or am I the mouse?"

"You tell me."

She was silent as we accelerated. The car leaned into the curves and at some points fishtailed toward the edge of the road, my edge, the steep one, as she carelessly sped around the switchback corners. We came up over a hill. The parking area at the rest rooms was just in front of us. This was where I supposed she would stop. I reached for the door handle. Without warning she took a sharp left and continued on. The road narrowed. The banks rose on either side as she climbed at a high rate of speed to the crest of the mountain.

"Genevieve. This is bullshit. We need to talk about this."

"We're going to talk, Phoebe. When I get to the top, we'll stop and talk."

My only thought was *if* we got to the top.

The road leveled out, and we were high atop a plateau that stretched in three directions. It all looked vaguely familiar, although I knew I had never been there before. The realization of that familiarity slammed me in the chest with such force, I looked at Genevieve to see if she had hit me. Both her hands were firmly clutching the steering wheel.

There were some things missing: Anna Wolf, the bear, and the ram. I had walked that road in my dream. Had felt the point of her staff against my back and shielded myself from the splinters of quartz that had hurled through the air each time the ram had brought its hooves down. Darkness had been replaced with the light that swallowed the stars that had been close enough to touch.

The quartz rocks that peppered the landscape caught the rays of the sun and shot prisms of light toward us and toward the sky. To my left a herd of horses started at our approach and ran, tails flagging, down into a ravine.

"Those are holdovers from Spanish ponies that were left to roam free."

"Stop the car, Genevieve. We're here."

"They're missing a vertebra, the final one in the spinal column."

"Stop the fucking car."

"We're almost there, Phoebe. We're almost there."

I couldn't straighten my thoughts out. The dust that swirled behind the car caught the wind and came in through the windows. My eyes watered, and my throat constricted. The next thing I knew I was thrown against the windshield as she hit the brakes. The last thing I remembered was a sickening thud as my head connected with the glass.

When I came to, I flopped backward, my head against the seat. I reached up and felt the warm, sticky blood flowing down my forehead. I tried to focus my eyes but couldn't get past the stabbing pain that was building behind them. The fractured windshield spiderwebbed out from where my head had damn near gone through the glass. I looked over. Genevieve was not in the car.

I reached for the door latch, pulled it up, and opened the door. Nausea was rising in my throat. A gust of wind hit my face, and I breathed deeply, trying to clear my head. Swinging my legs over, I reached up with my right hand, grabbed the top of the car, and pulled myself out. The muscles in my legs were putty and barely supported me. I inched around the door toward the hood of the car and leaned down over it. It was hot, too hot to use as a brace. I stood, staggered backward, and held on to the upper frame of the door.

Genevieve was standing in the distance, looking away from me. There was no way in hell she could make it to the car before I started it and left her on the plateau. I looked in and saw that the keys were not in the ignition. I was in deep shit and I knew it. I didn't know what she had, maybe a gun. My mind raced.

Adrenaline surged. I got down on my knees and looked under the front seat. A long leather bundle was shoved underneath. I pulled it out, certain of what I'd find inside. The soft leather stuck to the piercing pins as I unfolded the bundle. The blood, Monday's blood, was dead brown on the doeskin.

"There's nothing in the car that will help you, Phoebe."

Her voice scared the shit out of me. I rose quickly and bounced my head off the top of the car. I turned to face her.

"Walk with me a ways," she said softly.

"Let's talk. Right here."

"No. I told you there was something I had to show you and then we'd talk."

She reached out and grabbed my arm. Still unsteady on my feet, I stumbled after her. Her nails dug into my flesh as she tightened her grip.

"Did you know that another name for the Pryors is Land of the Eagle?"

"What the shit are you talking about, Genevieve?"

"This. All of this. Land of the Eagle."

I pulled away and straightened, facing her. "Cut the shit. I don't want some senseless garbage. What the hell are we doing up here?"

"This is where it happened. This is where I killed him."

"Monday?"

"You know exactly what I'm talking about, Phoebe. Up there. On the Overlook."

"Why? Shit. He was a maggot. Not worth—"

"Destroying my life over?" She laughed. "I thought the same thing. But I accomplished what I set out to do."

"Which was?"

"The artifacts." She looked at me. "That's what we came for, isn't it?"

"Where are they?"

"Up here. Come on and I'll show you."

Genevieve pushed me roughly in front of her. A sick dizziness rushed over me as I stumbled forward. I reached up with the sleeve of my jacket and wiped the blood from my forehead. I focused and stopped dead. Before me, as far as the eye could see, was sky, and directly in front of me was a drop-off of unimaginable depth.

"You're looking down four thousand feet to the Dry Head below.

The Crow called it the Place of Many Skulls. There was a buffalo jump down there centuries ago. At the base of it they slaughtered the buffalo and stacked the skulls. As with everything, the name was bastardized and it became the Dry Head. The artifacts are down there."

I took a step backward and bumped into her. My pulse was no longer inside my body but throbbing in the air around me. I'd played this scene out in my dreams. I could have given a shit what they called the place, and I sure as hell wasn't in the mood for rappelling for artifacts.

"Okay. Now you've shown me. Let's get out of here."

"Not yet."

I turned and faced her. She backed away a few feet and watched me intently.

"Don't you want to know why?"

"Not particularly. I'd like to leave. With or without you." I took another step forward and to the side.

"No!" she yelled and moved a step closer.

There was no way I was backing up to play elevator on a one-way trip four thousand feet down.

"Genevieve. I can help. Get you help. This isn't a lost cause. Hell, it was probably self-defense."

"No. I relished killing him. Delighted in it. I had finally found a home. My people.

"Oh, I know who I am. I've pulled bits and pieces together over the years. My adoptive parents knew that my father was from Montana and that I had spent some time with my Indian grandparents near Billings. When I came here I was struck by the strength of family that the Crow people based their existence on."

"Genevieve."

"Most of them live far below poverty. Ironic, isn't it, that they consider themselves rich because of family. I could never verify anything but I knew the Crow were my people. I knew I was home. You see, Phoebe, I'm that little girl that your doctor friend spoke to you about."

"It was you on the phone. Why the hell didn't you say something then? Genevieve, trust me."

She laughed and ran her hands through her hair. "So you can help me, right?"

"Kyle. He'll be there for you."

"No, Phoebe." The expression on her face softened into a heart-wrenching sadness. "No one will be there for me. They never have. Whatever might have been was taken away from me many years ago."

"It's never too late."

She looked beyond me and listened. I strained and hoped against hope that I was hearing what I thought I was hearing. An engine in the distance, the sound winding toward us up the hill.

"I want you to understand."

"Then talk to me. Talk to me, Genevieve." I listened and heard the sound draw closer. "I want to understand. Make me understand." I spoke slowly.

"He had all of those things. Those wonderful things that should never have had a price put on them. I tried to explain to you in the office that day . . ."

"I remember."

"He wasn't just going to sell some beaded trinkets, Phoebe. He was selling my heritage. The one that been stripped from, denied me. Because of him and people like him, when I heard the voices calling me home, I followed and nothing was there. It was gone."

"But now you're here. You've got friends . . ."

"I liked you the first time I met you. Maybe . . ."

"Maybe what?"

The sound drew closer still. I could see the bronze-colored roof of a vehicle crest the hill behind Genevieve and stop. The sound of the engine died.

"Another time? We could have been friends. Maybe it would have made a difference. I wanted you to understand. That's why I placed those pages in your house. In case something happened, I knew you would take care of them and remember."

"Genevieve, you're not making sense."

"Genevieve!" A voice screamed from behind.

She turned, looked briefly at Kyle as he approached, revolver drawn, and then looked back at me. She placed her hands on my shoulders. What blood I had left drained to my feet.

"For God's sake don't do this." My words came out in a whispered vibrato. "Please. He can help you. Help us."

"Remember, Phoebe."

"What?"

She placed her arms around me and pulled me to her. I felt the warmth of her breath as she kissed my cheek.

"The artifacts are down there. On the ledges. This is our secret, and if I didn't—"

My arms reached up and held her. I knew now what she was about to do.

"God don't. Please."

Without a word she stepped beside me, stretched her arms, and leaned silently forward and off the cliff. I dropped to my knees, covered my ears, and waited for the scream that was sure to come. It didn't. I collapsed, sobbing, into the earth. Somewhere outside of myself I could hear Kyle calling my name. The air split around me with a deafening screech. I looked up and saw an eagle diving toward me. I shielded my head from its talons as it screamed against the wind. The air vibrated around my face as its wings flapped, and then it was gone. She was gone.

33

*E*ach rock and rut the Blazer drove over shot pains through my head. I sat numbly as Kyle drove down the mountain. When we reached the foot, he stopped, pulled into an open space in a stand of willows, and parked.

"Stay put. There's a spring over here. You've got blood all over your face. We need to get that off." He reached into the glove compartment, pulled out a rag, and got out of the Blazer.

I opened the door, got out, walked over to a low flat boulder, and sat down. My head felt heavy, dizzy. Kyle approached with the wet rag and sat down beside me. The rag felt ice cold as he swabbed at my forehead. I flinched.

"That's a nasty cut. You're going to need stitches."

"She just vanished over the side. She leaned over and then she was gone."

"Phoebe—"

"Fuck. She just leaned over . . . I thought she was going to push me . . ."

"That crossed my mind."

"You had your gun out. Would you have shot her?"

"I don't know. All I could think about was you on the edge. Everything was in slow motion. I started walking toward both of you, and my feet were like cement."

"Why are you here? How did you know?" I reached up and held his forearm, stopping him from wiping at the cut.

"It all happened so fast. We got a call. Two calls. I was on the phone with Louis's brother-in-law. He's the one that had been calling. Seems like Louis overheard a conversation Genevieve was having with Thomas, of all people. It scared the shit out of him. He thought

Genevieve had killed James and the Cheyenne kid and he was next. So he split to Browning."

"Jesus. Have you talked to him?"

"Yeah. He'd told this whole thing to his sister and her husband, and they tried like hell to get him to call, but he wouldn't do it. He did agree to his brother-in-law calling me. Hell, he was so scared that Genevieve would come looking for him and that it would be his word against hers."

"Those kids saw what happened. It was Genevieve with Thomas on the mountain that night."

"I know. We've got Thomas in custody. Which brings me to the second call. Some kids were fishing early this morning and heard some guy wailing. Thought he was being killed or something. They followed the sound and found Thomas, slashing himself."

"He was trying to kill himself?"

"No. It's a tradition. When you're in mourning, you cut yourself. It's still done today. Some of the elders are missing parts of their fingers. They cut them off during mourning. Thomas was with Monday."

"You found Monday? Thomas dug—"

"Yeah. He did. Seems he thought Monday deserved a proper burial."

"Poor fool. He was a pawn for both of them, wasn't he?"

"All three of them used the guy."

"Three?"

"Looks that way. From what we can tell—he's not all that coherent—Genevieve and Thomas met Monday down on Montana the night Sharon Mills was on her way home. He showed them some things he had in duffel bags. He was fucking with her mind."

"How the hell did she think she could buy those things?"

"She knew she couldn't. She appealed to his conscience."

"He didn't have one."

"You got that right. How's your head?"

"On the outside? Numb. Inside, there's a rocket going off. How does it look?"

"I think they're going to have to shave some hair off the top to stitch it."

"Like hell they will. How did she end up on the mountain with Monday?"

"Thomas said she stuck him. I figure it was with the pins. That's when he staggered out of the shadows onto Sharon Mills's car. Only he wasn't dead. Near dead, but not quite. They hauled him up on the mountain. Thomas said Monday was *very mad*."

"He must have come to."

"Right. And that's when she finished him. They hid him in the Big Ice Cave. My bet is that the day you were meeting with Matthew and Steven, Thomas had gone up to give Monday his *proper burial*. When the kids left, there you were. In his delusion you were a threat. He'd already placed Monday's body in the outhouse."

"Where is he now?"

"At the hospital. He took traditional a little too far. He lost a lot of blood."

"What's going to happen to him, Kyle?"

"They'll probably put him somewhere."

"Did he help Mueller put that guy in my tree?"

"Mueller isn't talking, but I think it went down like this. Mueller approaches Thomas and manipulates him just enough to get him on his side. Then those two stupid kids decide to shake down Mueller. It'd be like trying to fill a cavity on a rattlesnake, only they didn't see that far. All they saw was some quick, easy cash. It cost 'em."

I leaned my head into his chest. His arm felt good around my shoulders.

"I liked her, Kyle. I really liked Genevieve."

"I know. Me too."

"She was sick. Shit. Why didn't anybody see it?"

"She was smart. Smart enough to hide it."

"It just doesn't seem fair somehow."

"Nothing ever does, Phoebe."

We sat in silence. Everything was magnified: the deep blue of the sky, the lay of the land washed with burnished earth colors, the scent of the high plains that seemed to call the birds into song. It seemed somehow illicit in its beauty. Genevieve was dead, and the world she'd spoken of in hushed tones the day we sat at the picnic tables in Pryor was going to go on without her.

"Come on. I have to get down low enough to use the radio. There should be quite a crowd around Monday about now. Phoebe, where are the artifacts? Did she say?"

I looked toward the sky and saw a hawk, something, circling high above. I could almost feel her breath against my cheek, hear her whisper in my ear.

"No, Kyle. I don't know where they are. She said nothing." I reached into my jacket pocket and took out the Ziploc bag. "I don't know what to do with these." I handed the bag to Kyle. He looked at it briefly and handed it back to me.

"Hang on to them," he said. "We'll figure it out later. When the time is right, you'll know what to do."

"Take me to where they found Monday."

"We're on our way."

The wind cuts through the late-morning sun as it sweeps across the valley. It follows the contour of the parched foothills, gathering the scents of the day as it courses its way up to the top of the Pryor Mountains and beyond. The strong smell of silver sage and high plains soil, mixed with the sickening stench of decaying flesh, rides the wind. It swirls around me and reaches deep into my gut. Saliva fills my mouth. I clench my teeth and try to keep the block of sick pushing up my throat from erupting.

Turning away, I take a deep breath through my mouth. I can taste the stink as I turn back and step to the scaffold. I reach out and touch the stiff hide, the coarse, tan hair compressing under my fingers. The hide slides easily and falls off the edge. The imitation Hudson Bay blanket is tucked tightly under the reclining form. Reaching chin high, I pull the blanket loose and stare at the black-painted face of Monday Brown. His long, silver hair, combed smooth and hanging free, lifts in the wind and dances across his face. His chest is bare. Deep, bloodless gashes on his right arm, three in all, stare back at me in ghoulish, lipless grins.

Hooves dangling from leather cords at each corner of the scaffold, antelope or deer probably, are singing their own song, a tuneless dirge, as they clack together. A woman is weeping somewhere behind me. I turn and see Monday's wife kneeling on the ground. Her onyx-eyed child is standing beside her, his hand resting softly on her shoulder.

I look toward the mountains and think of the old woman. Christ, did it happen? Can the dead reach from beyond to lead the living in defense of the ones they love? The wind lifts a feather from Monday's hair and carries it toward me. It lands in the dust at my feet, and as I kneel to pick it up I feel a gnarled hand on my shoulder. Age-thick-ened nails dig deep into my flesh. Adrenaline surges through me as I jerk away and rise. No one is within ten feet of where I'm standing. I look back at Monday Brown.

Two days ago, he was buried in a silver coffin with a white satin liner, his head resting on a cloud-soft smocked pillow. They closed the lid, lowered him six feet into the waiting ground, and covered him with dirt. No one tried to stop the people who walked past and spit on his grave.

Now, here in this heat, I've found him again, laid to rest for the second time. His body defiled in the *old way*. His face painted, his hair adorned, his wife and child mourning, in the *old way*. Son of a bitch that he was, he would have liked this way best.